TROUBLE FOR LUCIA

E. F. Benson

Chivers Press ● Thorndike Press
Bath, England ● Thorndike, Maine USA

This Large Print edition is published by Chivers Press, England, and by Thorndike Press, USA.

Published in 1997 in the U.K. by arrangement with the author's agent.

Published in 1997 in the U.S. by arrangement with HarperCollins Publishers, Inc.

U.K. Hardcover ISBN 0–7451–6997–X (Chivers Large Print)
U.K. Softcover ISBN 0–7451–6998–8 (Camden Large Print)
U.S. Softcover ISBN 0–7862–0959–3 (General Series Edition)

The text of this Large Print edition is unabridged.
Other aspects of the book may vary from the original edition.

Set in 16 pt. New Times Roman.

Printed in Great Britain on acid-free paper.

British Library Cataloguing in Publication Data available

Library of Congress Catalog Card Number: 96–90821

TROUBLE FOR LUCIA

CHAPTER ONE

Lucia Pillson, the Mayor-Elect of Tilling and her husband Georgie were talking together one October afternoon in the garden-room at Mallards. The debate demanded the exercise of their keenest faculties. Viz:

Should Lucia, when next month she entered on the supreme Municipal Office, continue to go down to the High Street every morning after breakfast with her market-basket, and make her personal purchases at the shops of the baker, the grocer, the butcher and wherever else the needs of the day's catering directed? There were pros and cons to be considered, and Lucia had been putting the case for both sides with the tedious lucidity of opposing counsel addressing the Court. It might be confidently expected that, when she had finished exploring the entire territory, she would be fully competent to express the verdict of the jury and the sentence of the judge. In anticipation of the numerous speeches she would soon be called upon to make as Mayor, she was cultivating, whenever she remembered to do so, a finished oratorical style, and a pedantic Oxford voice.

'I must be very careful, Georgie,' she said. 'Thoroughly democratic as you know I am in the truest sense of the word, I shall be entrusted, on the ninth of November next, with the duty of upholding the dignity and tradition of my high office. I'm not sure that I ought to go popping in and out of shops, as I have hitherto done, carrying my market-basket and bustling about just like anybody else. Let me put a somewhat similar case to you. Supposing you saw a newly-appointed Lord Chancellor trotting round the streets of Westminster in shorts, for the sake of exercise. What would you feel about it? What would your reactions be?'

'I hope you're not thinking of putting on shorts, are you?' asked Georgie, hoping to introduce a lighter tone.

'Certainly not,' said Lucia. 'A parallel case only. And then there's this. It would be intolerable to my democratic principles that, if I went into the grocer's to make some small purchase, other customers already there should stand aside in order that I might be served first. That would never do. Never!'

Georgie surveyed with an absent air the pretty piece of needlework on which he was engaged. He was embroidering the Borough arms of Tilling in coloured silks on the back of the white kid gloves which Lucia would wear at the inaugural ceremony, and he was not quite sure that he had placed the device exactly in the middle.

'How tar'some,' he said. 'Well, it will have to do. I daresay it will stretch right. About the Lord Chancellor in shorts. I don't think I should mind. It would depend a little on what sort of knees he had. As for other customers standing aside because you were the Mayor, I don't think you need be afraid of that for a moment. Most unlikely.'

Lucia became violently interested in her gloves.

'My dear, they look too smart for anything,' she said. 'Beautiful work, Georgie. Lovely. They remind me of the jewelled gloves you see in primitive Italian pictures on the hands of kneeling Popes and adoring Bishops.'

'Do you think the arms are quite in the middle?' he asked.

'It looks perfect. Shall I try it on?'

Lucia displayed the back of her gloved hand, leaning her forehead elegantly against the finger-tips.

'Yes, that seems all right,' said Georgie. 'Give it me back. It's not quite finished. About the other thing. It would be rather marked if you suddenly stopped doing your marketing yourself, as you've done it every day for the last two years or so. Except Sundays. Some people might say that you were swanky because you were Mayor. Elizabeth would.'

'Possibly. But I should be puzzled, dear, to name off-hand anything that mattered less to me than what Elizabeth Mapp-Flint said, poor woman. Give me your opinion, not hers.'

'You might drop the marketing by degrees, if you felt it was undignified,' said Georgie yawning. 'Shop every day this week, and only on Monday, Wednesday and Friday next week—'

'No, dear,' interrupted Lucia. 'That would be hedging, and I never hedge. One thing or the other.'

'A hedge may save you from falling into a ditch,' said Georgie brilliantly.

'*Georgino*, how epigrammatic! What does it mean exactly? What ditch?'

'Any ditch,' said Georgie. 'Just making a mistake and not being judicious. Tilling is a mass of pitfalls.'

'I don't mind about pitfalls so long as my conscience assures me that I am guided by right principles. I must set an example in my private as well as my public life. If I decide to go on with my daily marketing I shall certainly make a point of buying very cheap, simple provisions. Cabbages and turnips, for instance, not asparagus.'

'We've got plenty of that in the garden when it comes in,' said Georgie.

'—plaice, not soles. Apples,' went on Lucia, as if he hadn't spoken. 'Plain living in private—everybody will hear me buying cheap vegetables—Splendour, those lovely gloves, in public. And high thinking in both.'

'That would sound well in your inaugural speech,' said Georgie.

'I hope it will. What I want to do in our dear Tilling is to elevate the tone, to make it a real

4

centre of intellectual and artistic activity. That must go on simultaneously with social reforms and the well-being of the poorer classes. All the slums must be cleared away. There must be an end to overcrowding. Pasteurisation of milk, Georgie; a strict censorship of the films; benches in sunny corners. Of course, it will cost money. I should like to see the rates go up by leaps and bounds.'

'That won't make you very popular,' said Georgie.

'I should welcome any unpopularity that such reforms might earn for me. The decorative side of life, too. Flower boxes in the windows of the humblest dwellings. Cheap concerts of first-rate music. The revival of ancient customs, like beating the bounds. I must find out just what that is.'

'The town-council went in procession round the boundaries of the parish,' said Georgie, 'and the Mayor was bumped on the boundary stones. Hadn't we better stick to the question of whether you go marketing or not?'

Lucia did not like the idea of being bumped on boundary stones...

'Quite right, dear. I lose myself in my dreams. We were talking about the example we must set in plain living. I wish it to be known that I do my catering with economy. To be heard ordering neck of mutton at the butcher's.'

'I won't eat neck of mutton in order to be an

5

example to anybody,' said Georgie. 'And, personally, whatever you settle to do, I won't give up the morning shopping. Besides, one learns all the news then. Why, it would be worse than not having the wireless! I should be lost without it. So would you.'

Lucia tried to picture herself bereft of that eager daily interchange of gossip, when her Tilling circle of friends bustled up and down the High Street carrying their market-baskets and bumping into each other in the narrow doorways of shops. Rain or fine, with umbrellas and goloshes or with sunshades and the thinnest blouses, it was the bracing hour that whetted the appetite for the complications of life. The idea of missing it was unthinkable, and without the slightest difficulty she ascribed exalted motives and a high sense of duty to its continuance.

'You are right, dear,' she said. 'Thank you for your guidance! More than ever now in my new position, it will be incumbent on me to know what Tilling is thinking and feeling. My finger must be on its pulse. That book I was reading the other day, which impressed me so enormously—what on earth was it? A biography.'

'Catherine the Great?' asked Georgie. Lucia had dipped into it lately, but the suggestion was intended to be humorous.

'Yes: I shall forget my own name next. She always had her finger on the pulse of her

6

people: that I maintain was the real source of her greatness. She used to disguise herself, you remember, as a peasant woman—moujik, isn't it?—and let herself out of the back-door of the Winter Palace, and sat in the bars and cafes or wherever they drink vodka and tea—samovars—and hear what the common people were saying, astonishing her Ministers with her knowledge.'

Georgie felt fearfully bored with her and this preposterous rubbish. Lucia did not care two straws what 'the common people' were saying. She, in this hour of shopping in the High Street, wanted to know what fresh mischief Elizabeth Mapp-Flint was hatching, and what Major Benjy Mapp-Flint was at, and whether Diva Plaistow's Irish terrier had got mange, and if Irene Coles had obtained the sanction of the Town Surveying Department to paint a fresco on the front of her house of a nude Venus rising from the sea, and if Susan Wyse had really sat down on her budgerigar, squashing it quite flat. Instead of which she gassed about the duty of the Mayor-Elect of Tilling to have her finger on the pulse of the place, like Catherine the Great. Such nonsense was best met with a touch of sarcasm.

'That will be a new experience, dear,' he said. 'Fancy your disguising yourself as a gypsy-woman and stealing out through the back-door, and sitting in the bars of public-houses. I do call that thorough.'

7

'Ah, you take me too literally, Georgie,' she said. 'Only a loose analogy. In some respects I should be sorry to behave like that marvellous woman. But what a splendid notion to listen to all that the moujiks said when their tongues were unloosed with vodka. *In vino veritas*.'

'Not always,' said Georgie. 'For instance, Major Benjy was sitting boozing in the club this afternoon. The wind was too high for him to go out and play golf, so he spent his time in port ... Putting out in a gale, you see, or stopping in port. Quite a lot of port.'

Georgie waited for his wife to applaud this pretty play upon words, but she was thinking about herself and Catherine the Great.

'Well, wine wasn't making him truthful, but just the opposite,' he went on. 'Telling the most awful whoppers about the tigers he'd shot and his huge success with women when he was younger.'

'Poor Elizabeth,' said Lucia in an unsympathetic voice.

'He grew quite dreadful,' said Georgie, 'talking about his bachelor days of freedom. And he had the insolence to dig me in the ribs and whisper "We know all about that, old boy, don't we? Ha ha. What?"'

'Georgie, how impertinent,' cried Lucia. 'Why, it's comparing Elizabeth with me!'

'And me with him,' suggested Georgie.

'Altogether most unpleasant. Any more news?'

8

'Yes; I saw Diva for a moment. Paddy's not got mange. Only a little eczema. And she's quite determined to start her tea-shop. She asked me if I thought you would perform the opening ceremony and drink the first cup of tea. I said I thought you certainly would. Such *éclat* for her if you went in your robes! I don't suppose there would be a muffin left in the place.'

Lucia's brow clouded, but it made her happy to be on Mayoral subjects again.

'Georgie, I wish you hadn't encouraged her to hope that I would,' she said. 'I should be delighted to give Diva such a magnificent send-off as that, but I must be very careful. Supposing next day somebody opens a new boot-shop I shall have made a precedent and shall have to wear the first pair of shoes. Or a hat-shop. If I open one, I must open all, for I will not show any sort of favouritism. I will gladly, ever so gladly, go and drink the first cup of tea at Diva's, as Mrs Pillson, but not officially. I must be officially incognita.'

'She'll be disappointed,' said Georgie.

'Poor Diva, I fear so. As for robes, quite impossible. The Mayor never appears in robes except when attended by the whole Corporation. I can hardly request my Aldermen and Councillors to have tea with Diva in state. Of course it's most enterprising of her, but I can't believe her little tea-room will resemble the goldmine she anticipates.'

9

'I don't think she's doing it just to make money,' said Georgie, 'though, of course she wouldn't mind that.'

'What then? Think of the expense of cups and saucers and tables and teaspoons. The trouble, too. She told me she meant to serve the teas herself.'

'It's just that she'll enjoy so much,' said Georgie, 'popping in and out and talking to her customers. She's got a raving passion for talking to anybody, and she finds it such silent work living alone. She'll have constant conversation if her tea-room catches on.'

'Well, you may be right,' said Lucia. 'Oh, and there's another thing. My Mayoral banquet. I lay awake half last night—perhaps not quite so much—thinking about it, and I don't see how you can come to it.'

'That's sickening,' said Georgie. 'Why not?'

'It's very difficult. If I ask you, it will certainly set a precedent—'

'You think too much about precedents,' interrupted Georgie. 'Nobody will care.'

'But listen. The banquet is entirely official. I shall ask the Mayors of neighbouring boroughs, the Bishop, the Lord Lieutenant, the Vicar, who is my Chaplain, my Aldermen and Councillors, and Justices of the Peace. You, dear, have no official position. We are, so to speak, like Queen Victoria and the Prince Consort.'

'You said that before,' said Georgie, 'and I

10

looked it up. When she opened Parliament he drove with her to Westminster and sat beside her on a throne. A throne—'

'I wonder if that is so. Some of those lives of the Queen are very inaccurate. At that rate, the wife of the Lord Chancellor ought to sit on a corner of the Woolsack. Besides, where are you to be placed? You can't sit next me. The Lord Lieutenant must be on my right and the Bishop on my left—'

'If they come,' observed Georgie.

'Naturally they won't sit there if they don't. After them come the Mayors, Aldermen and Councillors. You would have to sit below them all, and that would be intolerable to me.'

'I shouldn't mind where I sat,' said Georgie.

'I should love you to be there, Georgie,' she said. 'But in what capacity? It's all official, I repeat. Think of tradition.'

'But there isn't any tradition. No woman has ever been Mayor of Tilling before: you've often told me that. However, don't let us argue about it. I expect Tilling will think it very odd if I'm not there. I shall go up to London that day, and then you can tell them I've been called away.'

'That would never do,' cried Lucia. 'Tilling would think it much odder if you weren't here on my great day.'

'Having dinner alone at Mallards,' said Georgie bitterly. 'The neck of mutton you spoke of.'

He rose.

'Time for my bath,' he said. 'And I shan't talk about it or think about it any more. I leave it to you.'

* * *

Georgie went upstairs, feeling much vexed. He undressed and put on his blue silk dressing-gown, and peppered his bath with a liberal allowance of verbena salts. He submerged himself in the fragrant liquid, and concentrated his mind on the subject he had resolved not to think about any more. Just now Lucia seemed able to apply her mind to nothing except herself and the duties or dignities of her coming office.

'"Egalo—megalo—mayoralo—mania", I call it,' Georgie said to himself in a withering whisper. 'Catherine the Great! Delirium! She thinks the whole town is as wildly excited about her being Mayor as she is herself. Whereas it's a matter of supreme indifference to them ... All except Elizabeth, who trembles with rage and jealousy whenever she sees Lucia ... But she always did that ... Bother! I've dropped my soap and it slips away like an eel ... All very tar'some. Lucia can't talk about anything else ... Breakfast, lunch, tea and dinner, there's nothing but that ... Mayoral complex ... It's a crashing bore, that's what it is ... Everlastingly reminding me that I've no official position ... Hullo, who's that? No, you

12

can't come in, whoever you are.'

A volley of raps had sounded at the door of the bathroom. Then Lucia's voice:

'No, I don't want to come in,' she said. 'But, *eureka*, Georgie. *Ho trovato: ho ben trovato!*'

'What have you found?' called Georgie, sitting up in his bath.

'It. Me. My banquet. You and my banquet. I'll tell you at dinner. Be quick.'

'Probably she'll let me hand the cheese,' thought Georgie, still feeling morose. 'I'm in no hurry to hear that.'

He padded back to his bedroom in his dressing-gown and green morocco slippers. A parcel had arrived for him while he was at his bath, and Foljambe, the parlour-maid valet had put it on his pink bed-quilt.

'It must be my new dinner-suit,' he said to himself. 'And with all this worry I'd quite forgotten about it.'

He cut the string and there it was: jacket and waistcoat and trousers of ruby-coloured velvet, with synthetic-onyx buttons, quite superb. It was Lucia's birthday present to him; he was to order just what dinner-suit he liked, and the bill was to be sent to her. She knew nothing more, except that he had told her that it would be something quite out of the common and that Tilling would be astonished. He was thrilled with its audacious beauty.

'Now let me think,' he meditated. 'One of my pleated shirts, and a black butterfly tie, and my

13

garnet solitaire. And my pink vest. Nobody will see it, but I shall know it's there. And red socks. Or daren't I?'

He swiftly invested himself in this striking creation. It fitted beautifully in front, and he rang the bell for Foljambe to see if it was equally satisfactory behind. Her masterful knock sounded on the door, and he said come in.

Foljambe gave a shrill ejaculation.

'Lor!' she said. 'Something fancy-dress, sir?'

'Not at all,' said Georgie. 'My new evening suit. Isn't it smart, Foljambe? Does it fit all right at the back?'

'Seems to,' said Foljambe, pulling his sleeve. 'Stand a bit straighter, sir. Yes, quite a good fit. Nearly gave me one.'

'Don't you like it?' asked Georgie anxiously.

'Well, a bit of a shock, sir. I hope you won't spill things on it, for it would be a rare job to get anything sticky out of the velvet, and you do throw your food about sometimes. But it is pretty now I begin to take it in.'

Georgie went into his sitting-room next door, where there was a big mirror over the fireplace, and turned on all the electric lights. He got up on a chair, so that he could get a more comprehensive view of himself, and revolved slowly in the brilliant light. He was so absorbed in his Narcissism that he did not hear Lucia come out of her bedroom. The door was ajar, and she peeped in. She gave a strangled scream at the sight of a large man in a glaring red suit standing on a chair with his back to her. It was unusual. Georgie whisked round at her cry.

'Look!' he said. 'Your delicious present. There it was when I came from my bath. Isn't it lovely?'

Lucia recovered from her shock.

'Positively Venetian, Georgie,' she said. 'Real Titian.'

'I think it's adorable,' said Georgie, getting down. 'Won't Tilling be excited? Thank you a thousand times.'

'And a thousand congratulations, Georgino,' she said. 'Oh, and my discovery! I am a genius, dear. There'll be a high table across the room at my banquet with two tables joining it at the corners going down the room. Me, of course, in the centre of the high table. We shall sit only on one side of these tables. And you can sit all by yourself exactly opposite me. Facing me. No official position, neither above or below the others. Just the Mayor's husband close to her materially, but officially in the air, so to speak.'

From below came the merry sound of little bells that announced dinner. Grosvenor, the other parlour-maid, was playing quite a sweet tune on them to-night, which showed she was pleased with life. When she was cross she made a snappy jangled discord.

'That solves everything!' said Georgie.

15

'Brilliant. How clever of you! I *did* feel a little hurt at the thought of not being there. Listen: Grosvenor's happy, too. We're all pleased.'

He offered her his beautiful velvet arm, and they went downstairs.

'And my garnet solitaire,' he said 'Doesn't it go well with my clothes? I must tuck my napkin in securely. It would be frightful if I spilt anything. I am glad about the banquet.'

'So am I, dear. It would have been horrid not to have had you there. But I had to reconcile the feelings of private life with the etiquette of public life. We must expect problems of the sort to arise while I'm Mayor—'

'Such good fish,' said Georgie, trying to divert her from the eternal subject.

Quite useless.

'Excellent, isn't it,' said Lucia. 'In the time of Queen Elizabeth, Georgie, the Mayor of Tilling was charged with supplying fish for the Court. A train of pack-mules was despatched to London twice a week. What a wonderful thing if I could get that custom restored! Such an impetus to the fishermen here.'

'The Court must have been rather partial to putrid fish,' said Georgie. 'I shouldn't care to eat a whiting that had been carried on a mule to London in hot weather, or in cold, for that matter.'

'Ah, I should not mean to go back to the mules,' said Lucia, 'though how picturesque to see them loaded at the river-bank, and starting

16

on their Royal errand. One would use the railway. I wonder if it could be managed. The Royal Fish Express.'

'Do you propose a special train full of soles and lobsters twice a week for Buckingham Palace or Royal Lodge?' he asked.

'A refrigerating van would be sufficient. I daresay if I searched in the archives I should find that Tilling had the monopoly of supplying the Royal table, and that the right has never been revoked. If so, I should think a petition to the King: "Your Majesty's loyal subjects of Tilling humbly pray that this privilege be restored to them". Or perhaps some preliminary enquiries from the Directors of the Southern Railway first. Such prestige. And a steady demand would be a wonderful thing for the fishing industry.'

'It's got enough demand already,' said Georgie. 'There isn't too much fish for us here as it is.'

'Georgie! Where's your political economy? Demand invariably leads to supply. There would be more fishing-smacks built, more men would follow the sea. Unemployment would diminish. Think of Yarmouth and its immense trade. How I should like to capture some of it for our Tilling! I mustn't lose sight of that among all the schemes I ponder over so constantly ... But I've had a busy day: let us relax a little and make music in the garden-room.'

17

She rose, and her voice assumed a careless lightness.

'I saw to-day,' she said, 'in one of my old bound-up volumes of duets, an arrangement for four hands of Glazonov's "Bacchanal". It looked rather attractive. We might run through it.'

Georgie had seen it, too, a week ago, and though most of Lucia's music was familiar, he felt sure they had never tried this. He had had a bad cold in the head, and, not being up to their usual walk for a day or two, he had played over the bass part several times while Lucia was out taking her exercise: some day it might come in useful. Then this very afternoon, busy in the garden, he had heard a long-continued soft-pedalled tinkle, and rightly conjectured that Lucia was stealing a march on him in the treble part ... Out they went to the garden-room, and Lucia found the "Bacchanal". His new suit made him feel very kindly disposed.

'You must take the treble, then,' he said. 'I could never read that.'

'How lazy of you, dear,' she said, instantly sitting down. 'Well, I'll try if you insist, but you mustn't scold me if I make a mess of it.'

It went beautifully. Odd trains of thought coursed through the heads of both. 'Why is she such a hypocrite?' he wondered. 'She was practising it half the afternoon.' ... Simultaneously Lucia was saying to herself, 'Georgie can't be reading it. He must have tried it before.' At the end were mutual congratulations: each thought that the other had read it wonderfully well. Then bed-time. She kissed her hand to him as she closed her bedroom door, and Georgie made a few revolutions in front of his mirror before divesting himself of the new suit. By a touching transference of emotions, Lucia had vivid dreams of heaving seas of ruby-coloured velvet, and Georgie of the new Cunard liner, *Queen Mary*, running aground in the river on a monstrous shoal of whiting and lobsters.

*   *   *

There was an early autumnal frost in the night, though not severe enough to blacken the superb dahlias in Lucia's garden and soon melting. The lawn was covered with pearly moisture when she and Georgie met at breakfast, and the red roofs of Tilling gleamed bright in the morning sun. Lucia had already engaged a shorthand and typewriting secretary to get used to her duties before the heavy Mayoral correspondence began to pour in, but to-day the post brought nothing but a few circulars at once committed to the waste-paper basket. But it would not do to leave Mrs Simpson completely idle, so, before setting out for the morning marketing, Lucia dictated invitations to Mrs Bartlett and the Padre, to Susan and Mr Wyse, to Elizabeth Mapp-Flint and Major Benjy for dinner and Bridge the following night. She would write in the invocations and signatures when she returned, and she apologized in each letter for the stress of work which had prevented her from writing with her own hand throughout.

'Georgie, I shall have to learn typing myself,' she said as they started. 'I can easily imagine some municipal crisis which would swamp Mrs Simpson, quick worker though she is. Or isn't there a machine called the dictaphone? . . . How deliciously warm the sun is! When we get back I shall make a water-colour sketch of my dahlias in the *giardino segreto*. Any night might see them blackened, and I should deplore not having a record of them. *Ecco*, there's Irene beckoning to us from her window. Something about the fresco, I expect.'

Irene Coles bounced out into the street.

'Lucia, beloved one,' she cried. 'It's too cruel! That lousy Town Surveying Department refuses to sanction my fresco-design of Venus rising from the sea. Come into my studio and look at my sketch of it, which they have sent back to me. Goths and Vandals and Mrs Grundys to a man and woman!'

The sketch was very striking. A nude, well-nourished, putty-coloured female, mottled with green shadows, was balanced on an oyster shell, while a prize-fighter, representing the wind and sprawling across the sky, propelled her with puffed cheeks up a river towards a red-roofed town on the shore which presented Tilling with pre-Raphaelite fidelity.

'Dear me! Quite Botticellian!' said Lucia.

'What?' screamed Irene. 'Darling, how can you compare my great deep-bosomed Venus, fit to be the mother of heroes, with Botticelli's anæmic flapper? What'll the next generation in Tilling be like when my Venus gets ashore?'

'Yes. Quite. So vigorous! So allegorical!' said Lucia. 'But, dear Irene, do you want everybody to be reminded of that whenever they go up and down the street?'

'Why not? What can be nobler than Motherhood?' asked Irene.

'Nothing! Nothing!' Lucia assured her. 'For a maternity home—'

Irene picked up her sketch and tore it across.

'I know what I shall do,' she said. 'I shall turn my wondrous Hellenic goddess into a Victorian mother. I shall dress her in a tartan shawl and skirt and a bonnet with a bow underneath her chin and button-boots and a parasol. I shall give my lusty South Wind a frock-coat and trousers and a top-hat, and send the design back to that foul-minded Department asking if I have now removed all objectionable features. Georgie, when next you come to see me, you won't need to blush.'

'I haven't blushed once!' said Georgie indignantly. 'How can you tell such fibs?'

*   *   *

21

'Dear Irene is so full of vitality,' said Lucia as they regained the street. 'Such ozone! She always makes me feel as if I was out in a high wind, and I wonder if my hair is coming down. But so easily managed with a little tact—Ah! There's Diva at her window. We might pop in on her for a minute, and I'll break it to her about a State-opening for her tea-rooms ... Take care, Georgie! There's Susan's Royce plunging down on us.'

Mrs Wyse's huge car, turning into the High Street, drew up directly between them and Diva's house. She let down the window and put her large round face where the window had been. As usual, she had on her ponderous fur-coat, but on her head was a quite new hat, to the side of which, like a cockade, was attached a trophy of bright blue, green and yellow plumage, evidently the wings, tail and breast of a small bird.

'Can I give you a lift, dear?' she said in a mournful voice. 'I'm going shopping in the High Street. You, too, of course, Mr Georgie, if you don't mind sitting in front.'

'Many thanks, dear Susan,' said Lucia, 'but hardly worth while, as we are in the High Street already.'

Susan nodded sadly to them, put up the window, and signalled to her chauffeur to proceed. Ten yards brought her to the grocer's, and the car stopped again.

22

'Georgie, it was the remains of the budgerigar tacked to her hat,' said Lucia in a thrilled whisper as they crossed the street. 'Yes, Diva: we'll pop in for a minute.'

'Wearing it,' said Diva in her telegraphic manner as she opened the front-door to them. 'In her hat.'

'Then is it true, Diva?' asked Lucia. 'Did she sit down on her budgerigar?'

'Definitely. I was having tea with her. Cage open. Budgerigar flitting about the room. A messy bird. Then Susan suddenly said "Tweet, tweet. Where's my blue Birdie?" Not a sign of it. "It'll be all right," said Susan. "In the piano or somewhere." So we finished tea. Susan got up and there was blue Birdie. Dead and as flat as a pancake. We came away at once.'

'Very tactful,' said Georgie. 'But the head wasn't on her hat, I'm pretty sure.'

'Having it stuffed, I expect. To be added later between the wings. And what about those new clothes, Mr Georgie?'

'How on earth did you hear that?' said Georgie in great astonishment. How news travelled in Tilling! Only last night, dining at home, he had worn the ruby-coloured velvet for the first time, and now, quite early next morning, Diva had heard about it. Really things were known in Tilling almost before they happened.

'My Janet was posting a letter, ten p.m.,' said Diva. 'Foljambe was posting a letter. They chatted. And are they really red?'

'You'll see before long,' said Georgie, pleased to know that interest in his suit was blazing already. 'Just wait and see.'

All this conversation had taken place on Diva's doorstep.

'Come in for a minute,' she said. 'I want to consult you about my parlour, when I make it into a tea-room. Shall take away those two big tables, and put in six little ones, for four at each. Then there's the small room at the back full of things I could never quite throw away. Bird-cages. Broken coal-scuttles. Old towel-horses. I shall clear them out now, as there's no rummage-sale coming on. Put that big cupboard there against the wall, and a couple of card tables. People might like a rubber after their tea if it's raining. Me always ready to make a fourth if wanted. Won't that be cosy?'

'Very cosy indeed,' said Lucia. 'But may you provide facilities for gambling in a public place, without risking a police-raid?'

'Don't see why not,' said Diva. 'I may provide chess or draughts, and what's to prevent people gambling at them? Why not cards? And you will come in your robes, won't you, on Mayoring day, to inaugurate my tea-rooms?'

'My dear, quite impossible,' said Lucia firmly. 'As I told Georgie, I should have to be attended by my Aldermen and Councillors, as if it was some great public occasion. But I'll come as Mrs Pillson, and everyone will say that the Mayor performed the opening ceremony. But, officially, I must be incognita.'

'Well, that's something,' said Diva. 'And may I put up some posters to say that Mrs Pillson will open it?'

'There can be no possible objection to that,' said Lucia with alacrity. 'That will not invalidate my incognita. Just some big lettering at the top "Ye Olde Tea-House", and, if you think my name will help, big letters again for "Mrs Pillson" or "Mrs Pillson of Mallards". Quite. Any other news? I know that your Paddy hasn't got mange.'

'Nothing, I think. Oh yes, Elizabeth was in here just now, and asked me who was to be your Mayoress?'

'My Mayoress?' asked Lucia. 'Aren't I both?'

'I'm sure I don't know,' said Diva. 'But she says she's sure all Mayors have Mayoresses.'

'Poor Elizabeth: she always gets things muddled. Oh, Diva, will you—No nothing: I'm muddled, too. Goodbye, dear. All too cosy for words. A month to-day, then, for the opening. Georgie, remind me to put that down.'

Lucia and her husband passed on up the street.

'Such an escape!' she said. 'I was on the point of asking Diva to dine and play Bridge to-morrow, quite forgetting that I'd asked the

Bartletts and the Wyses and the Mapp-Flints. You know, our custom of always asking husbands and wives together is rather Victorian. It dates us. I shall make innovations when the first terrific weeks of office are over. If we always ask couples, single people like Diva get left out.'

'So shall I if the others do it, too,' remarked Georgie. 'Look, we've nearly caught up Susan. She's going into the post-office.'

As Susan, a few yards ahead, stepped ponderously out of the Royce, her head brushed against the side of the door, and a wing from the cockade of bright feathers, insecurely fastened, fluttered down on to the pavement. She did not perceive her loss, and went into the office. Georgie picked up the plume.

'Better put it back on the seat inside,' whispered Lucia. 'Not tactful to give it her in public. She'll see it when she gets in.'

'She may sit down on it again,' whispered Georgie. 'Oh, the far seat: that'll do. She can't miss it.'

He placed it carefully in the car, and they walked on.

'It's always a joy to devise those little unseen kindnesses,' said Lucia. 'Poulterer's first, Georgie. If all my guests accept for to-morrow, I had better bespeak two brace of partridges.'

'Delicious,' said Georgie, 'but how about the plain living? Oh I see: that'll be after you

26

become Mayor ... Good morning, Padre.'

The Reverend Kenneth Bartlett stepped out of a shop in front. He always talked a mixture of faulty Scots and spurious Elizabethan English. It had been a playful diversion at first, but now it had become a habit, and unless carried away by the conversation he seldom spoke the current tongue.

'Guid morrow, richt worshipful leddy,' he said. 'Well met, indeed, for there's a sair curiosity abroad, and 'tis you who can still it. Who's the happy wumman whom ye'll hae for your Mayoress?'

'That's the second time I've been asked that this morning,' said Lucia. 'I've had no official information that I must have one.'

'A'weel. It's early days yet. A month still before you need her. But ye mun have one: Mayor and Mayoress, 'tis the law o' the land. I was thinking—'

He dropped his voice to a whisper.

'There's that helpmate of mine,' he said. 'Not that there's been any colloquy betune us. She just passed the remark this morning: "I wonder who Mistress Pillson will select for her Mayoress," and I said I dinna ken and left it there.'

'Very wise,' said Lucia encouragingly.

The Padre's language grew almost Anglicized.

'But it put an idea into my head, that my Evie might be willing to help you in any way

27

she could. She'd keep you in touch with all Church matters which I know you have at heart, and Sunday Schools and all that. Mind. I don't promise that she'd consent, but I think 'tis likely, though I wouldn't encourage false hopes. All confidential, of course; and I must be stepping.'

He looked furtively round as if engaged in some dark conspiracy and stepped.

'Georgie, I wonder if there can be any truth in it,' said Lucia. 'Of course, nothing would induce me to have poor dear little Evie as Mayoress. I would as soon have a mouse. Oh, there's Major Benjy: he'll be asking me next who my Mayoress is to be. Quick, into the poulterer's.'

They hurried into the shop. Mr Rice gave her a low bow.

'Good-morning, your worship—' he began.

'No, not yet, Mr Rice,' said Lucia. 'Not for a month yet. Partridges. I shall very likely want two brace of partridges to-morrow evening.'

'I've got some prime young birds, your worsh—ma'am,' said Mr Rice.

'Very well. Please earmark four birds for me. I will let you know the first thing to-morrow morning, if I require them.'

'Earmarked they are, ma'am,' said Mr Rice enthusiastically.

Lucia peeped cautiously out. Major Benjy had evidently seen them taking cover, and was regarding electric heaters in the shop next door

28

with an absent eye. He saw her look out and made a military salute.

'Good-morning,' he said cordially. 'Lovely day isn't it? October's my favourite month. Chill October, what? I was wondering, Mrs Pillson, as I strolled along, if you had yet selected the fortunate lady who will have the honour of being your Mayoress.'

'Good morning, Major. Oddly enough somebody else asked me that very thing a moment ago.'

'Ha! I bet five to one I know who that was. I had a word or two with the Padre just now, and the subject came on the *tapis*, as they say in France. I fancy he's got some notion that that good little wife of his—but that would be too ridiculous—'

'I've settled nothing yet,' said Lucia. 'So overwhelmed with work lately. Certainly it shall receive my attention. Elizabeth quite well? That's good.'

She hurried away with Georgie.

'The question of the Mayoress is in the air like influenza, Georgie,' she said. 'I must ring up the Town Hall as soon as I get in, and find out if I must have one. I see no necessity. There's Susan Wyse beckoning again.'

Susan let down the window of her car.

'Just going home again,' she said. 'Shall I give you a lift up the hill?'

'No, a thousand thanks,' said Lucia. 'It's only a hundred yards.'

Susan shook her head sadly.

'Don't overdo it, dear,' she said. 'As we get on in life we must be careful about hills.'

'This Mayoress business is worrying me, Georgie,' said Lucia when Susan had driven off. 'If it's all too true, and I must have one, who on earth shall I get? Everyone I can think of seems so totally unfit for it. I believe, do you know, that it must have been in Major Benjy's mind to recommend me to ask Elizabeth.'

'Impossible!' said Georgie. 'I might as well recommend you to ask Foljambe.'

CHAPTER TWO

Lucia found on her return to Mallards that Mrs Simpson had got through the laborious task of typing three identical dinner invitations for next day to Mrs Wyse, Mrs Bartlett and Mrs Mapp-Flint with husbands. She filled up in autograph 'Dearest Susan, Evie and Elizabeth' and was affectionately theirs. Rack her brains as she would she could think of no further task for her secretary, so Mrs Simpson took these letters to deliver them by hand, thus saving time and postage. 'And could you be here at nine-thirty to-morrow morning,' said Lucia, 'instead of ten in case there is a stress of work? Things turn up so suddenly, and it would never do to fall into arrears.'

Lucia looked at her engagement book. Its fair white pages satisfied her that there were none at present.

'I shall be glad of a few days' quiet, dear,' she said to Georgie. 'I shall have a holiday of painting and music and reading. When once the rush begins there will be little time for such pursuits. Yet I know there was something very urgent that required my attention. Ah, yes! I must find out for certain whether I must have a Mayoress. And I must get a telephone extension into the garden-room, to save running in and out of the house for calls.'

Lucia went in and rang up the clerk at the Town Hall. Yes: he was quite sure that every Mayor had a Mayoress, whom the Mayor invited to fill the post. She turned to Georgie with a corrugated brow.

'Yes, it is so,' she said. 'I shall have to find some capable obliging woman with whom I can work harmoniously. But who?'

The metallic clang of the flap of the letterbox on the front door caused her to look out of the window. There was Diva going quickly away with her scudding, bird-like walk. Lucia opened the note she had left, and read it. Though Diva was telegraphic in conversation, her epistolary style was flowing.

DEAREST LUCIA,
    I felt quite shy of speaking to you about it to-day, for writing is always the best, don't

you think, when it's difficult to find the right words or to get them out when you have, so this is to tell you that I am quite at your disposal, and shall to find the right words or to get them out when you have, so much longer in Tilling than you, dear, that perhaps I can be of some use in all your entertainments and other functions. Not that I would *ask* you to choose me as your Mayoress, for I shouldn't think of such a thing. So pushing! So I just want to say that I am quite at your service, as you may feel rather diffident about asking me, for it would be awkward for me to refuse, being such an old friend, if I didn't feel like it. But I should positively enjoy helping you, quite apart from my duty as a friend.

Ever yours,
DIVA.

'Poor dear, ridiculous little Diva!' said Lucia, handing Georgie this artless epistle. 'So ambitious and so pathetic! And now I shall hurry off to begin my sketch of the dahlias. I will not be interrupted by any further public business this morning. I must have a little time to myself—What's that?'

Again the metallic clang from the letter box, and Lucia, consumed with curiosity, again peeped out from a corner of the window and saw Mr Wyse with his malacca cane and his Panama hat and his black velveteen coat, walking briskly away.

'Just an answer to my invitation for tomorrow, I expect,' she said. 'Susan probably doesn't feel up to writing after the loss of her budgerigar. She had a sodden and battered look this morning, didn't you think, like a cardboard box that has been out in the rain. Flaccid. No resilience.'

Lucia had taken Mr Wyse's letter from the post-box, as she made these tonic remarks. She glanced through it, her mouth falling wider and wider open.

'Listen, Georgie!' she said:

DEAR AND WORSHIPFUL MAYOR-ELECT,

It has reached my ears (Dame Rumour) that during the coming year, when you have so self-sacrificingly consented to fill the highest office which our dear little Tilling can bestow, thereby honouring itself so far more than you, you will need some partner to assist you in your arduous duties. From little unconscious signs, little involuntary self-betrayals that I have observed in my dear Susan, I think I may encourage you to hope that she *might* be persuaded to honour herself and you by accepting the onerous post which I hear is yet unfilled. I have not had any word with her on the subject. Nor is she aware that I am writing to you. As you know, she has sustained a severe bereavement in the sudden death of her little

33

winged companion. But I have ventured to say to her 'Carissima sposa, you must buck up. You must not let a dead bird, however dear, stand between you and the duties and opportunities of life which may present themselves to you.' And she answered (whether she guessed the purport of my exhortation, I cannot say), 'I will make an effort, Algernon.' I augur favourably from that.

Of the distinction which renders her so suitable for the post of Mayoress I need not speak, for you know her character so well. I might remind you, however, that our late beloved Sovereign himself bestowed on her the insignia of the Order of Member of the British Empire, and that she would therefore bring to her new office a *cachet* unshared by any of the otherwise estimable ladies of Tilling. And in this distressing estrangement which now exists between the kingdoms of England and Italy, the fact that my dear Susan is sister-in-law to my dear sister Amelia, Contessa di Faraglione, might help to heal the differences between the countries. In conclusion, dear lady, I do not think you could do better than to offer my Susan the post for which her distinction and abilities so eminently fit her, and you may be sure that I shall use my influence with her to get her to accept it.

A rivederci, illustrissima Signora, ed anche presto!

A<small>LGERNON</small> W<small>YSE</small>.

P.S.: I will come round at any moment to confer with you.

P.P.S.: I reopen this to add that Susan has just received your amiable invitation for to-morrow, which we shall both be honoured to accept.

Lucia and Georgie looked at each other in silence at the end of the reading of this elegant epistle.

'Beautifully expressed, I must allow,' she said. 'Oh, Georgie, it is a frightful responsibility to have patronage of this crucial kind in one's gift! It is mine to confer not only an honour but an influence for good of a most far-reaching sort. A line from me and Susan is my Mayoress. But good Susan has not the energy, the decision which I should look for. I could not rely on her judgment.'

'She put Algernon up to writing that lovely letter,' said Georgie. 'How they're all struggling to be Mayoress!'

'I am not surprised, dear, at that,' said Lucia, with dignity. 'No doubt also Evie got the Padre to recommend her—'

'And Diva recommended herself,' remarked Georgie, 'as she hadn't got anyone to do it for her.'

'And Major Benjy was certainly going to say a word for Elizabeth, if I hadn't cut him short,' said Lucia. 'I find it all rather ugly, though, poor things, I sympathise with their ambitions which in themselves are noble. I shall have to draft two very tactful letters to Diva and Mr Wyse, before Mrs Simpson comes to-morrow. What a good thing I told her to come at half-past nine. But just for the present I shall dismiss it all from my mind, and seek an hour's peace with my paint-box and my *belli fiori*. What are you going to do till lunch?'

'It's my day for cleaning my bibelots,' said Georgie. 'What a rush it all is!'

Georgie went to his sitting-room and got busy. Soon he thought he heard another metallic clang from the post-box, and hurrying to the window, he saw Major Benjy walking briskly away from the door.

'That'll be another formal application, I expect,' he said to himself, and went downstairs to see, with his wash-leather in his hand. There was a letter in the post-box, but to his surprise it was addressed not to Lucia, but himself. It ran:

MY DEAR PILLSON,

My wife has just received Her Worship's most amiable invitation that we should dine *chez vous* to-morrow. I was on the point of writing to you in any case, so she begs me to say we shall be charmed.

Now, my dear old man (if you'll permit me to call you so) I've a word to say to you.

Best always, isn't it, to be frank and open. At least that's my experience in my twenty-five years of service in the King's (God bless him) army. So listen. *Re Mayoress*. It will be a tremendous asset to your wife's success in her most distinguished post, if she can get a wise and level-headed woman to assist her. A woman of commanding character, big-minded enough to disregard the little flurries and disturbances of her office, and above all one who has tact, and would never make mischief. Some of our mutual friends—I mention no names—are only too apt to scheme and intrigue and indulge in gossip and tittle-tattle. I can only put my finger on one who is entirely free from such failings, and that is my dear Elizabeth. I can't answer for her accepting the post. It's a lot to ask of any woman, but in my private opinion, if your wife approached Elizabeth in a proper spirit, making it clear how inestimable a help she (Elizabeth) would be to her, (the Mayor), I think we might hope for a favourable reply. Perhaps to-morrow evening I might have a quiet word with you. Sincerely yours,

BENJAMIN MAPP-FLINT (Major).

Georgie with his wash-leather hurried out to the *giardino segreto* where Lucia was drawing dahlias. He held the letter out to her, but she scarcely turned her head.

'No need to tell me, dear, that your letter is on behalf of another applicant. Elizabeth Mapp-Flint, I believe. Read it me while I go on drawing. Such exquisite shapes: we do not look at flowers closely enough.'

As Georgie read it she plied a steady pencil, but when he came to the sentence about approaching Elizabeth in a proper spirit, her hand gave a violent jerk.

'Georgie, it isn't true!' she cried. 'Show me … Yes. My india-rubber? Ah, there it is.'

Georgie finished the letter, and Lucia, having rubbed out the random line her pencil had made, continued to draw dahlias with concentrated attention.

'Lucia, it's too ridiculous of you to pretend to be absorbed in your sketch,' he said impatiently. 'What are you going to do?'

Lucia appeared to recall herself from the realms of peace and beauty.

'Elizabeth will be my Mayoress,' she said calmly. 'Don't you see, dear, she would be infinitely more tiresome if she wasn't? As Mayoress, she will be muzzled, so to speak. Officially, she will have to perform the tasks I allot to her. She will come to heel, and that will be very good for her. Besides, who else *is* there? Diva with her tea-shop? Poor Susan? Little mouse-like Evie Bartlett?'

'But can you see yourself approaching Elizabeth in a proper spirit?' he asked.

Lucia gave a gay trill of laughter.

38

'Certainly I cannot. I shall wait for her to approach me. She will have to come and implore me. I shall do nothing till then.'

Georgie pondered on this extraordinary decision.

'I think you're being very rash,' he said. 'And you and Elizabeth hate each other like poison—'

'Emphatically no,' said Lucia. 'I have had occasion sometimes to take her down a peg or two. I have sometimes felt it necessary to thwart her. But hate? Never. Dismiss that from your mind. And don't be afraid that I shall approach her in any spirit at all.'

'But what am I to say to Benjy when he asks me for a few private words to-morrow night?'

Lucia laughed again.

'My dear, they'll all ask you for a few private words to-morrow night. There's the Padre running poor little Evie. There's Mr Wyse running Susan. They'll all want to know whom I'm likely to choose, and to secure your influence with me. Be like Mr Baldwin and say your lips are sealed, or like some other Prime Minister, wasn't it? who said "Wait and see." Counting Diva, there are four applicants now—remind me to tell Mrs Simpson to enter them all—and I think the list may be considered closed. Leave it to me; be discreet ... And the more I think of it, the more clearly I perceive that Elizabeth Mapp-Flint must be my Mayoress. It is far better to have her on a lead, bound to me by ties of gratitude than skulking about like a pariah dog, snapping at me. True, she may not be capable of gratitude, but I always prefer to look for the best in people, like Mr Somerset Maugham in his delightful stories.'

*   *   *

Mrs Simpson arriving at half-past nine next morning had to wait a considerable time for Lucia's tactful letters to Diva and Mr Wyse; she and Georgie sat long after breakfast scribbling and erasing on half-sheets and envelopes turned inside out till they got thoroughly tactful drafts. Lucia did not want to tell Diva point-blank that she could not dream of asking her to be Mayoress, but she did not want to raise false hopes. All she could do was to thank her warmly for her offers of help ('So like you, dear Diva!') and to assure her that she would not hesitate to take advantage of them should occasion arise. To Mr Wyse she said that no one had a keener appreciation of Susan's great gifts (so rightly recognised by the King) than she; no one more deplored the unhappy international relations between England and Italy ... Georgie briefly acknowledged Major Benjy's letter and said he had communicated its contents to his wife, who was greatly touched. Lucia thought that these letters had better not reach their recipients till after her party, and Mrs Simpson posted them later in the day.

*   *   *

Lucia was quite right about the husbands of expectant Mayoresses wanting a private word with Georgie that evening. Major Benjy and Elizabeth arrived first, a full ten minutes before dinner-time and explained to Foljambe that their clocks were fast, while Georgie in his new red velvet suit was putting the menu-cards which Mrs Simpson had typed on the dinner-table. He incautiously put his head out of the dining-room door, while this explanation was going on, and Benjy spied him.

'Ha, a word with you, my dear old man,' he exclaimed, and joined Georgie, while Elizabeth was taken to the garden-room to wait for Lucia.

''Pon my soul, amazingly stupid of us to have come so early,' he said, closing the dining-room door behind him. 'I told Liz we should be too early—ah, our clocks were fast. Don't let me interrupt you; charming flowers, and, dear me, what a handsome suit. Just the colour of my wife's dress. However, that's neither here nor there. What I should like to urge on you is to persuade your wife to take advantage of Elizabeth's willingness to become Mayoress, for the good of the town. She's willing, I gather, to sacrifice her time and her leisure for

41

that. Mrs Pillson and Mrs Mapp-Flint would be an alliance indeed. But Elizabeth feels that her offer can't remain open indefinitely, and she rather expected to have heard from your wife to-day.'

'But didn't you tell me, Major,' asked Georgie, 'that your wife knew nothing about your letter to me? I understood that it was only your opinion that if properly approached—'

There was a tap at the door, and Mr Wyse entered. He was dressed in a brand new suit, never before seen in Tilling, of sapphire blue velvet, with a soft pleated shirt, a sapphire solitaire and bright blue socks. The two looked like two middle-aged male mannequins.

Mr Wyse began bowing.

'Mr Georgie!' he said. 'Major Benjy! The noise of voices. It occurred to me that perhaps we men were assembling here according to that pretty Italian custom, for a glass of vermouth, so my wife went straight out to the garden-room. I am afraid we are some minutes early. The Royce makes nothing of the steep hill from Starling Cottage.'

Georgie was disappointed at the ruby velvet not being the only sartorial sensation of the evening, but he took it very well.

'Good evening,' he said. 'Well, I do call that a lovely suit. I was just finishing the flowers, when Major Benjy popped in. Let us go out to the garden-room, where we shall find some sherry.'

Once again the door opened.

'Eh, here be all the laddies,' said the Padre. 'Mr Wyse; a handsome costume, sir. Just the colour of the dress wee wifie's donned for this evening. She's ganged awa' to the garden-room. I wanted a bit word wi' ye, Mr Pillson, and your parlour-maid told me you were here.'

'I'm afraid we must go out now to the garden-room, Padre,' said Georgie, rather fussed. 'They'll all be waiting for us.'

It was difficult to get them to move, for each of the men stood aside to let the others pass, and thus secure a word with Georgie. Eventually the Church unwillingly headed the procession, followed by the Army, lured by the thought of sherry, and Mr Wyse deftly closed the dining-room door again and stood in front of it.

'A word, Mr Georgie,' he said. 'I had the honour yesterday to write a note to your wife about a private matter—not private from you, of course—and I wondered whether she had spoken to you about it. I have since ascertained from my dear Susan—'

The door opened again, and bumped against his heels and the back of his head with a dull thud. Foljambe's face looked in.

'Beg your pardon, sir,' she said. 'Thought I heard you go.'

'We must follow the others,' said Georgie. 'Lucia will wonder what's happened to us.'

The wives looked enquiringly into the faces

43

of their husbands as they filed into the garden-room to see if there was any news. Georgie shook hands with the women and Lucia with the men. He saw how well his suit matched Elizabeth's gown, and Mr Wyse's might have been cut from the same piece as that of the Padre's wife. Another brilliant point of colour was furnished by Susan Wyse's budgerigar. The wing that had been flipped off yesterday had been re-stitched, and the head, as Diva had predicted, had been stuffed and completed the bird. She wore this notable decoration as a centre-piece on her ample bosom. Would it be tactful, wondered Georgie, to admire it, or would it be tearing open old wounds again? But surely when Susan displayed her wound so conspicuously, she would be disappointed if he appeared not to see it. He gave her a glass of sherry and moved aside with her.

'Perfectly charming, Mrs Wyse,' he said, looking pointedly at it. 'Lovely! Most successful!'

He had done right; Susan's great watery smile spread across her face.

'So glad you like it,' she said, 'and since I've worn it, Mr Georgie, I've felt comforted for Blue Birdie. He seems to be with me still. A very strong impression. Quite psychical.'

'Very interesting and touching,' said Georgie sympathetically.

'Is it not? I am hoping to get into rapport with him again. His pretty sweet ways! And

44

may I congratulate you, too? Such a lovely suit!'

'Lucia's present to me,' said Georgie, 'though I chose it.'

'What a coincidence!' said Susan. 'Algernon's new suit is my present to him and he chose it. There are brain-waves everywhere, Mr Georgie, beyond the farthest stars.'

Foljambe announced dinner. Never before had conversation, even at Lucia's table, maintained so serious and solid a tone. The ladies in particular, though the word Mayoress was never mentioned, vied with each other in weighty observations bearing on municipal matters, in order to show the deep interest they took in them. It was as if they even engaged on a self-imposed viva-voce examination to exhibit their qualifications for the unmentioned post. They addressed their answers to Lucia and of each other they were highly critical.

'No, dear Evie,' said Elizabeth, 'I cannot share your views about girl-guides. Boy scouts I wholeheartedly support. All that drill teaches them discipline, but the best discipline for girls is to help mother at home. Cooking, housework, lighting the fire, father's slippers. Don't you agree, dear hostess?'

'Eh, Mistress Mapp-Flint,' said the Padre, strongly upholding his wife. 'Ye havena' the tithe of my Evie's experience among the bairns of the parish. Half the ailments o' the lassies

45

come from being kept at home without enough exercise and air and chance to fend for themselves. Easy to have too much of mother's apron strings, and as fur father's slippers I disapprove of corporal punishment for the young of whatever sex.'

'Oh, Padre, how could you think I meant that!' exclaimed Elizabeth.

'And as for letting a child light a fire,' put in Susan, 'that's most dangerous. No match-box should ever be allowed within a child's reach. I must say too, that I wish the fire brigade in Tilling was better organized and more efficient. If once a fire broke out here the whole town would be burned to the ground.'

'Dear Susan, is it possible you haven't heard that there was a fire in Ford Place last week? Fancy! And you're strangely in error about the brigade's efficiency, for they were there in three minutes from the time the alarm was given, and the fire was extinguished in five minutes more.'

'Lucia, what is really wanted in Tilling,' said Susan, 'is better lighting of the streets. Coming home sometimes in the evening my Royce has to crawl down Porpoise Street.'

'More powerful lamps to your car would make that all right, dear,' said Elizabeth. 'Not a very great expense. The paving of the streets, to my mind, wants the most immediate attention. I nearly fell down the other day, stepping in a great hole. The roads, too: the road opposite my house is little better than a snipe-bog. Again and again I have written to the *Hampshire Argus* about it.'

Mr Wyse bowed across the table to her.

'I regret to say I have missed seeing your letters,' he said. 'Very careless of me. Was there one last week?'

Evie emitted the mouse-like squeak which denoted intense private amusement.

'I've missed them, too,' she said. 'I expect we all have. In any case, Elizabeth, Grebe is outside the parish boundaries. Nothing to do with Tilling. It's a County Council road you will find if you look at a map. Now the overcrowding in the town itself, Lucia, is another matter which does concern us. I have it very much at heart, as anybody must have who knows anything about it. And then there are the postal deliveries. Shocking. I wrote a letter the other day—'

This was one of the subjects which Susan Wyse had specially mugged up. By leaning forward and putting an enormous elbow on the table she interposed a mountain of healthy animal tissue between Evie and Lucia, and the mouse was obliterated behind the mountain.

'And only two posts a day, Lucia,' she said. 'You will find it terribly inconvenient to get only two and the second is never anything but circulars. There's not a borough in England so ill-served. I'm told that if a petition is sent to the Postmaster-General signed by fifty per cent of the population he is bound by law to

47

give us a third delivery. Algernon and I would be only too happy to get up this petition—'

Algernon from the other side of the table suddenly interrupted her.

'Susan, take care!' he cried. 'Your budgerigar: your raspberry soufflé!'

He was too late. The budgerigar dropped into the middle of Susan's bountifully supplied plate. She took it out, dripping with hot raspberry juice and wrapped it in her napkin, moaning softly to herself. The raspberry juice stained it red, as if Blue Birdie had been sat on again, and Foljambe very tactfully handed a plate to Susan on which she deposited it. After so sad and irrelevant an incident, it was hard to get back to high topics, and the Padre started on a lower level.

'A cosy little establishment will Mistress Diva Plaistow be running presently,' he said. 'She tells me that the opening of it will be the first function of our new Mayor. A find send-off indeed.'

A simultaneous suspicion shot through the minds of the candidates present that Diva (incredible as it seemed) might be in the running. Like vultures they swooped on the absent prey.

'A little too cosy for my tastes,' said Elizabeth. 'If all the tables she means to put into her tea-room were full, sardines in a tin wouldn't be the word. Not to mention that the occupants of two of the tables would be being kippered up the chimney, and two others in a gale every time the door was opened. And are you going to open it officially, dear Lucia?'

'Certainly not,' said Lucia. 'I told her I would drink the first cup of tea with pleasure, but as Mrs Pillson, not as Mayor.'

'Poor Diva can't *make* tea,' squeaked Evie. 'She never could. It's either hot water or pure tannin.'

'And she intends to make all the fancy pastry herself,' said Susan sorrowfully. 'Much better to stick to bread and butter and a plain cake. Very ambitious, I call it, but nowadays Diva's like that. More plans for all we know.'

'And quite a reformer,' said Elizabeth. 'She talks about a quicker train service to London. She knows a brother-in-law of one of the directors. Of course the thing is as good as done with a word from Diva. It looks terribly like paranoia coming on.'

*   *   *

The ladies left. Major Benjy drunk off his port in a great hurry, so as to get a full glass when it came round again.

'A very good glass of port,' he said. 'Well, I don't mind if I fill up. The longer I live with my Liz, Pillson, the more I am astonished at her masculine grasp of new ideas.'

'My Susan's remarks about an additional postal delivery and lighting of the streets

49

showed a very keen perception of the reforms of which our town most stands in need,' said Algernon. 'Her judgment is never at fault. I have often been struck—'

The Padre, speaking to Major Benjy, raised his voice for Georgie to hear and thumped the table.

'Wee wifie's energy is unbounded,' he said. 'Often I say to her: "Spare yourself a bitty" I've said, and always she's replied "Heaven fits the back to the burden" quo' she, "and if there's more work and responsibility to be undertaken, Evie's ready for it".'

'You mustn't let her overtax herself, Padre,' said Benjy with great earnestness. 'She's got her hands over full already. Not so young as she was.'

'Eh, that's what ails all the ladies of Tilling,' retorted the Padre, 'an' she'll be younger than many I could mention. An abounding vitality. If they made me Lord Archbishop to-morrow, she'd be a mother in Israel to the province, and no mistake.'

This was too much for Benjy. It would have been a gross dereliction of duty not to let loose his withering powers of satire.

'No no, Padre,' he said. 'Tilling can't spare you. Canterbury must find someone else.'

'Eh, well, and if the War Office tries to entice you away, Major, you must say no. That'll be a bargain. But the point of my observation was that my Evie is aye ready and willing for any

50

call that may come to her. That's what I'm getting at.'

'Ha, ha, Padre; let me know when you've got it, and then I'll talk to you. Well, if the port is standing idle in front of you—'

Georgie rose. He had had enough of these unsolicited testimonials, and when Benjy became satirical it was a symptom that he should have no more port.

'I think it's time we got to our Bridge,' he said. 'Lucia will scold me if I keep you here too long.'

They marched in a compact body to the garden-room, where Lucia had been keeping hopeful Mayoresses at bay with music, and two tables were instantly formed. Georgie and Elizabeth, rubies, played against the sapphires, Mr Wyse and Evie, and the other table was drab in comparison. The evening ended unusually late, and it was on the stroke of midnight when the three pairs, of guests unable to get a private word with either of their hosts, moved sadly away like a vanquished army. The Royce conveyed the Wyses to Porpoise Street, just round the corner, with Susan, faintly suggesting Salome, holding the plate with the blood-stained handkerchief containing the budgerigar; a taxi that had long been ticking conveyed the Mapp-Flints to the snipe-bog, and two pairs of goloshes took the Padre and his wife to the Vicarage.

Lucia's tactful letters were received next morning. Mr Wyse thought that all was not yet lost, though it surprised him that Lucia had not taken Susan aside last night and implored her to be Mayoress. Diva, on the other hand, with a more correct estimate of the purport of Lucia's tact, was instantly sure that all was lost, and exclaiming, 'Drat it, so that's that,' gave Lucia's note to Paddy to worry, and started out for her morning's shopping. There were plenty of absorbing interests to distract her. Susan, with the budgerigar cockade in her hat, looked out of the window of the Royce, but to Diva's amazement the colour of the bird's plumage had changed; it was flushed with red like a stormy sunset with patches of blue sky behind. Could Susan, for some psychical reason, have dyed it? ... Georgie and Lucia were approaching from Mallards, but Diva, after that tactful note, did not want to see her friend till she had thought of something pretty sharp to say. Turning towards the High Street she bumped baskets sharply with Elizabeth.

'Morning, dear!' said Elizabeth. 'Do you feel up to a chat?'

'Yes,' said Diva. 'Come in. I'll do my shopping afterwards. Any news?'

'Benjy and I dined with Worshipful last night. Wyses, Bartletts, Bridge. We all missed you.'

'Wasn't asked,' said Diva. 'A good dinner? Did you win?'

'Partridges a little tough,' said Elizabeth musingly. 'Old birds are cheaper, of course. I won a trifle, but nothing like enough to pay for our taxi. An interesting, curious evening. Rather revolting at times, but one mustn't be captious. Evie and Susan—oh, a terrible thing happened. Susan wore the bird as a breastplate, and it fell into the raspberry soufflé. Plop!'

Diva gave a sigh of relief.

'*That* explains it,' she said. 'Saw it just now and it puzzled me. Go on, Elizabeth.'

'Revolting, I was saying. Those two women. One talked about boy scouts, and the other about posts, and then one about overcrowding and the other about the fire brigade. I just sat and listened and blushed for them both. So cheap and obvious.'

'But what's so cheap and obvious and blush-making?' asked Diva. 'It only sounds dull to me.'

'All that fictitious interest in municipal matters. What has Susan cared hitherto for postal deliveries, or Evie for overcrowding? In a nutshell, they were trying to impress Lucia, and get her to ask them, at least one of them, to be Mayoress. And from what Benjy told me, their husbands were just as barefaced when we went into the garden-room. An evening of intrigue and self-advertisement. Pah!'

53

'Pah indeed!' said Diva. 'How did Lucia take it?'

'I really hardly noticed. I was too disgusted at all these underground schemings. So transparent! Poor Lucia! I trust she will get someone who will be of use to her. She'll be sadly at sea without a woman of sense and experience to consult.'

'And was Mr Georgie's dinner costume very lovely?' asked Diva.

Elizabeth half closed her eyes as if to visualise it.

'A very pretty colour,' she said. 'Just like the gown I had dyed red not long ago, if you happen to remember it. Of course he copied it.'

The front door-bell rang. It was quicker to answer it oneself, thought Diva, than to wait for Janet to come up from the kitchen, and she trundled off.

'Come in, Evie,' she said, 'Elizabeth's here.'

But Elizabeth would not wait, and Evie, in turn, gave her own impressions of the previous evening. They were on the same lines as Elizabeth's, only it had been Elizabeth and Susan who (instead of revolting her) had been so vastly comical with their sudden interest in municipal affairs:

'And, oh, dear me,' she said, 'Mr Wyse and Major Benjy were just as bad. It was like that musical thing where you have a tune in the treble, and the same tune next in the bass. Fugue; that's it. Those four were just like a

Bach concert. Kenneth and I simply sat listening. And I'm much mistaken if Lucia and Mr Georgie didn't see through them all.'

Diva had now got a complete idea of what had taken place; clearly there had been a six-part fugue.

'But she's got to choose somebody,' she said. 'Wonder who it'll be.'

'Perhaps you, he, he!' squeaked Evie for a joke.

'That it won't,' cried Diva emphatically, looking at the fragments of Lucia's tactful note scattered about the room. 'Sooner sing songs in the gutter. Fancy being at Lucia's beck and call, whenever she wants something done which she doesn't want to do herself. Not worth living at that price. No, thank you!'

'Just my fun,' said Evie. 'I didn't mean it seriously. And then there were other surprises. Mr Georgie in a red—'

'I know; the colour of Elizabeth's dyed one,' put in Diva.

'—and Mr Wyse in sapphire velvet,' continued Evie. 'Just like my second-best, which I was wearing.'

'No! I hadn't heard that,' said Diva. 'Aren't the Tilling boys getting dressy?'

*　　　*　　　*

The tension increased during the next week to a point almost unbearable, for Lucia, like the

55

Pythian Oracle in unfavourable circumstances, remained dumb, waiting for Elizabeth to implore her. The strain was telling and whenever the telephone bell rang in the houses of any of the candidates she or her husband ran to it to see if it carried news of the nomination. But, as at an inconclusive sitting of the Conclave of Cardinals for the election of the Pontiff, no announcement came from the precinct; and every evening, since the weather was growing chilly, a column of smoke curled out of the chimney of the garden-room. Was it that Lucia, like the Cardinals, could not make up her mind, or had she possibly chosen her Mayoress and had enjoined silence till she gave the word? Neither supposition seemed likely, the first, because she was so very decisive a person; the second, because it was felt that the chosen candidate could not have kept it to herself.

Then a series of curious things happened, and to the overwrought imagination of Tilling they appeared to be of the nature of omens. The church clock struck thirteen one noon, and then stopped with a jarring sound. That surely augured ill for the chances of the Padre's wife. A spring broke out in the cliff above the Mapp-Flints' house, and flowing through the garden, washed the asparagus bed away. That looked like Elizabeth's hopes being washed away too. Susan Wyse's Royce collided with a van in the High Street and sustained damage to a mud-guard; that looked bad for Susan. Then Elizabeth, distraught with anxiety, suddenly felt convinced that Diva had been chosen. What made this the more probable was that Diva had so emphatically denied to Evie that she would ever be induced to accept the post. It was like poor Diva to think that anybody would believe such a monstrous statement; it only convinced Elizabeth that she was telling a thumping lie, in order to conceal something. Probably she thought she was being Bismarckian, but that was an error. Bismarck had said that to tell the truth was a useful trick for a diplomatist, because others would conclude that he was not. But he had never said that telling lies would induce others to think that he was telling the truth.

The days went on, and Georgie began to have qualms as to whether Elizabeth would ever humble herself and implore the boon.

'Time's passing,' he said, as he and Lucia sat one morning in the garden-room. 'What on earth will you do, if she doesn't?'

'She will,' said Lucia, 'though I allow she has held out longer than I expected. I did not know how strong that false pride of hers was. But she's weakening. I've been sitting in the window most of the morning—such a multiplicity of problems to think over—and she has passed the house four times since breakfast. Once she began to cross the road to the front-door, but then she saw me, and walked away again. The sight of me, poor thing, must have made more vivid to her what she had to do. But she'll come to it. Let us discuss something more important. That idea of mine about reviving the fishing industry. The Royal Fish Express. I made a few notes—'

Lucia glanced once more out of the window.

'Georgie,' she cried. 'There's Elizabeth approaching again. That's the fifth time. Round and round like a squirrel in its cage.'

She glided to her ambush behind the curtain, and, peeping stealthily out, became like the reporter of the University boat-race on the wireless.

'She's just opposite, level with the front-door,' she announced. 'She's crossing the road. She's quickening up. She's crossed the road. She's slowing down on the front-door steps. She's raised her hand to the bell. She's dropped it again. She turned half-round—no, I don't think she saw me. Poor woman, what a tussle! Just pride. Georgie, she's rung the bell. Foljambe's opened the door; she must have been dusting the hall. Foljambe's let her in, and has shut the door. She'll be out here in a minute.'

Foljambe entered.

'Mrs Mapp-Flint, ma'am,' she said. 'I told her you were probably engaged, but she much wants to see you for a few moments on a private matter of great importance.'

Lucia sat down in a great hurry, and spread
58

some papers on the table in front of her.

'Go into the garden, will you, Georgie,' she said, 'for she'll never be able to get it out unless we're alone. Yes, Foljambe; tell her I can spare her five minutes.'

CHAPTER THREE

Five minutes later Elizabeth again stood on the doorstep of Mallards, uncertain whether to go home to Grebe by the Vicarage and tell inquisitive Evie the news, or *via* Irene and Diva. She decided on the latter route, unconscious of the vast issues that hung on this apparently trivial choice.

On this warm October morning, quaint Irene (having no garden) was taking the air on a pile of cushions on her doorstep. She had a camera beside her in case of interesting figures passing by, and was making tentative jottings in her sketch-book for her Victorian Venus in a tartan shawl. Irene noticed something peculiarly buoyant about Elizabeth's gait, as she approached, and with her Venus in mind she shouted to her:

'Stand still a moment, Mapp. Stand on one leg in a poised attitude. I want that prancing action. One arm forward if you can manage it without tipping up.'

Elizabeth would have posed for the devil in
59

this triumphant mood.

'Like that, you quaint darling?' she asked.

'Perfect. Hold it for a second while I snap you first.'

Irene focused and snapped.

'Now half a mo' more,' she said, seizing her sketch-book. 'Be on the point of stepping forward again.'

Irene dashed in important lines and curves.

'That'll do,' she said. 'I've got you. I never saw you so lissom and elastic. What's up? Have you been successfully seducing some young lad in the autumn of your life?'

'Oh, you shocking thing,' said Elizabeth. 'Naughty! But I've just been having such a lovely talk with our sweet Lucia. Shall I tell you about it, or shall I tease you?'

'Whichever you like,' said Irene, putting in a little shading. 'I don't care a blow.'

'Then I'll give you a hint. Make a pretty curtsey to the Mayoress.'

'Rubbish,' said Irene.

'No, dear. Not rubbish. Gospel.'

'My God, what an imagination you have,' said Irene. 'How do you *do* it? Does it just come to you like a dream?'

'Gospel, I repeat,' said Elizabeth. 'And such joy, dear, that you should be the first to hear about it, except Mr Georgie.'

Irene looked at her and was forced to believe. Unaffected bliss beamed in Mapp's face; she wasn't pretending to be pleased, she wallowed in a bath of exuberant happiness.

'Good Lord, tell me about it,' she said. 'Bring another cushion, Lucy,' she shouted to her six-foot maid, who was leaning out of the dining-room window, greedily listening.

'Well, dear, it was an utter surprise to me,' said Elizabeth. 'Such a notion had never entered my head. I was just walking up by Mallards: I often stroll by to look at the sweet old home that used to be mine—'

'You can cut all that,' said Irene.

'—and I saw Lucia at the window of the garden-room, looking, oh, so anxious and worn. She slipped behind a curtain and suddenly I felt that she needed me. A sort of presentiment. So I rang the bell—oh, and that was odd, too, for I'd hardly put my finger on it when the door was opened, as if kind Foljambe had been waiting for me—and I asked her if Lucia would like to see me.'

Elizabeth paused for a moment in her embroidery.

'So Foljambe went to ask her,' she continued, 'and came almost running back, and took me out to the garden-room. Lucia was sitting at her table apparently absorbed in some papers. Wasn't that queer, for the moment before she had been peeping out from behind the curtain? I could see she was thoroughly over-wrought and she gave me such an imploring look that I was quite touched.'

61

A wistful smile spread over Elizabeth's face.

'And then it came,' she said. 'I don't blame her for holding back: a sort of pride, I expect, which she couldn't swallow. She begged me to fill the post, and I felt it was my duty to do so. A dreadful tax, I am afraid, on my time and energies, and there will be difficult passages ahead, for she is not always very easy to lead. What Benjy will say to me I don't know, but I must do what I feel to be right. What a blessed thing to be able to help others!'

Irene was holding herself in, trembling slightly with the effort.

Elizabeth continued, still wistfully.

'A lovely little talk,' she said, 'and then there was Mr Georgie in the garden, and he came across the lawn to me with such questioning eyes, for I think he guessed what we had been talking about—'

Irene could contain herself no longer. She gave one maniac scream.

'Mapp, you make me sick,' she cried. 'I believe Lucia has asked you to be Mayoress, poor misguided darling, but it didn't happen like that. It isn't true, Mapp. You've been longing to be Mayoress: you've been losing weight, not a bad thing either, with anxiety. You asked her: you implored her. I am not arguing with you, I am telling you ... Hullo, here they both come. It will be pretty to see their gratitude to you. Don't go, Mapp.'

Elizabeth rose. Dignity prevented her from

making any reply to these gutter-snipe observations. She did it very well. She paused to kiss her hand to the approaching Lucia, and walked away without hurrying. But once round the corner into the High Street, she, like Foljambe, 'almost ran'.

Irene hailed Lucia.

'Come and talk for a minute, darling,' she said. 'First, is it all too true, Mayoress Mapp, I mean? I see it is. You had far better have chosen me or Lucy. And what a liar she is! Thank God I told her so. She told me that you had at last swallowed your pride, and asked her—'

'What?' cried Lucia.

'Just that; and that she felt it was her duty to help you.'

Lucia, though trembling with indignation, was magnificent.

'Poor thing!' she said. 'Like all habitual liars, she deceives herself far more often than she deceives others.'

'But aren't you going to *do* anything?' asked Irene, dancing wild fandangoes on the doorstep. 'Not tell her she's a liar? Or, even better, tell her you never asked her to be Mayoress at all! Why not? There was no one there but you and she.'

'Dear Irene, you wouldn't want me to lower myself to her level?'

'Well, for once it wouldn't be a bad thing. You can become lofty again immediately

63

afterwards. But I'll develop the snap-shot I made of her, and send it to the press as a photograph of our new Mayoress.'

Within an hour the news was stale. But the question of how the offer was made and accepted was still interesting, and fresh coins appeared from Elizabeth's mint: Lucia, it appeared had said 'Beloved friend, I could never have undertaken my duties without your support' or words to that effect, and Georgie had kissed the hand of the Mayoress-Elect. No repudiation of such sensational pieces came from head-quarters and they passed into a sort of doubtful currency. Lucia merely shrugged her shoulders, and said that her position forbade her directly to defend herself. This was thought a little excessive; she was not actually of Royal blood. A brief tranquillity followed, as when a kettle, tumultuously boiling, is put on the hob to cool off, and the *Hampshire Argus* merely stated that Mrs Elizabeth Mapp-Flint (née Mapp) would be Mayoress of Tilling for the ensuing year.

Next week the kettle began to lift its lid again, for in the same paper there appeared a remarkable photograph of the Mayoress. She was standing on one foot, as if skating, with the other poised in the air behind her. Her face wore a beckoning smile, and one arm was stretched out in front of her in eager solicitation. Something seemed bound to happen. It did.

Diva by this time had furnished her tea-room, and was giving dress-rehearsals, serving tea herself to a few friends and then sitting down with them, very hot and thirsty. To-day Georgie and Evie were being entertained, and the Padre was expected. Evie did not know why he was late: he had been out in the parish all day, and she had not seen him since after breakfast.

'Nothing like rehearsals to get things working smoothly,' said Diva, pouring her tea into her saucer and blowing on it. 'There are two jams, Mr Georgie, thick and clear, or is that soup?'

'They're both beautifully clear,' said Georgie politely, 'and such hot, crisp toast.'

'There should have been pastry-fingers as well,' said Diva, 'but they wouldn't rise.'

'Tar'some things,' said Georgie with his mouth full.

'Stuck to the tin and burned,' replied Diva. 'You must imagine them here even for a shilling tea. And cream for eighteen-penny teas with potted meat sandwiches. Choice of China or Indian. Tables for four can be reserved, but not for less ... Ah, here's the Padre. Have a nice cup of tea, Padre, after all those funerals and baptisms.'

'Sorry I'm late, Mistress Plaistow,' said he, 'and I've a bit o' news, and what d'ye think that'll be about? Shall I tease you, as Mistress Mapp-Flint says?'

'You won't tease me,' said Georgie, 'because I know it's about that picture of Elizabeth in the *Hampshire Argus*. And I can tell you at once that Lucia knew nothing about it, whatever Elizabeth may say, till she saw it in the paper. Nothing whatever, except that Irene had taken a snap-shot of her.'

'Well, then, you know nowt o' my news. I was sitting in the club for a bitty, towards noon, when in came Major Benjy, and picked up the copy of the *Hampshire Argus* where was the portrait of his guid wife. I heard a sort o' gobbling turkey-cock noise and there he was, purple in the face, wi' heathen expressions streaming from him like torrents o' spring. Out he rushed with the paper in his hand—club-property, mind you, and not his at all—and I saw him pelting down the road to Grebe.'

'No!' cried Diva.

'Yes, Mistress Plaistow. A bit later as I was doing my parish visiting, I saw the Major again with the famous cane riding-whip in his hand, with which, we've all heard often enough, he hit the Indian tiger in the face while he snatched his gun to shoot him. "No one's going to insult my wife, while I'm above ground," he roared out, and popped into the office o' the *Hampshire Argus*.'

'Gracious! What a crisis!' squeaked Evie.

'And that's but the commencement, mem! The rest I've heard from the new Editor, Mr McConnell, who took over not a week ago. Up

66

came a message to him that Major Mapp-Flint would like to see him at once. He was engaged, but said he'd see the Major in a quarter of an hour, and to pass the time wouldn't the Major have a drink. Sure he would, and sure he'd have another when he'd made short work of the first, and, to judge by the bottle, McConnell guessed he'd had a third, but he couldn't say for certain. Be that as it may, when he was ready to see the Major, either the Major had forgotten what he'd come about, or thought he'd be more prudent not to be so savage, for a big man is McConnell, a very big man indeed, and the Major was most affable, and said he'd just looked in to pay a call on the newcomer.'

'Well, that was a come-down,' ejaculated Georgie.

'And further to come down yet,' said the Padre, 'for they had another drink together, and the poor Major's mind must have got in a fair jumble. He'd come out, ye see, to give the man a thrashing, and instead they'd got very pleasant together, and now he began talking about bygones being bygones. That as yet was Hebrew-Greek to McConnell, for it was the Art-Editor who'd been responsible for the picture of the Mayoress and McConnell had only just glanced at it, thinking there were some queer Mayoresses in Hampshire, and then, oh, dear me, if the Major didn't ask him to step round and have a bit of luncheon with

67

him, and as for the riding-whip it went clean out of his head and he left it in the waiting-room at the office. There was Mistress Elizabeth when they got to Grebe, looking out o' the parlour window and waiting to see her brave Benjy come marching back with the riding-whip shewing a bit of wear and tear, and instead there was the Major with no riding-whip at all, arm in arm with a total stranger saying as how this was his good friend Mr McConnell, whom he'd brought to take pot-luck with them. Dear, oh dear, what wunnerful things happen in Tilling, and I'll have a look at that red conserve.'

'Take it all,' cried Diva. 'And did they have lunch?'

'They did that,' said the Padre, 'though a sorry one it was. It soon came out that Mr McConnell was the Editor of the *Argus*, and then indeed there was a terrifying glint in the lady's eye. He made a hop and a skip of it when the collation was done, leaving the twa together, and he told me about it a' when I met him half an hour ago and 'twas that made me a bit late, for that's the kind of tale ye can't leave in the middle. God knows what'll happen now, and the famous riding-whip somewhere in the newspaper office.'

The door-bell had rung while this epic was being related, but nobody noticed it. Now it was ringing again, a long, uninterrupted tinkle, and Diva rose.

'Shan't be a second,' she said. 'Don't discuss it too much till I get back.'

She hurried out.

'It must be Elizabeth herself,' she thought excitedly. 'Nobody else rings like that. Using up such a lot of current, instead of just dabbing now and then.'

She opened the door. Elizabeth was on the threshold smiling brilliantly. She carried in her hand the historic riding-whip. Quite unmistakable.

'Dear one!' she said. 'May I pop in for a minute. Not seen you for so long.'

Diva overlooked the fact that they had had a nice chat this morning in the High Street, for there was a good chance of hearing more. She abounded in cordiality.

'Do come in,' she said. 'Lovely to see you after all this long time. Tea going on. A few friends.'

Elizabeth sidled into the tea-room: the door was narrow for a big woman.

'Evie dearest! Mr Georgie! Padre!' she saluted. 'How de do everybody. How cosy! Yes, Indian, please, Diva.'

She laid the whip down by the corner of the fireplace. She beamed with geniality. What turn could this humiliating incident have taken, everybody wondered, to make her so jocund and gay? In sheer absorption of constructive thought the Padre helped himself to another dollop of red jam and ate it with his

69

teaspoon. Clearly she had reclaimed the riding-whip from the *Argus* office but what next? Had she administered to Benjy the chastisement he had feared to inflict on another? Meantime, as puzzled eyes sought each other in perplexity, she poured forth compliments.

'What a banquet, Diva!' she exclaimed. 'What a pretty tablecloth! If this is the sort of tea you will offer us when you open, I shan't be found at home often. I suppose you'll charge two shillings at least, and even then you'll be turning people away.'

Diva recalled herself from her speculations.

'No: this will be only a shilling tea,' she said, 'and usually there'll be pastry as well.'

'Fancy! And so beautifully served. So dainty. Lovely flowers on the table. Quite like having tea in the garden with no earwigs ... I had an unexpected guest to lunch to-day.'

Cataleptic rigidity seized the entire company.

'Such a pleasant fellow,' continued Elizabeth. 'Mr McConnell, the new Editor of the *Argus*. Benjy paid a morning call on him at the office and brought him home. He left his tiger-riding-whip there, the forgetful boy, so I went and reclaimed it. Such a big man: Benjy looked like a child beside him.'

Elizabeth sipped her tea. The rigidity persisted.

'I never by any chance see the *Hampshire Argus*,' she said. 'Not set eyes on it for years, for it used to be very dull. All advertisements. But with Mr McConnell at the helm, I must take it in. He seemed so intelligent.'

Imperceptibly the rigidity relaxed, as keen brains dissected the situation ... Elizabeth had sent her husband out to chastise McConnell for publishing this insulting caricature of herself. He had returned, rather tipsy, bringing the victim to lunch. Should the true version of what had happened become current, she would find herself in a very humiliating position with a craven husband and a monstrous travesty unavenged. But her version was brilliant. She was unaware that the *Argus* had contained any caricature of her, and Benjy had brought his friend to lunch. A perfect story, to the truth of which, no doubt, Benjy would perjure himself. Very clever! Bravo Elizabeth!

Of course there was a slight feeling of disappointment, for only a few minutes ago some catastrophic development seemed likely, and Tilling's appetite for social catastrophe was keen. The Padre sighed and began in a resigned voice 'A'weel, all's well that ends well', and Georgie hurried home to tell Lucia what had really happened and how clever Elizabeth had been. She sent fondest love to Worshipful, and as there were now four of them left, they adjourned to Diva's card-room for a rubber of Bridge.

*   *   *

71

Diva's Janet came up to clear tea away, and with her the bouncing Irish terrier, Paddy, who had only got a little eczema. He scouted about the room, licking up crumbs from the floor and found the riding-whip. It was of agreeable texture for the teeth, just about sufficiently tough to make gnawing a pleasure as well as a duty. He picked it up, and, the back-door being open, took it into the wood-shed and dealt with it. He went over it twice, reducing it to a wet and roughly minced sawdust. There was a silver cap on it, which he spurned and when he had triturated or swallowed most of the rest, he rolled in the debris and shook himself. Except for the silver cap, no murderer could have disposed of a corpse with greater skill.

Upstairs the geniality of the tea-table had crumbled over cards. Elizabeth had been losing and she was feeling hot. She said to Diva 'This little room—so cosy—is quite stifling, dear. May we have the window open?' Diva opened it as a deal was in progress, and the cards blew about the table: Elizabeth's remnant consisted of Kings and aces, but a fresh deal was necessary. Diva dropped a card on the floor, face upwards, and put her foot on it so nimbly that nobody could see what it was. She got up to fetch the book of rules to see what ought to happen next, and, moving her foot disclosed an ace. Elizabeth demanded another fresh deal. That was conceded, but it left a friction. Then towards the end of a hand, Elizabeth saw that she had revoked, long, long ago, and detection was awaiting her. 'I'll give you the last trick,' she said, and attempted to jumble up together all the cards. 'Na, na, not so fast, Mistress,' cried the Padre, and he pounced on the card of error. 'Rather like cheating: rather like Elizabeth' was the unspoken comment, and everyone remembered how she had tried the same device about eighteen months ago. The atmosphere grew acid. The Padre and Evie had to hurry off for a choir-practice, for which they were already late, and Elizabeth finding she had not lost as much as she feared lingered for a chat.

'Seen poor Susan Wyse lately?' she asked Diva.

Diva was feeling abrupt. It *was* cheating to try to mix up the cards like that.

'This morning,' she said. 'But why "poor"? You're always calling people "poor". She's all right.'

'Do you think she's got over the budgerigar?' asked Elizabeth.

'Quite. Wearing it to-day. Still raspberry-coloured.'

'I wonder if she has got over it,' mused Elizabeth. 'If you ask me, I think the budgerigar has got over her.'

'Not the foggiest notion what you mean,' said Diva.

'Just what I say. She believes she is getting in

touch with the bird's spirit. She told me so herself. She thinks that she hears that tiresome little squeak it used to make, only she now calls it singing.'

'Singing in the ears, I expect,' interrupted Diva. 'Had it sometimes myself. Wax. Syringe.'

'—and the flutter of its wings,' continued Elizabeth. 'She's trying to get communications from it by automatic script. I hope our dear Susan won't go dotty.'

'Rubbish!' said Diva severely, her thoughts going back again to that revoke. She moved her chair up to the fire, and extinguished Elizabeth by opening the evening paper.

The Mayoress bristled and rose.

'Well, we shall see whether it's rubbish or not,' she said. 'Such a lovely game of Bridge, but I must be off. Where's Benjy's riding-whip?'

'Wherever you happened to put it, I suppose,' said Diva.

Elizabeth looked in the corner by the fireplace.

'That's where I put it,' she said. 'Who can have moved it?'

'You, of course. Probably took it into the card-room.'

'I'm perfectly certain I didn't,' said Elizabeth, hurrying there. 'Where's the switch, Diva?'

'Behind the door.'

'What an inconvenient place to put it. It ought to have been the other side.'

Elizabeth cannoned into the card-table and a heavy fall of cards and markers followed.

'Afraid I've upset something,' she said. 'Ah, I've got it.'

'I said you'd taken it there yourself,' said Diva. 'Pick those things up.'

'No, not the riding-whip; the switch,' she said.

Elizabeth looked in this corner and that, and under tables and chairs, but there was no sign of what she sought. She came out, leaving the light on.

'Not here,' she said. 'Perhaps the Padre has taken it. Or Evie.'

'Better go round and ask them,' said Diva.

'Thank you, dear. Or might I use your telephone? It would save me a walk.'

The call was made, but they were both at choir-practice.

'Or Mr Georgie, do you think?' asked Elizabeth. 'I'll just enquire.'

Now one of Diva's most sacred economies was the telephone. She would always walk a reasonable distance herself to avoid these outlays which, though individually small, mounted up so ruinously.

'If you want to telephone to all Tilling, Elizabeth,' she said, 'you'd better go home and do it from there.'

'Don't worry about that,' said Elizabeth

effusively; 'I'll pay you for the calls now, at once.'

She opened her bag, dropped it, and a shower of coins of low denomination scattered in all directions on the parquet floor.

'Clumsy of me,' she said, pouncing on the bullion. 'Ninepence in coppers, two sixpences and a shilling, but I know there was a threepenny bit. It must have rolled under your pretty sideboard. Might I have a candle, dear?'

'No,' said Diva firmly. 'If there's a threepenny bit, Janet will find it when she sweeps in the morning. You must get along without it till then.'

'There's no "if" about it, dear. There *was* a threepenny bit. I specially noticed it because it was a new one. With your permission I'll ring up Mallards.'

Foljambe answered. No; Mr Georgie had taken his umbrella when he went out to tea, and he couldn't have brought back a riding-whip by mistake ... Would Foljambe kindly make sure by asking him ... He was in his bath ... Then would she just call through the door. Mrs Mapp-Flint would hold the line.

As Elizabeth waited for the answer, humming a little tune, Janet came in with Diva's glass of sherry. She put up two fingers and her eyebrows to enquire whether she should bring two glasses, and Diva shook her head. Presently Georgie came to the telephone himself.

'Wouldn't have bothered you for words, Mr Georgie,' said Elizabeth. 'Foljambe said you were in your bath. She must have made a mistake.'

'I was just going,' said Georgie rather crossly, for the water must be getting cold. 'What is it?'

'Benjy's riding-whip has disappeared most mysteriously, and I can't rest till I trace it. I thought you might possibly have taken it away by mistake.'

'What, the tiger one?' said Georgie, much interested in spite of the draught round his ankles. 'What a disaster. But I haven't got it. What a series of adventures it's had! I saw you bring it into Diva's; I noticed it particularly.'

'Thank you,' said Elizabeth, and rang off.

'And now for the police-station,' said Diva, sipping her delicious sherry. 'That'll be your fourth call.'

'Third, dear,' said Elizabeth, uneasily wondering what Georgie meant by the series of adventures. 'But that would be premature for the present. I must search a little more here, for it must be somewhere. Oh, here's Paddy. Good dog! Come to help Auntie Mayoress to find pretty riding-whip? Seek it, Paddy.'

Paddy, intelligently following Elizabeth's pointing hand, thought it must be a leaf of Diva's evening paper, which she had dropped on the floor, that Auntie Mayoress wanted. He pounced on it, and worried it.

'Paddy, you fool,' cried Diva. 'Drop it at once. Torn to bits and all wet. Entirely your fault, Elizabeth.' She rose, intensely irritated.

'You must give it up for the present,' she said to Elizabeth who was poking about among the logs in the wood-basket. 'All most mysterious, I allow, but it's close on my supper-time, and that interests me more.'

Elizabeth was most reluctant to return to Benjy with the news that she had called for the riding-whip at the office of the *Argus* and had subsequently lost it.

'But it's Benjy's most cherished relic,' she said. 'It was the very riding-whip with which he smacked the tiger over the face, while he picked up his rifle and then shot him.'

'Such a lot of legends aren't there?' said Diva menacingly. 'And if other people get talking there may be one or two more, just as remarkable. And I want my supper.'

Elizabeth paused in her search. This dark saying produced an immediate effect.

'Too bad of me to stop so long,' she said. 'And thanks, dear, for my delicious tea. It would be kind of you if you had another look round.'

Diva saw her off. The disappearance of the riding-whip was really very strange: positively spooky. And though Elizabeth had been a great nuisance, she deserved credit and sympathy for her ingenious version of the awkward incident ... She looked for the pennies which Elizabeth had promised to pay at once for those telephone calls, but there was no trace of them, and all her exasperation returned.

'Just like her,' she muttered. 'That's the sort of thing that really annoys me. So mean!'

It was Janet's evening out, and after eating her supper, Diva returned to the tea-room for a few games of patience. It was growing cold; Janet had forgotten to replenish the wood-basket, and Diva went out to the wood-shed with an electric torch to fetch in a few more logs. Something gleamed in the light, and she picked up a silver cap, which seemed vaguely familiar. A fragment of chewed wood projected from it, and looking more closely she saw engraved on it the initials B. F.

'Golly! It's it,' whispered the awe-struck Diva. 'Benjamin Flint, before he Mapped himself. But why here? And how?'

An idea struck her, and she called Paddy, but Paddy had no doubt gone out with Janet. Forgetting about fresh logs but with this relic in her hand, Diva returned to her room, and warmed herself with intellectual speculation.

Somebody had disposed of all the riding-whip except this metallic fragment. By process of elimination (for she acquitted Janet of having eaten it), it must be Paddy. Should she ring up Elizabeth and say that the riding-whip had been found? That would not be true, for all that had been found was a piece of overwhelming evidence that it never would be found. Besides, who could tell what Elizabeth had said to Benjy by this time? Possibly (even probably, considering what Elizabeth was) she would not tell him that she had retrieved it from the office of the *Argus*, and thus escape his just censure for having lost it.

'I believe,' thought Diva, 'that it might save developments which nobody can foresee, if I said nothing about it to anybody. Nobody knows except Paddy and me. *Silentio*, as Lucia says, when she's gabbling fit to talk your head off. Let them settle it between themselves, but nobody shall suspect *me* of having had anything to do with it. I'll bury it in the garden before Janet comes back. Rather glad Paddy ate it. I was tired of Major Benjy showing me the whip, and telling me about it over and over again. Couldn't be true, either. I'm killing a lie.'

With the help of a torch and a trowel Diva put the relic beyond reasonable risk of discovery. This was only just done when Janet returned with Paddy.

'Been strolling in the garden,' said Diva with chattering teeth. 'Such a mild night. Dear Paddy! Such a clever dog.'

*　　　*　　　*

Elizabeth pondered over the mystery as she walked briskly home, and when she came to discuss it with Benjy after dinner they presently became very friendly. She reminded him that he had behaved like a poltroon this morning, and, like a loyal wife, she had shielded him from exposure by her ingenious explanations. She disclosed that she had retrieved the riding-whip from the *Argus* office, but had subsequently lost it at Diva's tea-rooms. A great pity, but it still might turn up. What they must fix firmly in their minds was that Benjy had gone to the office of the *Argus* merely to pay a polite call on Mr McConnell, and that Elizabeth had never seen the monstrous caricature of herself in that paper.

'That's settled then,' she said, 'and it's far the most dignified course we can take. And I've been thinking about more important things than these paltry affairs. There's an election to the Town Council next month. One vacancy. I shall stand.'

'Not very wise, Liz,' he said. 'You tried that once, and came in at the bottom of the poll.'

'I know that. Lucia and I polled exactly the same number of votes. But times have changed now. She's Mayor and I'm Mayoress. It's of her I'm thinking. I shall be much more assistance to her as a Councillor. I shall be a support to her at the meetings.'

'Very thoughtful of you,' said Benjy. 'Does she see it like that?'

'I've not told her yet. I shall be firm in any case. Well, it's bedtime; such an exciting day!

Dear me, if I didn't forget to pay Diva for a few telephone calls I made from her house. Dear Diva, and her precious economies!'

And in Diva's back garden, soon to tarnish by contact with the loamy soil, there lay buried, like an unspent shell with all its explosive potentialities intact, the silver cap of the vanished relic.

* * *

Mayoring day arrived and Lucia, formally elected by the Town Council, assumed her scarlet robes. She swept them a beautiful curtsey and said she was their servant. She made a touching allusion to her dear friend the Mayoress, whose loyal and loving support would alone render her own immense responsibilities a joy to shoulder, and Elizabeth, wreathed in smiles, dabbed her handkerchief on the exact piece of her face where tears, had there been any, would have bedewed it. The Mayor then entertained a large party to lunch at the King's Arms Hotel, preceding them in state while church bells rang, dogs barked, cameras clicked, and the sun gleamed on the massive maces borne before her. There were cheers for Lucia led by the late Mayor and cheers for the Mayoress led by her present husband.

In the afternoon Lucia inaugurated Diva's tea-shop, incognita as Mrs Pillson. The populace of Tilling was not quite so thrilled as she had expected at the prospect of taking its tea in the same room as the Mayor, and no one saw her drink the first cup of tea except Georgie and Diva, who kept running to the window on the look-out for customers. Seeing Susan in her Royce, she tapped on the pane, and got her to come in so that they could inaugurate the card-room with a rubber of Bridge. Then suddenly a torrent of folk invaded the tea-room and Diva had to leave an unfinished hand to help Janet to serve them.

'Wish they'd come sooner,' she said, 'to see the ceremony. Do wait a bit; if they ease off we can finish our game.'

She hurried away. A few minutes afterwards she opened the door and said in a thrilling whisper, 'Fourteen shilling ones, and two eighteen-penny's.'

'Splendid!' said everybody, and Susan began telling them about her automatic script.

'I sit there with my eyes shut and my pencil in my hand,' she said, 'and Blue Birdie on the table by me. I get a sort of lost feeling, and then Blue Birdie seems to say "Tweet, tweet", and I say "Good morning, dear". Then my pencil begins to move. I never know what it writes. A queer, scrawling hand, not a bit like mine.'

The door opened and Diva's face beamed redly.

'Still twelve shilling ones,' she said, 'though six of the first lot have gone. Two more

83

eighteen-penny, but the cream is getting low, and Janet's had to add milk.'

'Where had I got to?' said Susan. 'Oh, yes. It goes on writing till Blue Birdie seems to say "Tweet, tweet" again, and that means it's finished and I say "Good-bye, dear".'

'What sort of things does it write?' asked Lucia.

'All sorts. This morning it kept writing *mère* over and over again.'

'That's very strange,' said Lucia eagerly. 'Very. I expect Blue Birdie wants to say something to me.'

'No,' said Susan. 'Not your sort of Mayor. The French word *mère*, just as if Blue Birdie said "Mummie". Speaking to me evidently.'

This did not seem to interest Lucia.

'And anything of value?' she asked.

'It's all of value,' said Susan.

A slight crash sounded from the tea-room.

'Only a tea-cup,' said Diva, looking in again. 'Rather like breaking a bottle of wine when you launch a ship.'

'Would you like me to show myself for a minute?' asked Lucia. 'I will gladly walk through the room if it would help.'

'So good of you, but I don't want any help except in handling things. Besides, I told the reporter of the *Argus* that you had had your tea, and were playing cards in here.'

'Oh, not quite wise, Diva,' said Lucia. 'Tell him I wasn't playing for money. Think of the

84

example.'

'Afraid he's gone,' said Diva. 'Besides, it wouldn't be true. Two of your Councillors here just now. Shillings. Didn't charge them. Advertisement.'

The press of customers eased off, and, leaving Janet to deal with the remainder, Diva joined them, clinking a bag of bullion.

'Lots of tips,' she said. 'I never reckoned on that. Mostly twopences, but they'll add up. I must just count the takings, and then let's finish the rubber.'

The takings exceeded all expectation; quite a pile of silver; a pyramid of copper.

'What will you do with all that money now the banks are closed?' asked Georgie lightly. 'Such a sum to have in the house. I should bury it in the garden.'

Diva's hand gave an involuntary twitch as she swept the coppers into a bag. Odd that he should say that!

'Safe enough,' she replied. 'Paddy sleeps in my room, now that I know he hasn't got mange.'

*   *   *

The Mayoral banquet followed in the evening. Unfortunately, neither the Lord Lieutenant nor the Bishop nor the Member of Parliament were able to attend, but they sent charming letters of regret, which Lucia read before her

Chaplain, the Padre, said Grace. She wore her Mayoral chain of office round her neck, and her chain of inherited seed-pearls in her hair, and Georgie, as arranged, sat alone on the other side of the table directly opposite her. He was disadvantageously placed with regard to supplies of food and drink, for the waiter had to go round the far end of the side-tables to get at him, but he took extra large helpings when he got the chance, and had all his wine-glasses filled. He wore on the lapel of his coat a fine green and white enamel star, which had long lain among his bibelots, and which looked like a foreign order. At the far end of the room was a gallery, from which ladies, as if in purdah, were allowed to look on. Elizabeth sat in the front row, and waggled her hand at the Mayor, whenever Lucia looked in her direction, in order to encourage her. Once, when a waiter was standing just behind Lucia, Elizabeth felt sure that she had caught her eye, and kissed her hand to her. The waiter promptly responded, and the Mayoress, blushing prettily, ceased to signal ... There were flowery speeches made and healths drunk, and afterwards a musical entertainment. The Mayor created a precedent by contributing to this herself and giving (as the *Hampshire Argus* recorded in its next issue) an exquisite rendering on the piano of the slow movement of Beethoven's Moonlight Sonata. It produced a somewhat pensive effect, and she went back to her presiding place again amid respectful applause and a shrill, solitary cry of 'Encore!' from Elizabeth. The spirits of her guests revived under the spell of lighter melodies, and at the end Auld Lang Syne was sung with crossed hands by all the company, with the exception of Georgie, who had no neighbours. Lucia swept regal curtsies to right and left, and a loop of the seed-pearls in her hair got loose and oscillated in front of her face.

The Mayor and her Prince Consort drove back to Mallards, Lucia strung up to the highest pitch of triumph, Georgie intensely fatigued. She put him through a catechism of self-glorification in the garden-room.

'I think I gave them a good dinner,' she said. 'And the wine was excellent, wasn't it?'

'Admirable,' said Georgie.

'And my speech. Not too long?'

'Not a bit. Exactly right.'

'I thought they drank my health very warmly. *Non e vero?*'

'Very. *Molto,*' said Georgie.

Lucia struck a chord on the piano before she closed it.

'Did I take the Moonlight a little too quick?' she asked.

'No. I never heard you play it better.'

'I felt the enthusiasm tingling round me,' she said. 'In the days of horse-drawn vehicles, I am sure they would have taken my horses out of the shafts and pulled us up home. But impossible with a motor.'

Georgie yawned.

'They might have taken out the carburetter,' he said wearily.

She glanced at some papers on her table.

'I must be up early to-morrow,' she said, 'to be ready for Mrs Simpson ... A new era, Georgie. I seem to see a new era for our dear Tilling.'

CHAPTER FOUR

Lucia did not find her new duties quite as onerous as she expected, but she made them as onerous as she could. She pored over plans for new houses which the Corporation was building, and having once grasped the difference between section and elevation was full of ideas for tasteful weathercocks, lightning conductors and balconies. With her previous experience in Stock Exchange transactions to help her, she went deeply into questions of finance and hit on a scheme of borrowing money at three and a half per cent for a heavy outlay for the renewal of drains, and investing it in some thoroughly sound concern that brought in four and a half per cent. She explained this masterpiece to Georgie.

'Say we borrow ten thousand pounds at three and a half,' she said, 'the interest on that will be three hundred and fifty pounds a year. We invest it, Georgie,—follow me closely here—at four and a half, and it brings us in four hundred and fifty pounds a year. A clear gain of one hundred pounds.'

'That does seem brilliant,' said Georgie. 'But wait a moment. If you re-invest what you borrow, how do you pay for the work on your drains?'

Lucia's face grew corrugated with thought.

'I see what you're driving at, Georgie,' she said slowly. 'Very acute of you. I must consider that further before I bring my scheme before the Finance Committee. But in my belief—of course this is strictly private—the work on the drains is not so very urgent. We might put it off for six months, and in the meantime reap our larger dividends. I'm sure there's something to be done on those lines.'

*　　　*　　　*

Then with a view to investigating the lighting of the streets, she took Georgie out for walks after dinner on dark and even rainy evenings.

'This corner now,' she said as the rain poured down on her umbrella. 'A most insufficient illumination. I should never forgive myself if some elderly person tripped up here in the dark and stunned himself. He might remain undiscovered for hours.'

'Quite,' said Georgie, 'But this is very cold-catching. Let's get home. No elderly person will come out on such a night. Madness.'

'It is a little wet,' said Lucia, who never caught cold. 'I'll go to look at that alley by Bumpus's buildings another night, for there's a memorandum on Town Development plans waiting for me, which I haven't mastered. Something about residential zones and industrial zones, Georgie. I mustn't permit a manufactory to be opened in a residential zone: for instance, I could never set up a brewery or a blacksmith's forge in the garden at Mallards—'

'Well, you don't want to, do you?' said Georgie.

'The principle, dear, is the interesting thing. At first sight it looks rather like a curtailment of the liberty of the individual, but if you look, as I am learning to do, below the surface, you will perceive that a blacksmith's forge in the middle of the lawn would detract from the tranquillity of adjoining residences. It would injure their amenities.'

Georgie plodded beside her, wishing Lucia was not so excruciatingly didactic, but trying between sneezes to be a good husband to the Mayor.

'And mayn't you reside in an industrial zone?' he asked.

'That I must look into. I should myself certainly permit a shoe-maker to live above his shop. Then there's the general business zone. I

90

trust that Diva's tea-rooms in the High Street are in order: it would be sad for her if I had to tell her to close them ... Ah, our comfortable garden-room again! You were asking just now about residence in an industrial zone. I think I have some papers here which will tell you that. And there's a coloured map of zones somewhere, green for industrial, blue for residential and yellow for general business, which would fascinate you. Where is it now?'

'Don't bother about it to-night,' said Georgie. 'I can easily wait till to-morrow. What about some music? There's that Scarlatti duet.'

'*Ah, divino Scarlattino!*' said Lucia absently, as she turned over her papers. 'Eureka! Here it is! No, that's about slums, but also very interesting ... What's a "messuage"?'

'Probably a misprint for message,' said he. 'Or massage.'

'No, neither makes sense: I must put a query to that.'

Georgie sat down at the piano, and played a few fragments of remembered tunes. Lucia continued reading: it was rather difficult to understand, and the noise distracted her.

'Delicious tunes,' she said, 'but would it be very selfish of me, dear, to ask you to stop while I'm tackling this? So important that I should have it at my fingers' ends before the next meeting, and be able to explain it. Ah, I see ... no, that's green. Industrial. But in half an hour

91

or so—'

Georgie closed the piano.

'I think I shall go to bed,' he said. 'I may have caught cold.'

'Ah, now I see,' cried Lucia triumphantly. 'You can reside in any zone. That is only fair: why should a chemist in the High Street be forced to live half a mile away? And very clearly put. I could not have expressed it better myself. Good-night, dear. A few drops of camphor on a lump of sugar. Sleep well.'

* * *

The Mayoress was as zealous as the Mayor. She rang Lucia up at breakfast time every morning, and wished to speak to her personally.

'Anything I can do for you, dear Worship?' she asked. 'Always at your service, as I needn't remind you.'

'Nothing whatever, thanks,' answered Lucia. 'I've a Council meeting this afternoon—'

'No points you'd like to talk over with me? Sure?'

'Quite,' said Lucia firmly.

'There are one or two bits of things I should like to bring to your notice,' said the baffled Elizabeth, 'for of course you can't keep in touch with everything. I'll pop in at one for a few minutes and chance finding you

92

disengaged. And a bit of news.'

Lucia went back to her congealed bacon.

'She's got quite a wrong notion of the duties of a Mayoress, Georgie,' she said. 'I wish she would understand that if I want her help I shall ask for it. She has nothing to do with my official duties, and as she's not on the Town Council, she can't dip her oar very deep.'

'She's hoping to run you,' said Georgie. 'She hopes to have her finger in every pie. She will if she can.'

'I have got to be very tactful,' said Lucia thoughtfully. 'You see the only object of my making her Mayoress was to dope her malignant propensities, and if I deal with her too rigorously I should merely stimulate them ... Ah, we must begin our régime of plain living. Let us go and do our marketing at once, and then I can study the *agenda* for this afternoon before Elizabeth arrives.'

Elizabeth had some assorted jobs for Worship to attend to. Worship ought to know that a car had come roaring down the hill into Tilling yesterday at so terrific a pace that she hadn't time to see the number. A van and Susan's Royce had caused a complete stoppage of traffic in the High Street; anyone with only a few minutes to spare to catch a train must have missed it. 'And far worse was a dog that howled all last night outside the house next Grebe,' said Elizabeth. 'Couldn't sleep a wink.'

'But I can't stop it,' said Lucia.

93

'No? I should have thought some threatening notice might be served on the owner. Or shall I write a letter to the *Argus*, which we both might sign. More weight. Or I would write a personal note to you which you might read to the Council. Whichever you like, Worship. You to choose.'

Lucia did not find any of these alternatives attractive, but made a business-like note of them all.

'Most valuable suggestions,' she said. 'But I don't feel that I could move officially about the dog. It might be a cat next, or a canary.'

Elizabeth was gazing out of the window with that kind, meditative smile which so often betokened some atrocious train of thought.

'Just little efforts of mine, dear Worship, to enlarge your sphere of influence,' she said. 'Soon, perhaps, I may be able to support you more directly.'

Lucia felt a qualm of sickening apprehension.

'That would be lovely,' she said. 'But how, dear Elizabeth, could you do more than you are doing?'

Elizabeth focused her kind smile on dear Worship's face. A close up.

'Guess, dear!' she said.

'Couldn't,' said Lucia.

'Well, then, there's a vacancy in the Borough Council, and I'm standing for it. Oh, if I got in! At hand to support you in all your Council meetings. You and me! Just think!'

Lucia made one desperate attempt to avert this appalling prospect, and began to gabble.

'That would be wonderful,' she said, 'and how well I know that it's your devotion to me that prompts you. How I value that! But somehow it seems to me that your influence, your tremendous influence, would be lessened rather than the reverse, if you became just one out of my twelve Councillors. Your unique position as Mayoress would suffer. Tilling would think of you as one of a body. You, my right hand, would lose your independence. And then, unlikely, even impossible as it sounds, supposing you were not elected? A ruinous loss of prestige—'

Foljambe entered.

'Lunch,' she said, and left the door of the garden-room wide open.

Elizabeth sprang up with a shrill cry of astonishment.

'No idea it was lunch-time,' she cried. 'How naughty of me not to have kept my eye on the clock, but time passed so quickly, as it always does, dear, when I'm talking to you. But you haven't convinced me; far from it. I must fly; Benjy will call me a naughty girl for being so late.'

Lucia remembered that the era of plain living had begun. Hashed mutton and treacle pudding. Perhaps Elizabeth might go away if she knew that. On the other hand, Elizabeth

95

had certainly come here at one o'clock in order to be asked to lunch, and it would be wiser to ask her.

'Ring him up and say you're lunching here,' she decided. 'Do.'

Elizabeth recollected that she had ordered hashed beef and marmalade pudding at home.

'I consider that a command, dear Worship,' she said. 'May I use your telephone?'

* * *

All these afflictions strongly reacted on Georgie. Mutton and Mapp and incessant conversation about municipal affairs were making home far less comfortable than he had a right to expect. Then Lucia sprang another conscientious surprise on him, when she returned that afternoon positively invigorated by a long Council meeting.

'I want to consult you, Georgie,' she said. 'Ever since the *Hampshire Argus* reported that I played Bridge in Diva's card-room, the whole question has been on my mind. I don't think I ought to play for money.'

'You can't call threepence a hundred money,' said Georgie.

'It is not a large sum, but emphatically it *is* money. It's the principle of the thing. A very sad case—all this is very private—has just come to my notice. Young Twistevant, the grocer's son, has been backing horses, and is in debt with his last quarter's rent unpaid. Lately married and a baby coming. All the result of gambling.'

'I don't see how the baby is the result of gambling,' said Georgie. 'Unless he bet he wouldn't have one.'

Lucia gave the wintry smile that was reserved for jokes she didn't care about.

'I expressed myself badly,' she said. 'I only meant that his want of money, when he will need it more than ever, is the result of gambling. The principle is the same whether it's threepence or a starving baby. And Bridge surely, with its call both on prudence and enterprise, is a sufficiently good game to play for love: for love of Bridge. Let us set an example. When we have our next Bridge party, let it be understood that there are no stakes.'

'I don't think you'll get many Bridge parties if that's understood,' said Georgie. 'Everyone will go seven no trumps at once.'

'Then they'll be doubled,' cried Lucia triumphantly.

'And redoubled. It wouldn't be any fun. Most monotonous. The dealer might as well pick up his hand and say Seven no-trumps, doubled and redoubled, before he looked at it.'

'I hope we take a more intelligent interest in the game than *that*,' said Lucia. 'The judgment in declaring, the skill in the play of the cards, the various systems so carefully thought out—surely we shan't cease to practise them just because a few pence are no longer at stake? Indeed, I think we shall have far pleasanter games. They will be more tranquil, and on a loftier level. The question of even a few pence sometimes produces acrimony.'

'I can't agree,' said Georgie. 'Those acrimonies are the result of pleasant excitement. And what's the use of keeping the score, and wondering if you dare finesse, if it leads to nothing? You might try playing for twopence a hundred instead of threepence—'

'I must repeat that it's the principle,' interrupted Lucia. 'I feel that in my position it ought to be known that though I play cards, which I regard as quite a reasonable relaxation, I no longer play for money. I feel sure we should find it just as exciting. Let us put it to the test. I will ask the Padre and Evie to dine and play to-morrow, and we'll see how it goes.'

It didn't go. Lucia made the depressing announcement during dinner, and a gloom fell on the party as they cut for partners. For brief bright moments one or other of them forgot that there was nothing to be gained by astuteness except the consciousness of having been clever, but then he (or she) remembered, and the gleam faded. Only Lucia remained keen and critical. She tried with agonised anxiety to recollect if there was another trump in and decided wrong.

'Too stupid of me, Padre,' she said. 'I ought to have known. I should have drawn it, and

98

then we made our contract. Quite inexcusable. Many apologies.'

'Eh, it's no matter; it's no matter whatever,' he said. 'Just nothing at all.'

Then came the adding-up. Georgie had not kept the score and everyone accepted Lucia's addition without a murmur. At half-past ten instead of eleven, it was agreed that it was wiser not to begin another rubber, and Georgie saw the languid guests to the door. He came back to find Lucia replaying the last hand.

'You could have got another trick, dear,' she said. 'Look; you should have discarded instead of trumping. A most interesting manoeuvre. As to our test, I think they were both quite as keen as ever, and for myself I never had a more enjoyable game.'

*   *   *

The news of this depressing evening spread apace through Tilling, and a small party assembled next day at Diva's for shilling teas and discussions.

'I winna play for nowt,' said the Padre. 'Such a mirthless evening I never spent. And by no means a well-furnished table at dinner. An unusual parsimony.'

Elizabeth chimed in.

'I got hashed mutton and treacle pudding for lunch a few days ago,' she said. 'Just what I should have had at home except that it was beef and marmalade.'

'Perhaps you happened to look in a few minutes before unexpectedly,' suggested Diva who was handing crumpets.

There was a nasty sort of innuendo about this.

'I haven't got any cream, dear,' retorted Elizabeth. 'Would you kindly—'

'It'll be an eighteen-penny tea then,' Diva warned her, 'though you'll get potted meat sandwiches as well. Shall it be eighteen-pence?'

Elizabeth ignored the suggestion.

'As for playing Bridge for nothing,' she resumed, 'I won't. I've never played it before, and I'm too old to learn now. Dear Worship, of course, may do as she likes, so long as she doesn't do it with me.'

Diva finished her serving and sat down with her customers. Janet brought her cream and potted-meat sandwiches, for of course she could eat what she liked, without choosing between a shilling and an eighteen-penny tea.

'Makes it all so awkward,' she said. 'If one of us gives a Bridge-party, must the table at which Lucia plays do it for nothing?'

'The other table, too, I expect,' said Elizabeth bitterly, watching Diva pouring quantities of cream into her tea. 'Worship mightn't like to know that gambling was going on in her presence.'

'That I won't submit to,' cried Evie. 'I won't, I won't. She may be Mayor but she isn't

100

Mussolini.'

'I see nought for it,' said the Padre, 'but not to ask her. I play my Bridge for diversion and it doesna' divert me to exert my mind over the cards and not a bawbee or the loss if it to show for all my trouble.'

Other customers came in; the room filled up and Diva had to get busy again. The office boy from the *Hampshire Argus* and a friend had a good blow-out, and ate an entire pot of jam, which left little profit on their teas. On the other hand, Evie and the Padre and Elizabeth were so concerned about the Bridge crisis that they hardly ate anything. Diva presented them with their bills, and they each gave her a tip of twopence, which was quite decent for a shilling tea, but the office boy and his friend, in the bliss of repletion, gave her threepence. Diva thanked them warmly.

Evie and the Padre continued the subject on the way home.

'Such hard luck on Mr Georgie,' she said. 'He's as bored as anybody with playing for love. I saw him yawn six times the other night and he never added up. I think I'll ask him to a Bridge-tea at Diva's, just to see if he'll come without Lucia. Diva would be glad to play with us afterwards, but it would never do to ask her to tea first.'

'How's that?' asked the Padre.

'Why she would be making a profit by being our guest. And how could we tip her for four teas, when she had had one of them herself? Very awkward for her.'

'A'weel, then let her get her own tea,' said the Padre, 'though I don't think she's as delicate of feeling as all that. But ask the puir laddie by all means.'

Georgie was duly rung up and a slightly embarrassing moment followed. Evie thought she had said with sufficient emphasis 'So pleased if *you* will come to Diva's tomorrow for tea and Bridge,' but he asked her to hold on while he saw if Lucia was free. Then Evie had to explain it didn't matter whether Lucia was free or not, and Georgie accepted.

'I felt sure it would happen,' he said to himself, 'but I think I shan't tell Lucia. Very likely she'll be busy.'

Vain was the hope of man. As they were moderately enjoying their frugal lunch next day, Lucia congratulated herself on having a free afternoon.

'Positively nothing to do,' she said. 'Not a committee to attend, nothing. Let us have one of our good walks, and pop in to have tea with Diva afterwards. I want to encourage her enterprise.'

'A walk would be lovely,' said Georgie, 'but Evie asked me to have tea at Diva's and play a rubber afterwards.'

'I don't remember her asking me,' said Lucia. 'Does she expect me?'

'I rather think Diva's making our fourth,'

faltered Georgie.

Lucia expressed strong approval.

'A very sensible innovation,' she said. 'I remember telling you that it struck me as rather *bourgeois*, rather Victorian, always to have husbands and wives together. No doubt also, dear Evie felt sure I should be busy up till dinner-time. Really very considerate of her, not to give me the pain of refusing. How I shall enjoy a quiet hour with a book.'

'She doesn't like it at all the same,' thought Georgie, as, rather fatigued with a six mile tramp in a thick sea mist, he tripped down the hill to Diva's, 'and I shouldn't wonder if she guessed the reason...' The tea-room was crowded, so that Diva could not have had tea with them even if she had been asked. She presented the bill to Evie herself (three eighteen-penny teas) and received the generous tip of fourpence a head.

'Thank you, dear Evie,' she said pocketing the extra shilling. 'I do call that handsome. I'll join you in the card-room as soon as ever I can.'

They had most exciting games at the usual stakes. It was impossible to leave the last rubber unfinished, and Georgie had to hurry over his dressing not to keep Lucia waiting. Her eye had that gimlet-like aspect, which betokened a thirst for knowledge.

'A good tea and a pleasant rubber?' she asked.

'Both,' said Georgie. 'I enjoyed myself.'

'So glad. And many people having tea?'

'Crammed. Diva couldn't join us till close on six.'

'How pleasant for Diva. And did you play for stakes, dear, or for nothing?'

'Stakes,' said Georgie. 'The usual threepence.'

'Georgie, I'm going to ask a favour of you,' she said. 'I want you to set an example—poor young Twistevant, you know—I want it to be widely known that I do not play cards for money. You diminish the force of my example, dear, if you continue to do so. The lime-light is partially, at any rate, on you as well as me. I ask you not to.'

'I'm afraid I can't consent,' said Georgie. 'I don't see any harm in it—Naturally you will do as you like—'

'Thank you, dear,' said Lucia.

'No need to thank me. And I shall do as I like.'

Grosvenor entered.

'*Silentio!*' whispered Lucia. 'Yes, Grosvenor?'

'Mrs Mapp-Flint has rung up'—began Grosvenor.

'Tell her I can't attend to any business this evening,' said Lucia.

'She doesn't want you to, ma'am. She only wants to know if Mr Pillson will dine with her the day after to-morrow and play Bridge.'

'Thank her,' said Georgie firmly. 'Delighted.'

* * *

Card-playing circles in Tilling remained firm: there was no slump. If, in view of her exemplary position, Worship declined to play Bridge for money, far be it from us, said Tilling, to seek to persuade her against the light of conscience. But if Worship imagined that Tilling intended to follow her example, the sooner she got rid of that fond illusion the better. Lucia sent out invitations for another Bridge party at Mallards but everybody was engaged. She could not miss the significance of that, but she put up a proud front and sent for the latest book on Bridge and studied it incessantly, almost to the neglect of her Mayoral Duties, in order to prove that what she cared for was the game in itself. Her grasp of it, she declared, improved out of all knowledge, but she got no opportunities of demonstrating that agreeable fact. Invitations rained on Georgie, for it was clearly unfair that he should get no Bridge because nobody would play with the Mayor, and he returned these hospitalities by asking his friends to have tea with him at Diva's rooms, with a rubber afterwards, for he could not ask three gamblers to dinner and leave Lucia to study Bridge problems by herself, while the rest of the party played. Other entertainers followed his example, for it was far less trouble to order tea at Diva's and find the card-room ready, and as Algernon Wyse expressed it, 'ye olde tea-house' became quite like Almack's. This was good business for the establishment, and Diva bitterly regretted that it had not occurred to her from the first to charge card-money. She put the question one day to Elizabeth.

'All those markers being used up so fast,' she said, 'and I shall have to get new cards so much oftener than I expected. Twopence, say, for card-money, don't you think?'

'I shouldn't dream of it, dear,' said Elizabeth very decidedly. 'You must be doing very well as it is. But I should recommend some fresh packs of cards. A little greasy, when last I played. More daintiness, clean cards, sharp pencils and so on are well worth while. But card-money, no!'

*　　　*　　　*

The approach of the election to the vacancy on the Town Council diverted the Mayor's mind from her abstract study of Bridge. Up to within a few days of the date on which candidates' names must be sent in, Elizabeth was still the only aspirant. Lucia found herself faced by the prospect of her Mayoress being inevitably elected, and the thought of that filled her with the gloomiest apprehensions. She wondered if

106

Georgie could be induced to stand. It was his morning for cleaning his *bibelots*, and she went up to his room with offers of help.

'I so often wish, dear,' she said pensively, attacking a snuff-box, 'that you were more closely connected with me in my municipal work. And such an opportunity offers itself just now.'

'Do be careful with that snuff-box,' said he. 'Don't rub it hard. What's this opportunity?'

'The Town Council. There's a vacancy very soon. I'm convinced, dear, that with a little training, such as I could give you, you would make a marvellous Councillor, and you would find the work most absorbing.'

'I think it would bore me stiff,' he said. 'I'm no good at slums and drains.'

Lucia decided to disclose herself.

'Georgie, it's to help me,' she said. 'Elizabeth at present is the only candidate, and the idea of having her on the Council is intolerable. And with the prestige of your being my husband I don't doubt the result. Just a few days of canvassing; you with your keen interest in human nature will revel in it. It is a duty, it seems to me, that you owe to yourself. You would have an official position in the town. I have long felt it an anomaly that the Mayor's husband had none.'

Georgie considered. He had before now thought it would be pleasant to walk in Mayoral processions in a purple gown. And bored though he was with Lucia's municipal gabble, it would be different when, with the weight of his position to back him, he could say that he totally disagreed with her on some matter of policy, and perhaps defeat some project of hers at a Council Meeting. Also, it would be a pleasure to defeat Elizabeth at the poll...

'Well, if you'll help me with the canvassing—' he began.

'Ah, if I only could!' she said. 'But, dear, my position precludes me from taking any active part. It is analogous to that of the King, who, officially, is outside politics. The fact that you are my husband—what a blessed day was that when our lives were joined—will carry immense weight. Everyone will know that your candidature has my full approval. I shouldn't wonder if Elizabeth withdrew when she learns you are standing against her.'

'Oh, very well,' said he. 'But you must coach me on what my programme is to be.'

'Thank you, dear, a thousand times! You must send in your name at once. Mrs Simpson will get you a form to fill up.'

Several horrid days ensued and Georgie wended his dripping way from house to house in the most atrocious weather. His ticket was better housing for the poorer classes, and he called at rows of depressing dwellings, promising to devote his best energies to procuring the tenants bath-rooms, plumbing, bicycle-sheds and open spaces for their children to play in. A disagreeable sense oppressed him that the mothers, whose household jobs he was interrupting, were much bored with his visits, and took very little interest in his protestations. In reward for these distasteful exertions Lucia relaxed the Spartan commissariat—indeed, she disliked it very much herself and occasionally wondered if her example was being either followed or respected—and she gave him Lucullan lunches and dinners. Elizabeth, of course, at once got wind of his candidature and canvassing, but instead of withdrawing, she started a hurricane campaign of her own. Her ticket was the reduction of rates, instead of this rise in them which these idiotic schemes for useless luxuries would inevitably produce.

The result of the election was to be announced by the Mayor from the steps of the Town Hall. Owing to the howling gale, and the torrents of rain the street outside was absolutely empty save for the figure of Major Benjy clad in a sou'wester hat, a mackintosh and waders, crouching in the most sheltered corner he could find beneath a dripping umbrella. Elizabeth had had hard work to induce him to come at all: he professed himself perfectly content to curb his suspense in comfort at home by the fire till she returned with the news, and all the other inhabitants of Tilling felt they could wait till next morning ...

Then Lucia emerged from the Town Hall with a candidate on each side of her, and in a piercing scream, to make her voice heard in this din of the elements, she announced the appalling figures. Mrs Elizabeth Mapp-Flint, she yelled, had polled eight hundred and five votes, and was therefore elected.

Major Benjy uttered a hoarse 'Hurrah!' and trying to clap his hands let go of his umbrella which soared into the gale and was seen no more ... Mr George Pillson, screamed Lucia, had polled four hundred and twenty-one votes. Elizabeth, at the top of her voice, then warmly thanked the burgesses of Tilling for the confidence which they had placed in her, and which she would do her best to deserve. She shook hands with the Mayor and the defeated candidate, and instantly drove away with her husband. As there were no other burgesses to address Georgie did not deliver the speech which he had prepared: indeed it would have been quite unsuitable, since he had intended to thank the burgesses of Tilling in similar terms. He and Lucia scurried to their car, and Georgie put up the window.

'Most mortifying,' he said.

'My dear, you did your best,' said Lucia, pressing his arm with a wet but sympathetic hand. 'In public life, one has to take these little reverses—'

'Most humiliating,' interrupted Georgie. 'All that trouble thrown away. Being triumphed over by Elizabeth when you led me to expect quite the opposite. She'll be far more swanky now than if I hadn't put up.'

'No, Georgie, there I can't agree,' said Lucia. 'If there had been no other candidate, she would have said that nobody felt he had the slightest chance against her. That would have been much worse. Anyhow she knows now that four hundred and—what was the figure?'

'Four hundred and twenty-one,' said Georgie.

'Yes, four hundred and twenty-one thoughtful voters in Tilling—'

'—against eight hundred and five thoughtless ones,' said Georgie. 'Don't let's talk any more about it. It's a loss of prestige for both of us. No getting out of it.'

Lucia hurried indoors to tell Grosvenor to bring up a bottle of champagne for dinner, and to put on to the fire the pretty wreath of laurel leaves which she had privily stitched together for the coronation of her new Town Councillor.

'What's that nasty smell of burning evergreen?' asked Georgie morosely, as they went into the dining-room.

*　　*　　*

In the opinion of friends the loss of prestige had been entirely Lucia's. Georgie would never have stood for the Council unless she had urged him, and it was a nasty defeat which, it was hoped, might do the Mayor good. But the Mayoress's victory, it was feared, would have the worst effect on her character. She and Diva met next morning in the pouring rain to do their shopping.

'Very disagreeable for poor Worship,' said Elizabeth 'and not very friendly to me to put up another candidate—'

'Rubbish,' said Diva. 'She's made you Mayoress. Quite enough friendliness for one year, I should have thought.'

'And it was out of friendliness that I accepted. I wanted to be of use to her, and stood for the Council for the same reason—'

'Only she thought Mr Georgie would be of more use than you,' interrupted Diva.

'Somebody in her pocket—Take care, Diva. Susan's van.'

The Royce drew up close to them, and Susan's face loomed in the window.

'Good morning, Elizabeth,' she said. 'I've just heard—'

'Thanks, dear, for your congratulations,' said Elizabeth. 'But quite a walk-over.'

Susan's face shewed no sign of comprehension.

'What did you walk over?' she asked. 'In this rain, too?—Oh, the election to the Town Council. How nice for you! When are you going to reduce the rates?'

A shrill whistle, and Irene's huge red

umbrella joined the group.

'Hullo, Mapp!' she said. 'So you've got on the map again. Ha, ha! How dare you stand against Georgie when my Angel wanted him to get in?'

Irene's awful tongue always deflated Elizabeth.

'Dear quaint one!' she said. 'What a lovely umbrella.'

'I know that. But how dare you?'

Elizabeth was stung into sarcasm.

'Well, we don't all of us think that your Angel must always have her way, dear,' she replied, 'and that we must lie down flat for her to trample us into the mire.'

'But she raised you out of the mire, woman,' cried Irene, 'when she made you Mayoress. She took pity on your fruitless efforts to become somebody. Wait till you see my fresco.'

Elizabeth was sorry she had been so courageous!

'Painting a pretty fresco, dear?' she asked. 'How I shall look forward to seeing it!'

'It may be a disappointment to you,' said Irene. 'Do you remember posing for me on the day Lucia made you Mayoress? It came out in the *Hampshire Argus*. Well, it's going to come out again in my fresco. Standing on an oyster shell with Benjy blowing you along. Wait and see.'

This was no brawl for an M.B.E. to be mixed up in, and Susan called 'Home!' to her chauffeur, and shut the window. Even Diva thought she had better move on.

'Bye-bye,' she said. 'Must get back to my baking.'

Elizabeth turned on her with a frightful grin.

'Very wise,' she said. 'If you had got back earlier to your baking yesterday, we should have enjoyed your jam-puffs more.'

'That's too much!' cried Diva. 'You ate three.'

'And bitterly repented it,' said Elizabeth.

Irene hooted with laughter and went on down the street. Diva crossed it, and Elizabeth stayed where she was for a moment to recover her poise. Why did Irene always cause her to feel like a rabbit with a stoat in pursuit? She bewildered and disintegrated her; she drained her of all power of invective and retort. She could face Diva, and had just done so with signal success, but she was no good against Irene. She plodded home through the driving rain, menaced by the thought of that snap-shot being revived again in fresco.

CHAPTER FIVE

Nobody was more conscious of this loss of prestige than Lucia herself, and there were losses in other directions as well. She had hoped that her renunciation of gambling would have induced card-playing circles to follow her example. That hope was frustrated; Bridge-parties with the usual stakes were as numerous as ever, but she was not asked to them. Another worry was that the humiliating election rankled in Georgie's mind and her seeking his advice on municipal questions, which was intended to show him how much she relied on his judgment, left him unflattered. When they sat after dinner in the garden-room (where, alas, no eager gamblers now found the hours pass only too quickly) her lucid exposition of some administrative point failed to rouse any real enthusiasm in him.

'And if everything isn't quite clear,' she said, 'mind you interrupt me, and I'll go over it again.'

But no interruption ever came; occasionally she thought she observed that slight elongation of the face that betokens a suppressed yawn, and at the end, as likely as not, he made some comment which shewed he had not listened to a word she was saying. To-night, she was not sorry he asked no questions about the contentious conduct of the catchment board, as she was not very clear about it herself. She became less municipal.

'How these subjects get between one and the lighter side of life!' she said. 'Any news to-day?'

'Only that turn-up between Diva and Elizabeth,' he said.

'Georgie, you never told me! What about?'

'I began to tell you at dinner,' said Georgie, 'only you changed the subject to the water-rate. It started with jam-puffs. Elizabeth ate three one afternoon at Diva's, and said next morning that she bitterly repented it. Diva says she'll never serve her a tea again, until she apologizes, but I don't suppose she means it.'

'Tell me more!' said Lucia, feeling the old familiar glamour stealing over her. 'And how is her tea-shop getting on?'

'Flourishing. The most popular house in Tilling. All so pleasant and chatty, and a rubber after tea on most days. Quite a centre.'

Lucia wrestled with herself for an intense moment.

'There's a point on which I much want your advice,' she began.

'Do you know, I don't think I can hope to understand any more municipal affairs to-night,' said Georgie firmly.

'It's not that sort, dear,' she said, wondering how to express herself in a lofty manner. 'It is this: You know how I refused to play Bridge any more for money. I've been thinking deeply over that decision. Deeply. It was meant to set an example, but if nobody follows an example, Georgie, one has to consider the wisdom of continuing to set it.'

'I always thought you'd soon find it very tar'some not to get your Bridge,' said Georgie. 'You used to enjoy it so.'

'Ah, it's not *that*,' said Lucia, speaking in her

116

best Oxford voice. 'I would willingly never see a card again if that was all, and indeed the abstract study of the game interests me far more. But I did find a certain value in our little Bridge-parties quite apart from cards. Very suggestive discussions, sometimes about local affairs, and now more than ever it is so important for me to be in touch with the social as well as the municipal atmosphere of the place. I regret that others have not followed my example, for I am sure our games would have been as thrilling as ever, but if others won't come into line with me, I will gladly step back into the ranks again. Nobody shall be able to say of me that I caused splits and dissensions. "One and all", as you know, is my favourite motto.'

Georgie didn't know anything of the sort, but he let it pass.

'Capital!' he said. 'Everybody will be very glad.'

'And it would give me great pleasure to reconcile that childish quarrel between Diva and Elizabeth,' continued Lucia. 'I'll ask Elizabeth and Benjy to have tea with us there to-morrow; dear Diva will not refuse to serve a guest of *mine*, and their little disagreement will be smoothed over. A rubber afterwards.'

Georgie looked doubtful.

'Perhaps you had better tell them that you will play for the usual stakes,' he said. 'Else they might say they were engaged again.'

Lucia, with her vivid imagination, visualised the horrid superior grin which, at the other end of the telephone, would spread over Elizabeth's face, when she heard that, and felt that she would scarcely be able to get the words out. But she steeled herself and went to the telephone.

*   *   *

Elizabeth and Benjy accepted, and, after a reconciliatory eighteen-penny tea, at which Elizabeth ate jam-puffs with gusto ('Dear Diva, what delicious, light pastry,' she said. 'I wonder it doesn't fly away') the four retired into the card-room. As if to welcome Lucia back into gambling circles, the God of Chance provided most exciting games. There were slams declared and won, there was doubling and redoubling and rewards and vengeances. Suddenly Diva looked in with a teapot in her hand and a most anxious expression on her face. She closed the door.

'The Inspector of Police wants to see you, Lucia,' she whispered.

Lucia rose, white to the lips. In a flash there came back to her all her misgivings about the legality of Diva's permitting gambling in a public room, and now the police were raiding it. She pictured headlines in the *Hampshire Argus* and lurid paragraphs ... Raid on Mrs Godiva Plaistow's gaming rooms ... The list of the gamblers caught there. The Mayor and Mayoress of Tilling ... A retired Major. The Mayor's husband. The case brought before the Tilling magistrates with the Mayor in the dock instead of on the Bench. Exemplary fines. Her own resignation. Eternal infamy...

'Did he ask for me personally?' said Lucia.

'Yes. Knew that you were here,' wailed Diva. 'And my tea-shop will be closed. Oh, dear me, if I'd only heeded your warning about raids! Or if we'd only joined you in playing Bridge for nothing!'

Lucia rose to the topmost peak of magnanimity, and refrained from rubbing that in.

'Is there a back way out, Diva?' she asked. 'Then they could all go. I shall remain and receive my Inspector here. Just sitting here. Quietly.'

'But there's no back way out,' said Diva. 'And you can't get out of the window. Too small.'

'Hide the cards!' commanded Lucia, and they all snatched up their hands. Georgie put his in his breast-pocket. Benjy put his on the top of the large cupboard. Elizabeth sat on hers. Lucia thrust hers up the sleeve of her jacket.

'Ask him to come in,' she said. 'Now all talk!'

The door opened, and the Inspector stood majestically there with a blue paper in his hand.

119

'Indeed, as you say, Major Mapp-Flint,' said Lucia in an unwavering Oxford voice, 'the League of Nations has collapsed like a card-house—I should say a ruin—Yes, Inspector, did you want me?'

'Yes, your Worship. I called at Mallards, and was told I should catch you here. There's a summons that needs your signature. I hope your Worship will excuse my coming, but it's urgent.'

'Quite right, Inspector,' said Lucia. 'I am always ready to be interrupted on magisterial business. I see. On the dotted line. Lend me your fountain-pen, Georgie.'

As she held out her hand for it, all her cards tumbled out of her sleeve. A draught eddied through the open door and Benjy's *cache* on the cupboard fluttered into the air. Elizabeth jumped up to gather them, and the cards on which she was sitting fell on to the floor.

Lucia signed with a slightly unsteady hand, and gave the summons back to the Inspector.

'Thank you, your Worship,' he said. 'Very sorry to interrupt your game, ma'am.'

'Not at all,' said Lucia. 'You were only doing your duty.'

He bowed and left the room.

'I must apologise to you all,' said Lucia without a moment's pause, 'but my good Inspector has orders to ask for me whenever he wants to see me on any urgent matter. Dear me! All my cards exposed on the table and

120

Elizabeth's and Major Benjy's on the floor. I am afraid we must have a fresh deal.'

Nobody made any allusion to the late panic, and Lucia dealt again.

Diva looked in again soon, carrying a box of chocolates.

'Any more Inspectors, dear?' asked Elizabeth acidly. 'Any more raids? Your nerves seem rather jumpy.'

Diva was sorely tempted to retort that their nerves seemed pretty jumpy too, but it was bad for business to be sharp with patrons.

'No, and I'm giving him such a nice tea,' she said meekly. 'But it was a relief, wasn't it? A box of chocolates for you. Very good ones.'

The rubber came to an end, with everybody eating chocolates, and a surcharged chat on local topics succeeded. It almost intoxicated Lucia, who, now for weeks, had not partaken of that heady beverage, and she felt more than ever like Catherine the Great.

'A very recreative two hours,' she said to Georgie as they went up the hill homewards, 'though I still maintain that our game would have been just as exciting without playing for money. And that farcical interlude of my Inspector! Georgie, I don't mind confessing that just for one brief moment it *did* occur to me that he was raiding the premises—'

'Oh, I know that,' said Georgie. 'Why, you asked Diva if there wasn't a back way out, and told us to hide our cards and talk. I was the only one of us who knew how absurd it all was.'

'But how you bundled your cards into your pocket! We were all a little alarmed. All. I put it down to Diva's terror-stricken entrance with her teapot dribbling at the spout—'

'No! I didn't see that,' said Georgie.

'Quite a pool on the ground. And her lamentable outcry about her tea-rooms being closed. It was suggestion, dear. Very sensitive people like myself respond automatically to suggestion ... And most interesting about Susan and her automatic script. She thinks, Elizabeth tells me, that Blue Birdie controls her when she's in trance, and is entirely wrapped up in it.'

'She's hardly ever seen now,' said Georgie. 'She never plays Bridge, nor comes to Diva's for tea, and Algernon usually does her marketing.'

'I must really go to one of her *séances*, if I can find a free hour some time,' said Lucia. 'But my visit must be quite private. It would never do if it was known that the Mayor attended *séances* which do seem alin to necromancy. Necromancy, as you may know, is divining through the medium of a corpse.'

'But that's a human corpse, isn't it?' asked he.

'I don't think you can make a distinction—Oh! Take care!'

She pulled Georgie back, just as he was stepping on to the road from the pavement. A boy on a bicycle, riding without lights, flew down the hill, narrowly missing him.

'Most dangerous!' said Lucia. 'No lights and excessive speed. I must ring up my Inspector and report that boy—I wonder who he was.'

'I don't see how you can report him unless you know,' suggested Georgie.

Lucia disregarded such irrelevancy. Her eyes followed the boy as he curved recklessly round the sharp corner into the High Street.

'Really I feel more envious than indignant,' she said. 'It must be so exhilarating. Such speed! What Lawrence of Arabia always loved. I feel very much inclined to learn bicycling. Those smart ladies of the nineties use to find it very amusing. Bicycling-breakfasts in Battersea Park and all that. Our brisk walks, whenever I have time to take them, are so limited: in these short afternoons we can hardly get out into the country before it is time to turn again.'

The idea appealed to Georgie, especially when Lucia embellished it with mysterious and conspiratorial additions. No one must know that they were learning until they were accomplished enough to appear in the High Street in complete control of their machines. What a sensation that would cause! What envious admiration! So next day they motored out to a lonely stretch of road a few miles away, where a man from the bicycle shop, riding a man's bicycle and guiding a woman's, had a

123

clandestine assignation with them. He held Georgie on, while Chapman, Lucia's chauffeur, clung to her, and for the next few afternoons they wobbled about the road with incalculable swoopings. Lucia was far the quicker of the two in acquiring the precarious balance, and she talked all the time to Chapman.

'I'm beginning to feel quite secure,' she said. 'You might let go for one second. No: there's a cart coming. Better wait till it has passed. Where's Mr Georgie? Far behind, I suppose.'

'Yes, ma'am. Ever so far.'

'Oh, what a jolt!' she cried, as her front wheel went over a loose stone. 'Enough to unseat anybody. I put on the brake, don't I?'

After ringing the bell once or twice, Lucia found the brake. The bicycle stopped dead, and she stepped lightly off.

'So powerful,' she said remounting. 'Now both hands off for a moment, Chapman.'

*　　*　　*

The day came when Georgie's attendant still hovered close to him, but when Lucia outpaced Chapman altogether. A little way in front of her a man near the edge of the road, with a saucepan of tar bubbling over a pot of red-hot coals, was doctoring a telegraph post. Then something curious happened to the co-ordination between Lucia's brain and muscles.

The imperative need of avoiding the fire-pot seemed to impel her to make a bee-line for it. With her eyes firmly fixed on it, she felt in vain for that powerful brake, and rode straight into the fire-pot, upsetting the tar and scattering the coals.

'Oh, I'm so sorry,' she said to the operator. 'I'm rather new at it. Would half-a-crown? And then would you kindly hold my bicycle while I mount again?'

The road was quite empty after that, and Lucia sped prosperously along, wobbling occasionally for no reason, but rejoicing in the comparative swiftness. Then it was time to turn. This was impossible without dismounting, but she mounted again without much difficulty, and there was a lovely view of Tilling rising red-roofed above the level land. Telegraph post after telegraph post flitted past her, and then she caught sight of the man with the fire-pot again. Lucia felt that he was observing her, and once more something curious occurred to her co-ordinations, and with it the familiar sense of exactly the same situation having happened before. Her machine began to swoop about the road; she steadied it, and with the utmost precision went straight into the fire-pot again.

'You seem to make a practice of it,' remarked the operator severely.

'Too awkward of me,' said Lucia. 'It was the very last thing I wanted to do. Quite the last.'

'That'll be another half-crown,' said the victim, 'and now I come to look at you, it was you and your pals cocked up on the Bench, who fined me five bob last month, for not being half as unsteady as you.'

'Indeed! How small the world is,' said Lucia with great dignity and aloofness, taking out her purse. Indeed it was a strange coincidence that she should have disbursed to the culprit of last month exactly the sum that she had fined him for drunkenness. She thought there was something rather psychic about it, but she could not tell Georgie, for that would have disclosed to him that in the course of her daring, unaccompanied ride she had twice upset a fire-pot and scattered tar and red-hot coals on the highway. Soon she met him still outward bound and he, too, was riding unsupported.

'I've made such strides to-day,' he called out. 'How have you got on?'

'Beautifully! Miles!' said Lucia, as they passed each other. 'But we must be getting back. Let me see you turn, dear, without dismounting. Not so difficult.'

The very notion of attempting that made Georgie unsteady, and he got off.

'I don't believe she can do it herself,' he muttered, as he turned his machine and followed her. The motor was waiting for them, and just as she was getting in, he observed a blob of tar on one of her shoes. She wiped it off on the grass by the side of the road.

*   *   *

Susan had invited them both to a necromantic *séance* after tea that evening. She explained that she would not ask them to tea, because before these sittings she fasted and meditated in the dark for an hour. When they got home from their ride, Georgie went to his sitting-room to rest, but Lucia, fresh as a daisy, filled up time by studying a sort of catechism from the Board of the Southern Railway in answer to her suggestion of starting a Royal Fish Express with a refrigerating van to supply the Court. They did not seem very enthusiastic; they put a quantity of queries. Had Her Worship received a Royal command on the subject? Did she propose to run the R.F.E. to Balmoral when the Court was in Scotland, because there were Scotch fishing ports a little closer? Had she worked out the cost of a refrigerating van? Was the supply of fish at Tilling sufficient to furnish the Royal Table as well as the normal requirements of the district? Did her Worship—

Grosvenor entered. Mr Wyse had called, and would much like, if quite convenient, to have a few words with Lucia before the *séance*. That seemed a more urgent call, for all these fish questions required a great deal of thought, and must be gone into with Mrs Simpson next

127

morning, and she told Grosvenor that she could give him ten minutes. He entered, carrying a small parcel wrapped up in brown paper.

'So good of you to receive me,' he said. 'I am aware of the value of your time. A matter of considerable delicacy. My dear Susan tells me that you and your husband have graciously promised to attend her *séance* to-day.'

Lucia referred to her engagement book.

'Quite correct,' she said. 'I found I could just fit it in. Five-thirty p.m. is my entry.'

'I will speak but briefly of the ritual of these *séances*,' said Mr Wyse. 'My Susan sits at the table in our little dining-room, which you have, alas too rarely, honoured by your presence on what I may call less moribund occasions. It is furnished with a copious supply of scribbling paper and of sharpened pencils for her automatic script. In front of her is a small shrine, I may term it, of ebony—possibly ebonite—with white satin curtains concealing what is within. At the commencement of the *séance*, the lights are put out, and my Susan draws the curtains aside. Within are the mortal remains—or such as could be hygienically preserved—of her budgerigar. She used to wear them in her hat or as a decoration for the bosom. They once fell into a dish, a red dish, at your hospitable table.'

'I remember. Raspberry something,' said Lucia.

'I bow to your superior knowledge,' said Mr Wyse. 'Then Susan goes into a species of trance, and these communications through automatic script begin. Very voluminous sometimes, and difficult to decipher. She spends the greater part of the day in puzzling them out, not always successfully. Now, *adorabile Signora—*'

'Oh, Mr Wyse,' cried Lucia, slightly startled.

'Dear lady, I only meant Your Worship,' he explained.

'I see. Stupid of me,' she said. 'Yes?'

'I appeal to you,' continued he. 'To put the matter in a nutshell, I fear my dear Susan will get unhinged, if this goes on. Already she is sadly changed. Her strong commonsense, her keen appreciation of the comforts and interests of life, her fur-coat, her Royce, her shopping, her Bridge; all these are tasteless to her. Nothing exists for her except these communings.'

'But how can I help you?' asked Lucia...

Mr Wyse tapped the brown paper parcel.

'I have brought here,' he said, 'the source of all our trouble: Blue Birdie. I abstracted it from the shrine while my dear Susan was meditating in the drawing-room. I want it to disappear in the hope that when she discovers it has gone, she will have to give up the *séance*, and recover her balance. I would not destroy it: that would be going too far. Would you therefore, dear lady, harbour the Object in some place unknown to me, so that when Susan asks me, as she undoubtedly will, if I know where it is, I may be able to tell her that I do not? A shade jesuitical perhaps, but such jesuitry, I feel, is justifiable.'

Lucia considered this. 'I think it is, too,' she said. 'I will put it somewhere safe. Anything to prevent our Susan becoming unhinged. That must never happen. By the way, is there a slight odour?'

'A reliable and harmless disinfectant,' said Mr Wyse. 'There was a faint smell in the neighbourhood of the shrine which I put down to imperfect taxidermy. A thousand thanks, Worshipful Lady. One cannot tell what my Susan's reactions may be, but I trust that the disappearance of the Object may lead to a discontinuance of the *séances*. In fact, I do not see how they could be held without it.'

Lucia had ordered a stack of black japanned boxes to hold documents connected with municipal departments. The arms of the Borough and her name were painted on them, with the subject with which they were concerned. There were several empty ones, and when Mr Wyse had bowed himself out, she put Blue Birdie into the one labelled 'Museum', which seemed appropriate. 'Burial Board' would have been appropriate, too, but there was already an agenda-paper in that.

Presently she and Georgie set forth for Starling Cottage.

Susan and Algernon were ready for them in the dining-room. The shrine with drawn curtains was on the table. Susan had heated a shovel and was burning incense on it.

'Blue Birdie came from the Spice Islands,' she explained, waving the shovel in front of the shrine. 'Yesterday my hand wrote "sweet gums" as far as I could read it, over and over again, and I think that's what he meant. And I've put up a picture of St Francis preaching to the birds.'

Certainly Susan, as her husband had said, was much changed. She looked dotty. There was an ecstatic light in her eye, and a demented psychical smile on her mouth. She wore a wreath in her hair, a loose white gown, and reminded Lucia of an immense operatic Ophelia. But critical circumstances always developed Lucia's efficiency, and she nodded encouragingly to Algernon as Susan swept fragrantly about the room.

'So good of you to let us come, dear Susan,' she said. 'I have very great experience in psychical phenomena: adepts—do you remember the Guru at Riseholme, Georgie?— adepts always tell me that I should be a marvellous medium if I had time to devote myself to the occult.'

Susan held up her hand.

'Hush,' she whispered. 'Surely I heard "Tweet, Tweet," which means Blue Birdie is here. Good afternoon, darling.'

131

She put the fire-shovel into the fender.

'Very promising,' she said. 'Blue Birdie doesn't usually make himself heard so soon, and it always means I'm going into trance. It must be you, Lucia, who have contributed to the psychic force.'

'Very likely,' said Lucia, 'the Guru always said I had immense power.'

'Turn out the lights then, Algernon, all but the little ruby lamp by my paper, and I will undraw the curtains of the shrine. Tweet, Tweet! There it is again, and that lost feeling is coming over me.'

Lucia had been thinking desperately, while Ophelia got ready, with that intense concentration which, so often before, had smoothed out the most crumpled situations. She gave a silvery laugh.

'I heard it, I heard it,' she exclaimed to Algernon's great surprise. '*Buona sera*, Blue Birdie. Have you come to see Mummie and Auntie Lucia from Spicy Islands? ... Oh, I'm sure I felt a little brush of soft feathers on my cheek.'

'No! did you really?' asked Susan with the slightest touch of jealousy in her voice. 'My pencil, Algernon.'

Lucia gave a swift glance at the shrine, as Susan drew the curtains, and was satisfied that the most spiritually enlightened eye could not see that it was empty. But dark though the room was, it was as if fresh candles were being

132

profusely lit in her brain, as on some High Altar dedicated to Ingenuity. She kept her eyes fixed on Susan's hand poised over her paper. It was recording very little: an occasional dot or dash was all the inspiration Blue Birdie could give. For herself, she exclaimed now and then that she felt in the dark the brush of the bird's wing, or heard that pretty note. Each time she saw that the pencil paused. Then the last and the greatest candle was lit in her imagination, and she waited calm and composed for the conclusion of the *séance*, when Susan would see that the shrine was empty.

They sat in the dim ruby light for half an hour, and Susan, as if not quite lost, gave an annoyed exclamation.

'Very disappointing,' she said. 'Turn on the light, Algernon. Blue Birdie began so well and now nothing is coming through.'

Before he could get to the switch, Lucia, with a great gasp of excitement, fell back in her chair, and covered her eyes with her hands.

'Something wonderful has happened,' she chanted. 'Blue Birdie has left us altogether. What a manifestation!'

Still not even peeping, she heard Susan's voice rise to a scream.

'But the shrine's empty!' she cried. 'Where is Blue Birdie, Algernon?'

'I have no idea,' said the Jesuit. 'What has happened?'

Lucia still sat with covered eyes.

'Did I not tell you before the light was turned on that there had been a great manifestation?' she asked. 'I *knew* the shrine would be empty! Let me look for myself.'

'Not a feather!' she said. 'The dematerialization is complete. Oh, what would not the President of the Psychical Research have given to be present! Only a few minutes ago, Susan and I—did we not, Susan?—heard his little salutation, and I, at any rate, felt his feathers brush my cheek. Now no trace! Never, in all my experience, have I seen anything so perfect.'

'But what does it mean?' asked the distraught Susan, pulling the wreath from her dishevelled hair. Lucia waved her hands in a mystical movement.

'Dear Susan,' she said, beginning to gabble, 'listen! All these weeks your darling's spirit has been manifesting itself to you, and to me also to-night, with its pretty chirps and strokes of the wing, in order to convince you of its presence, earth-bound and attached to its mortal remains. Now on the astral plane Blue Birdie has been able so to flood them with spiritual reality that they have been dissolved, translated—ah, how badly I put it—into spirit. Blue Birdie has been helping you all these weeks to realise that all is spirit. Now you have this final, supreme demonstration. Rapt with all of him that was mortal into a higher sphere!'

'But won't he ever come back?' asked Susan.

'Ah, you would not be so selfish as to wish that!' said Lucia. 'He is free; he is earth-bound no longer, and, by this miracle of dematerialization, has given you proof of that. Let me see what his last earthly communication with you was.'

Lucia picked up the sheet on which Susan had automatically recorded a few undecipherable scribbles.

'I knew it!' she cried. 'See, there is nothing but those few scrawled lines. Your sweet bird's spirit was losing connection with the material sphere; he was rising above it. How it all hangs together!'

'I shall miss him dreadfully,' said Susan in a faltering voice.

'But you mustn't, you mustn't. You cannot grudge him his freedom. And, oh, what a privilege to have assisted at such a demonstration! Ennobling! And if my small powers added to yours, dear, helped toward such a beautiful result, why that is *more* than a privilege.'

Georgie felt sure that there was hocus-pocus somewhere, and that Lucia had had a hand in it, but his probings, as they walked away, only elicited from her idiotic replies such as 'Too marvellous! What a privilege!'

It soon became known in marketing circles next morning that very remarkable necromancy had occurred at Starling Cottage, that Blue Birdie had fluttered about the darkened room, uttering his sharp cries, and had several times brushed against the cheek of the Mayor. Then, wonder of wonders, his mortal remains had vanished. Mr Wyse walked up and down the High Street, never varying his account of the phenomena, but unable to explain them, and for the first time for some days Susan appeared in her Royce, but without any cockade in her hat.

There was something mysterious and incredible about it all, but it did not usurp the entire attention of Tilling, for why did Elizabeth, from whom violent sarcasm might have been expected, seem to shun conversation? She stole rapidly from shop to shop, and, when cornered by Diva, coming out of the butcher's, she explained, scarcely opening her lips at all, that she had a relaxed throat, and must only breathe through her nose.

'I should open my mouth wide,' said Diva severely, 'and have a good gargle,' but Elizabeth only shook her head with an odd smile, and passed on. 'Looks a bit hollow-cheeked, too,' thought Diva. By contrast, Lucia was far from hollow-cheeked; she had a swollen face, and made no secret of her appointment with the dentist to have 'it' out. From there she went home, with the expectation of receiving, later in the day, a denture comprising a few molars with a fresh attachment added.

She ate her lunch, in the fashion of a rabbit, with her front teeth.

'Such a skilful extraction, Georgie,' she said, 'but a little sore.'

As she had a Council meeting that afternoon, Georgie went off alone in the motor for his assignation with the boy from the bicycle shop. The *séance* last evening still puzzled him, but he felt more certain than ever that her exclamations that she heard chirpings and felt the brush of Birdie's wing were absolute rubbish; so, too, was her gabble that her psychic powers added to Susan's, had brought about the dematerialization. 'All bosh,' he said aloud in an annoyed voice, 'and it only confirms her complicity. It's very unkind of her not to tell me how she faked it, when she knows how I would enjoy it.'

His bicycle was ready for him; he mounted without the slightest difficulty, and the boy was soon left far behind. Then with secret trepidation he observed not far ahead a man with a saucepan of tar simmering over a fire-pot. As he got close, he was aware of a silly feeling in his head that it was exercising a sort of fascination over his machine, but by keeping his eye on the road he got safely by it, though with frightful wobbles, and dismounted for a short rest.

'Well, that's a disappointment,' observed the operator. 'You ain't a patch on the lady who knocked down my fire-pot twice yesterday.'

Suddenly Georgie remembered the dab of tar on Lucia's shoe, and illumination flooded his brain.

'No! Did she indeed?' he said with great interest. 'The same lady twice? That was bad riding!'

'Oh, something shocking. Not that I'd ever seek to hinder her, for she gave me half-a-crown per upset. Ain't she coming today?'

As he rode home Georgie again meditated on Lucia's secretiveness. Why could she not tell him about her jugglings at the *séance* yesterday and about her antics with the fire-pot? Even to him she had to keep up this incessant flow of triumphant achievement both in occult matters and in riding a bicycle. Now that they were man and wife she ought to be more open with him. 'But I'll tickle her up about the fire-pot,' he thought vindictively.

When he got home he found Lucia just returned from a most satisfactory Council meeting.

'We got through our business most expeditiously,' she said, 'for Elizabeth was absent, and so there were fewer irrelevant interruptions. I wonder what ailed her: nothing serious I hope. She was rather odd in the High Street this morning. No smiles: she scarcely opened her mouth when I spoke to her. And did you make good progress on your bicycle this afternoon?'

'Admirable,' said he. 'Perfect steering. There was a man with a fire-pot tarring a telegraph-post—'

'Ah, yes,' interrupted Lucia. 'Tar keeps off insects that burrow into the wood. Let us go and have tea.'

'—and an odd feeling came over me,' he continued firmly, 'that just because I must avoid it, I should very likely run into it. Have you ever felt that? I suppose not.'

'Yes, indeed I have in my earlier stages,' said Lucia cordially. 'But I can give you an absolute cure for it. Fix your eyes straight ahead, and you'll have no bother at all.'

'So I found. The man was a chatty sort of fellow. He told me that some learner on a bicycle had knocked over the pot twice yesterday. Can you imagine such awkwardness? I am pleased to have got past that stage.'

Lucia did not show by the wink of an eyelid that this arrow had pierced her, and Georgie, in spite of his exasperation, could not help admiring such nerve.

'Capital!' she said. 'I expect you've quite caught me up by your practice to-day. Now after my Council meeting I think I must relax. A little music, dear?'

A melodious half-hour followed. They were both familiar with Beethoven's famous Fifth Symphony, as arranged for four hands on the piano, and played it with ravishing sensibility.

'*Caro*, how it takes one out of all petty carpings and schemings!' said Lucia at the end. 'How all our smallnesses are swallowed up in that broad cosmic splendour! And how beautifully you played, dear. Inspired! I almost stopped in order to listen to you.'

Georgie writhed under these compliments: he could hardly switch back to dark hints about *séances* and fire-pots after them. In strong rebellion against his kindlier feelings towards her, he made himself comfortable by the fire, while Lucia again tackled the catechism imposed on her by the Directors of the Southern Railway. Fatigued by his bicycle-ride, Georgie fell into a pleasant slumber.

Presently Grosvenor entered, carrying a small packet, neatly wrapped up and sealed. Lucia put her finger to her lip with a glance at her sleeping husband, and Grosvenor withdrew in tiptoe silence. Lucia knew what this packet must contain; she could slip the reconstituted denture into her mouth in a moment, and there would be no more rabbit-nibbling at dinner. She opened the packet and took out of the cotton-wool wrapping what it contained.

It was impossible to suppress a shrill exclamation, and Georgie awoke with a start. Beneath the light of Lucia's reading-lamp there gleamed in her hand something dazzling, something familiar.

'My dear, what *have* you got?' he cried.

'Why, it's Elizabeth's front teeth! It's Elizabeth's widest smile without any of her face! But how? Why? Blue Birdie's nothing to this.'

Lucia made haste to wrap up the smile again. 'Of course it is,' she said. 'I knew it was familiar, and the moment you said "smile" I recognised it. That explains Elizabeth's shut mouth this morning. An accident to her smile, and now by some extraordinary mistake the dentist has sent it back to me. Me of all people! What are we to do?'

'Send it back to Elizabeth,' suggested Georgie, 'with a polite note saying it was addressed to you, and that you opened it. Serve her right, the deceitful woman! How often has she said that she never had any bother with her teeth, and hadn't been to a dentist since she was a child, and didn't know what toothache meant. No wonder; that kind doesn't ache.'

'Yes, that would serve her right—' began Lucia.

She paused. She began to think intensely. If Elizabeth's entire smile had been sent to her, where, except to Elizabeth, had her own more withdrawn aids to mastication been sent? Elizabeth could not possibly identify those four hinterland molars, unless she had been preternaturally observant, but the inference would be obvious if Lucia personally sent her back her smile.

'No, Georgie; that wouldn't be kind,' she

said. 'Poor Elizabeth would never dare to smile at me again, if she knew I knew. I don't deny she richly deserves it for telling all those lies, but it would be an unworthy action. It is by a pure accident that we know, and we must not use it against her. I shall instantly send this box back to the dentist's.'

'But how do you know who her dentist is?' asked Georgie.

'Mr Fergus,' said Lucia, 'who took my tooth so beautifully this morning; there was his card with the packet. I shall merely say that I am utterly at a loss to understand why this has been sent me, and not knowing what the intended destination was, I return it.'

Grosvenor entered again. She bore a sealed packet precisely similar to that which now again contained Elizabeth's smile.

'With a note, ma'am,' she said. 'And the boy is waiting for a packet left here by mistake.'

'Oh, do open it,' said Georgie gaily. 'Somebody else's teeth, I expect. I wonder if we shall recognise them. Quite a new game, and most exciting.'

Hardly were the words out of his mouth when he perceived what must have happened. How on earth could Lucia get out of such an awkward situation? But it took far more than that to disconcert the Mayor of Tilling. She gave Grosvenor the other packet.

'A sample or two of tea that I was expecting,' she said in her most casual voice. 'Yes, from

Twistevant's.' And she put the sample into a drawer of her table.

Who could fail to admire, thought Georgie, this brazen composure?

CHAPTER SIX

Elizabeth's relaxed throat had completely braced itself by next morning, and at shopping time she was profuse in her thanks to Diva.

'I followed your advice, dear, and gargled well when I got home,' she said, 'and not a trace of it this morning ... Ah, here's Worship and Mr Georgie. I was just telling Diva how quickly her prescription cured my poor throat; I simply couldn't speak yesterday. And I hope you're better, Worship. It must be a horrid thing to have a tooth out.'

Lucia and Georgie scrutinized her smile ... There was no doubt about it.

'Ah, you're one of the lucky ones,' said Lucia in tones of fervent congratulation. 'How I envied you your beautiful teeth when Mr Fergus said he must take one of mine out.'

'I envy you too,' said Georgie. 'We all do.'

These felicitations seemed to speed Elizabeth's departure. She shut off her smile, and tripped across the street to tell the Padre that her throat was well again, and that she would be able to sing alto as usual in the choir on Sunday. With a slightly puzzled face he joined the group she had just left.

'Queer doings indeed!' he said in a sarcastic voice. 'Everything in Tilling seems to be vanishing. There's Mistress Mapp-Flint's relaxed throat, her as couldn't open her mouth yesterday. And there's Mistress Wyse's little bird. Dematerialized, they say. Havers! And there's Major Benjy's riding-whip. Very strange indeed. I canna' make nothing of it a'.'

The subject did not lead to much. Lucia had nothing to say about Blue Birdie, nor Diva about the riding-whip. She turned to Georgie.

'My tulip bulbs have just come for my garden,' she said. 'Do spare a minute and tell me where and how to plant them. Doing it all myself. No gardener. Going to have an open-air tea-place in the Spring. Want it to be a bower.'

The group dispersed. Lucia went to the bicycle shop to order machines for the afternoon. She thought it would be better to change the *venue* and appointed the broad, firm stretch of sands beyond the golf links, where she and Georgie could practise turning without dismounting, and where there would be no risk of encountering fire-pots. Georgie went with Diva into her back-garden.

'Things,' explained Diva, 'can be handed out of the kitchen window. So convenient. And where shall I have the tulips?'

'All along that bed,' said Georgie. 'Give me a

trowel and the bulbs. I'll show you.'

Diva stood admiringly by.

'What a neat hole!' she said.

'Press the bulb firmly down, but without force,' said Georgie.

'I see. And then you cover it up, and put the earth back again—'

'And the next about three inches away—'

'Oh dear, oh dear. What a quantity it will take!' said Diva. 'And *do* you believe in Elizabeth's relaxed throat. I don't. I've been wondering—'

Through the open window of the kitchen came the unmistakable sound of a kettle boiling over.

'Shan't be a minute,' she said. 'Stupid Janet. Must have gone to do the rooms and left it on the fire.'

She trundled indoors. Georgie dug another hole for a bulb, and the trowel brought up a small cylindrical object, blackish of hue, but of smooth, polished surface, and evidently no normal product of a loamy soil. It was metal, and a short stub of wood projected from it. He rubbed the soil off it, and engraved on it were two initials, B. F. Memory poised like a hawk and swooped.

'It's it!' he said to himself. 'Not a doubt about it. Benjamin Flint.'

He slipped it into his pocket while he considered what to do with it. No; it would never do to tell Diva what he had found. Relics

145

did not bury themselves, and who but Diva could have buried this one? Evidently she wanted to get rid of it, and it would be heartless as well as unnecessary to let her know that she had not succeeded. Bury it again then? There are feats of which human nature is incapable, and Georgie dug a hole for the next tulip.

Diva whizzed out again, and went on talking exactly where she had left off before the kettle boiled over, but repeating the last word to give him the context.

'—wondering if it was not teeth in some way. She often says they're so marvellous, but people who have really got marvellous teeth *don't* speak about them. They let them talk for themselves. Or bite. Tilling's full of conundrums as the Padre said. Especially since Lucia's become Mayor. She's more dynamic than ever and makes things happen all round her. What a gift! Oh, dear me, I'm talking to her husband. You don't mind, Mr Georgie? She's so central.'

Georgie longed to tell her how central Lucia had been about Elizabeth's relaxed throat, but that wouldn't be wise.

'Mind? Not a bit,' he said. 'And she would love to know that you feel that about her. Well, good luck to the tulips, and don't dig them up to see how they're getting on. It doesn't help them.'

'Of course not. Won't it be a bower in the Spring? And Irene is going to paint a signboard

146

for me. Sure to be startling. But nothing nude, I said, except hands and faces.'

* * *

Irene was doing physical jerks on her doorstep as Georgie passed her house on his way home.

'Come in, King of my heart,' she called. 'Oh, Georgie, you're a public temptation, you are, when you've got on your mustard-coloured cape and your blue tam-o'-shanter. Come in, and let me adore you for five minutes—only five—or shall I show you the new design for my fresco?'

'I should like that best,' said Georgie severely.

Irene had painted a large sketch in oils to take the place of that which the Town Surveying Department had prohibited. Tilling, huddling up the hill and crowned by the church formed the background, and in front, skimming up the river was a huge oyster-shell, on which was poised a substantial Victorian figure in shawl and bonnet and striped skirt, instead of the nude, putty-coloured female. It reproduced on a large scale the snap-shot of Elizabeth which had appeared in the *Hampshire Argus*, and the face, unmistakably Elizabeth's, wore a rapturous smile. One arm was advanced, and one leg hung out behind, as if she was skating. An equally solid gentleman, symbolizing wind, sprawled, in a frock-coat and top-hat, on a cloud behind her and with puffed cheeks propelled her upstream.

'Dear me, most striking!' said Georgie. 'But isn't it very like that photograph of Elizabeth in the *Argus*? And won't people say that it's Major Benjy in the clouds?'

'Why, of course they will, stupid, unless they're blind,' cried Irene. 'I've never forgiven Mapp for being Mayoress and standing against you for the Town Council. This will take her down a peg, and all for the sake of Lucia.'

'It's most devoted of you, Irene,' he said, 'and such fun, too, but do you think—'

'I never think,' cried Irene. 'I *feel*, and that's how I feel. I'm the only person in this petty, scheming world of Tilling who acts on impulse. Even Lucia schemes sometimes. And as you've introduced the subject—'

'I haven't introduced any subject yet,' said Georgie.

'Just like you. You wouldn't. But Georgie, what a glorious picture, isn't it? I almost think it has gained by being Victorianized; there's a devilish reserved force about the Victorians which mere nudity lacks. A nude has all its cards on the table. I've a good mind to send it to the Royal Academy instead of making a fresco of it. Just to punish the lousy Grundys of Tilling.'

'That would serve them right,' agreed Georgie.

*   *   *

The afternoon bicycling along the shore was a great success. The tide was low, exposing a broad strip of firm, smooth sand. Chapman and the bicycle boy no longer ran behind, and, now that there was so much room for turning, neither of the athletes found the least difficulty in doing so, and their turns soon grew, as Lucia said, as sharp as a needle. The rocks and groins provided objects to be avoided, and they skimmed close by them without collision. They mounted and dismounted, masters of the arts of balance and direction; all those secret practisings suddenly flowered.

'It's time to get bicycles of our own,' said Lucia as they turned homewards. 'We'll order them to-day, and as soon as they come we'll do our morning shopping on them.'

'I shall be very nervous,' said Georgie.

'No need, dear. I pass you as being able to ride through any traffic, and to dismount quickly and safely. Just remember not to look at anything you want to avoid. The head turned well away.'

'I am aware of that,' said Georgie, much nettled by this patronage. 'And about you. Remember about your brake and your bell. You confuse them sometimes. Ring your bell, dear! Now put on your brake. That's better.'

They joined the car and drove back along

149

Fire-Pot Road. Work was still going on there, and Lucia, in a curious fit of absence of mind, pointed to the bubbling saucepan of tar.

'And to think that only a few days ago,' she said, 'I actually—My dear, I'll confess, especially as I feel sure you've guessed. I upset that tar-pot. Twice.'

'Oh, yes, I knew that,' said Georgie. 'But I'm glad you've told me at last. I'll tell you something, too. Look at this. Tell me what it is.'

He took out of his pocket the silver top of Benjy's riding-whip, which he had excavated this morning. Foljambe had polished it up. Lucia's fine eyebrows knit themselves in recollective agony.

'Familiar, somehow,' she mused. 'Ah! Initials. B. F. Why, it's Benjy's! Newspaper Office! Riding-whip! Disappearance! Georgie, how did you come by it?'

Georgie's account was punctuated by comments from Lucia.

'Only the depth of a tulip bulb . . . Not nearly deep enough, such want of thoroughness . . . Diva must have buried it herself, I think . . . So you were quite right not to have told her; very humiliating. But, how did the top come to be snapped off? Do you suppose she broke it off, and buried the rest somewhere else, like murderers cutting up their victims? And look at the projecting end! It looks as if it had been bitten off, and why should Diva do that? If it

150

had been Elizabeth with her beautiful teeth, it would have been easier to understand.'

'All very baffling,' said Georgie, 'but anyhow I've traced the disappearances a step further. I shall turn my attention to Blue Birdie next.'

Lucia thought she had done enough confession for one day.

'Yes, do look into it, Georgie,' she said. 'Very baffling, too. But Mr Wyse is most happy about the effect of my explanation upon Susan. She has accepted my theory that Blue Birdie has gone to a higher sphere.'

'That seems to me a very bad sign,' said Georgie. 'It looks as if she was seriously deranged. And, candidly, do you believe it yourself?'

'So difficult, isn't it,' said Lucia in a philosophical voice, 'to draw hard and fast lines between what one rationally believes, and what one trusts is true, and what seems to admit of more than one explanation. We must have a talk about that some day. A wonderful sunset!'

*   *   *

The bicycles arrived a week later, nickel-plated and belled and braked; Lucia's had the Borough Arms of Tilling brilliantly painted on the tool-bag behind her saddle. They were brought up to Mallards after dark; and next

151

morning, before breakfast, the two rode about the garden paths, easily passing up the narrow path into the kitchen garden, and making circles round the mulberry tree on the lawn ('Here we go round the mulberry tree' light-heartedly warbled Lucia) and proving themselves adepts. Lucia could not eat much breakfast with the first public appearance so close, and Georgie vainly hoped that tropical rain would begin. But the sun continued to shine, and at the shopping hour they mounted and bumped slowly down the cobbles of the steep street into the High Street, ready to ring their bells. Irene was the first to see them, and she ran by Lucia's side.

'Marvellous, perfect person,' she cried, putting out her hand as if to lay it on Lucia's. 'What is there you can't do?'

'Yes, dear, but don't touch me,' screamed Lucia in panic. 'So rough just here.' Then they turned on to the smooth tarmac of the High Street.

Evie saw them next.

'Dear, oh, dear, you'll both be killed!' she squealed. 'There's a motor coming at such a pace. Kenneth, they're riding bicycles!'

They passed superbly on. Lucia dismounted at the post-office; Georgie, applying his brake with exquisite delicacy, halted at the poulterer's with one foot on the pavement. Elizabeth was in the shop and Diva came out of the post-office.

'Good gracious me,' she cried. 'Never knew you could. And all this traffic!'

'Quite easy, dear,' said Lucia. 'Order a chicken, Georgie, while I get some stamps.'

She propped her bicycle against the kerb; Georgie remained sitting till Mr Rice came out of the poulterer's with Elizabeth.

'What a pretty bicycle!' she said, green with jealousy. 'Oh, there's Worship, too. Well, this is a surprise! So accomplished!'

They sailed on again. Georgie went to the lending library, and found that the book Lucia wanted had come, but he preferred to have it sent to Mallards: hands, after all, were meant to take hold of handles. Lucia went on to the grocer's, and by the time he joined her there, the world of Tilling had collected: the Padre and Evie, Elizabeth and Benjy and Mr Wyse, while Susan looked on from the Royce.

'Such a saving of time,' said Lucia casually to the admiring assembly. 'A little spin in the country, Georgie, for half an hour?'

They went unerringly down the High Street, leaving an amazed group behind.

'Well, there's a leddy of pluck,' said the Padre. 'See, how she glides along. A mistress of a' she touches.'

Elizabeth was unable to bear it, and gave an acid laugh. 'Dear Padre!' she said. 'What a fuss about nothing! When I was a girl I learned to ride a bicycle in ten minutes. The easiest thing in the world.'

'Did ye, indeed, mem,' said the Padre, 'and that was very remarkable, for in those days, sure, there was only those great high machines, which you rode straddle.'

'Years and years after that,' said Elizabeth, moving away.

He turned to Evie.

'A bicycle would be a grand thing for me in getting about the parish,' he said. 'I'll step into the bicycle shop, and see if they've got one on hire for to learn on.'

'Oh, Kenneth, I should like to learn, too,' said Evie. 'Such fun!'

*　　　*　　　*

Meantime the pioneers, rosy with success, had come to the end of the High Street. From there the road sloped rapidly downhill. 'Now we can put on the pace a little, Georgie,' said Lucia, and she shot ahead. All her practisings had been on the level roads of the marsh or on the sea-shore, and at once she was travelling much faster than she had intended, and with eyes glued on the curving road, she fumbled for her brake. She completely lost her head. All she could find in her agitation was her bell, and, incessantly ringing it, she sped with ever increasing velocity down the short steep road towards the bridge over the railway. A policeman on point duty stepped forward, with the arresting arm of the law held out to stop

154

her, but as she took no notice he stepped very hastily back again, for to commit suicide and possibly manslaughter, was a more serious crime than dangerous riding. Lucia's face was contorted with agonised apprehension, her eyes stared, her mouth was wide open, and all the young constable could do by way of identification was to notice, when the unknown female had whisked by him, that the bicycle was new and that there was the Borough coat of arms on the tool-bag. Lucia passed between a pedestrian and a van, just avoiding both: she switch-backed up and down the railway-bridge, still ringing her bell ... Then in front of her lay the long climb of the Tilling hill, and as the pace diminished she found her brake. She dismounted, and waited for Georgie. He had lost sight of her in the traffic, and followed her cautiously in icy expectation of finding her and that beautiful new bicycle flung shattered on the road. Then he had one glimpse of her swift swallow-flight up the steep incline of the railway-bridge. Thank God she was safe so far! He traversed it himself and then saw her a hundred yards ahead up the hill. Long before he reached her his impetus was exhausted, and he got off.

'Don't hurry, dear,' she called to him in a trembling voice. 'You were right, quite right to ride cautiously. Safety first *always*.'

'I felt very anxious about you,' said Georgie, panting as he joined her. 'You oughtn't to have

155

gone so fast. You deserve to be summoned for dangerous riding.'

A vision, vague and bright, shot through Lucia's brain. She could not conceive a more enviable piece of publicity than, at her age, to be summoned for so athletic a feat. It was punishable, no doubt, by law, but like a *crime passionel*, what universal admiration it would excite! What a dashing Mayor!

'I confess I was going very fast,' she said, 'but I felt I had such complete control of my machine. And so exhilarating. I don't suppose anybody has ever ridden so fast down Landgate Street. Now, if you're rested, shall we go on?'

They had a long but eminently prudent ride, and after lunch a well-earned siesta. Lucia, reposing on the sofa in the garden-room, was awakened by Grosvenor's entry from a frightful nightmare that she was pedalling for all she was worth down Beachy Head into the arms of a policeman on the shore.

'Inspector Morrison, ma'am,' said Grosvenor. 'He'll call again if not convenient.'

Nightmare vanished: the vague vision grew brighter. Was it possible? ...

'Certainly, at once,' she said springing up and Inspector Morrison entered.

'Sorry to disturb your Worship,' he said, 'but one of my men has reported that about eleven a.m. to-day a new bicycle with the arms of Tilling on the tool-bag was ridden at a dangerous speed by a female down Landgate Street. He made enquiries at the bicycle shop and found that a similar machine was sent to your house yesterday. I therefore ask your permission to question your domestics—'

'Quite right to apply to me, Inspector,' said Lucia. 'You did your duty. Certainly I will sign the summons.'

'But we don't know who it was yet, ma'am. I should like to ask your servants to account for their whereabouts at eleven a.m.'

'No need to ask them, Inspector,' said Lucia. 'I was the culprit. Please send the summons round here and I will sign it.'

'But, your Worship—'

Lucia was desperately afraid that the Inspector might wriggle out of summoning the Mayor and that the case would never come into Court. She turned a magisterial eye on him.

'I will not have one law for the rich and another for the poor in Tilling,' she said. 'I was riding at a dangerous speed. It was very thoughtless of me, and I must suffer for it. I ask you to proceed with the case in the ordinary course.'

*   *   *

This one appearance of Lucia and Georgie doing their shopping on bicycles had been enough to kindle the spark of emulation in the breasts of the more mature ladies of Tilling. It looked so lissom, so gaily adolescent to weave your way in and out of traffic and go for a spin in the country, and surely if Lucia could, they could also. Her very casualness made it essential to show her that there was nothing remarkable about her unexpected feat. The bicycle shop was besieged with enquiries for machines on hire and instructors. The Padre and Evie were the first in the field, and he put off his weekly visit to the workhouse that afternoon from half-past two till half-past three, and they hired the two bicycles which Lucia and Georgie no longer needed. Diva popped in next, and was chagrined to find that the only lady's bicycle was already bespoken, so she engaged it for an hour on the following morning. Georgie that day did quite complicated shopping alone, for Lucia was at a committee meeting at the Town Hall. She rode there—a distance of a hundred and fifty yards—to save time, but the gain was not very great, for she had to dismount twice owing to the narrow passage between posts for the prevention of vehicular traffic. Georgie, having returned from his shopping, joined her at the Town Hall when her meeting was over, and, with brakes fully applied, they rode down into the High Street, *en route* for another dash into the country. Susan's Royce was drawn up at the bicycle shop.

'Georgie, I shan't have a moment's peace,'

said Lucia, 'until I know whether Susan has ambitions too. I must just pop in.'

Both the Wyses were there. Algernon was leaning over Susan's shoulder as she studied a catalogue of the newest types of tricycles...

*   *   *

The Mayoress alone remained scornful and aloof. Looking out from her window one morning, she observed Diva approaching very slowly up the trafficless road that ran past Grebe buttressed up by Georgie's late instructor, who seemed to have some difficulty in keeping her perpendicular. She hurried to the garden-gate, reaching it just as Diva came opposite.

'Good morning, dear,' she said. 'Sorry to see that you're down with it, too.'

'Good morning dear,' echoed Diva, with her eyes glued to the road in front of her. 'I haven't the slightest idea what you mean.'

'But is it wise to take such strenuous exercise?' asked Elizabeth. 'A great strain surely on both of you.'

'Not a bit of a strain,' called Diva over her shoulder. 'And my instructor says I shall soon get on ever so quick.'

The bicycle gave a violent swerve.

'Oh, take care,' cried Elizabeth in an anxious voice, 'or you'll get off ever so quick.'

'We'll rest a bit,' said Diva to her instructor,

and she stepped from her machine and went back to the gate to have it out with her friend. 'What's the matter with you,' she said to Elizabeth, 'is that you can't bear us following Lucia's lead. Don't deny it. Look in your own heart, and you'll find it's true, Elizabeth. Get over it, dear. Make an effort. Far more Christian!'

'Thank you for your kind interest in my character, Diva,' retorted Elizabeth. 'I shall know now where to come when in spiritual perplexity.'

'Always pleased to advise you,' said Diva. 'And now give me a treat. You told us all you learned to ride in ten minutes when you were a girl. I'll give you my machine for ten minutes. See if you can ride at the end of it! A bit coy, dear? Not surprised. And rapid motion might be risky for your relaxed throat.'

There was a moment's pause. Then both ladies were so pleased at their own brilliant dialectic that Elizabeth said she would pop in to Diva's establishment for tea, and Diva said that would be charming.

*   *   *

In spite of Elizabeth (or perhaps even because of her) this revival of the bicycling nineties grew most fashionable. Major Benjy turned traitor and was detected by his wife surreptitiously practising with the gardener's bicycle on the cinder path in the kitchen garden. Mr Wyse suddenly appeared on the wheel riding in the most elegant manner. Figgis, his butler, he said, happened to remember that he had a bicycle put away in the garage and had furbished it up. Mr Wyse introduced a new style: he was already an adept and instead of wearing a preoccupied expression, made no more of it than if he was strolling about on foot. He could take a hand off his handle-bar, to raise his hat to the Mayor, as if one hand was all he needed. When questioned about this feat, he said that it was not really difficult to take both hands off without instantly crashing, but Lucia, after several experiments in the garden, concluded that Mr Wyse, though certainly a very skilful performer, was wrong about that. To crown all, Susan, after a long wait at the corner of Porpoise Street, where a standing motor left only eight or nine feet of the roadway clear, emerged majestically into the High Street on a brand new tricycle. 'Those large motors,' she complained to the Mayor, 'ought not to be allowed in our narrow streets.'

* * *

The Town Hall was crowded to its utmost capacity on the morning that Lucia was summoned to appear before her own Court for dangerous riding. She had bicycled there, now negotiating the anti-vehicular posts with the utmost precision, and, wearing her semi-official hat, presided on the Borough Bench. She and her brother magistrates had two cases to try before hers came on, of which one was that of a motor-cyclist whose brakes were out of order. The Bench, consulting together, took a grave view of the offence, and imposed a penalty of twenty shillings. Lucia in pronouncing sentence, addressed some severe remarks to him: he would have been unable to pull up, she told him, in case of an emergency, and was endangering the safety of his fellow citizens. The magistrates gave him seven days in which to pay. Then came the great moment. The Mayor rose, and in a clear unfaltering voice, said:

'Your Worships, I am personally concerned in the next case, and will therefore quit my seat on the Bench. Would the senior of Your Worships kindly preside in my temporary absence?'

She descended into the body of the Town Hall.

'The next case before your Worships,' said the Town Clerk, 'is one of dangerous riding of a push-bicycle on the part of Mrs Lucia Pillson. Mrs Lucia Pillson.'

She pleaded guilty in a voice of calm triumph, and the Bench heard the evidence. The first witness was a constable, who swore that he would speak the truth, the whole truth

162

and nothing but the truth. He was on point duty by the railway-bridge at 11 a.m. on Tuesday the twelfth instant. He observed a female bicyclist approaching at a dangerous speed down Landgate Street, when there was a lot of traffic about. He put out his arm to stop her, but she dashed by him. He estimated her speed at twenty miles an hour, and she seemed to have no control over her machine. After she had passed, he observed a tool-bag on the back of the saddle emblazoned with the Borough coat-of-arms. He made enquiries at the bicycle shop and ascertained that a machine of this description had been supplied the day before to Mrs Pillson of Mallards House. He reported to his superior.

'Have you any questions, your Worsh—to ask the witness?' asked the Town Clerk.

'None,' said Lucia eagerly. 'Not one.'

The next witness was the pedestrian she had so nearly annihilated. Lucia was dismayed to see that he was the operator with the fire-pot. He began to talk about his experiences when tarring telegraph-posts some while ago, but, to her intense relief, was promptly checked and told he must confine himself to what occurred at 11 a.m. on Tuesday. He deposed that at that precise hour, as he was crossing the road by the railway-bridge, a female bicyclist dashed by him at a speed which he estimated at over twenty miles an hour. A gratified smile illuminated the Mayor's face, and she had no

163

questions to ask him.

That concluded the evidence, and the Inspector of Police said there were no previous convictions against the accused.

The Bench consulted together: there seemed to be some difference of opinion as to the amount of the fine. After a little discussion the temporary Chairman told Lucia that she also would be fined twenty shillings. She borrowed it from Georgie, who was sitting near, and so did not ask for time in which to pay. With a superb air she took her place again on the Bench.

Georgie waited for her till the end of the sitting, and stood a little in the background, but well in focus, while Lucia posed on the steps of the Town Hall, in the act of mounting her bicycle, for the photographer of the *Hampshire Argus*. His colleague on the reporting staff had taken down every word uttered in this *cause célèbre* and Lucia asked him to send proofs to her, before it went to press. It was a slight disappointment that no reporters or photographers had come down from London, for Mrs Simpson had been instructed to inform the Central News Agency of the day and hour of the trial ... But the Mayor was well satisfied with the local prestige which her reckless athleticism had earned for her. Elizabeth, indeed, had attempted to make her friends view the incident in a different light, and she had a rather painful scene on the

164

subject with the Padre and Evie.

'All too terrible,' she said. 'I feel that poor Worship has utterly disgraced herself, and brought contempt on the dignified office she holds. Those centuries of honourable men who have been Mayors here must turn in their graves. I've been wondering whether I ought not, in mere self-respect, to resign from being Mayoress. It associates me with her.'

'That's not such a bad notion,' said the Padre, and Evie gave several shrill squeaks.

'On the other hand, I should hate to desert her in her trouble,' continued the Mayoress. 'So true what you said in your sermon last Sunday, Padre, that it's our duty as Christians always to stand by our friends, whenever they are in trouble and need us.'

'So because she needs you, which she doesn't an atom,' burst out Evie, 'you come and tell us that she's disgraced herself, and made everybody turn in their graves. Most friendly, Elizabeth.'

'And I'm of wee wifie's opinion, mem,' said the Padre, with the brilliant thought of Evie becoming Mayoress in his mind, 'and if you feel you canna' preserve your self-respect unless you resign, why, it's your Christian duty to do so, and I warrant that won't incommode her, so don't let the standing by your friends deter you. And if you ask me what I think of Mistress Lucia's adventure, 'twas a fine spunky thing to have gone flying down the Landgate

165

Street at thirty miles an hour. You and I daurna do it, and per-adventure we'd be finer folk if we daur. And she stood and said she was guilty like a God-fearing upstanding body and she deserves a medal, she does. Come awa', wifie: we'll get to our bicycle-lesson.'

The Padre's view was reflected in the town generally, and his new figure of thirty miles an hour accepted. Though it was a very lawless and dangerous feat, Tilling felt proud of having so spirited a Mayor. Diva indulged in secret visions of record-breaking when she had learned to balance herself, and Susan developed such a turn of speed on her tricycle that Algernon called anxiously after her 'Not so fast, Susan, I beg you. Supposing you met something.' The Padre scudded about his parish on the wheel, and, as the movement grew, Lucia offered to coach anybody in her garden. It became fashionable to career up and down the High Street after dark, when traffic was diminished, and the whole length of it resounded with tinkling bells and twinkled with bicycle lamps. There were no collisions, for everyone was properly cautious, but on one chilly evening the flapping skirt of Susan's fur coat got so inextricably entangled in the chain of her tricycle that she had to shed it, and Figgis trundled coat and tricycle back to Porpoise Street in the manner of a wheel-barrow.

As the days grew longer and the weather

warmer, picnic-parties were arranged to points of interest within easy distance, a castle, a church or a Martello tower, and they ate sandwiches and drank from their thermos flasks in ruined dungeons or on tombstones or by the edge of a moat. The party, by reason of the various rates of progress which each found comfortable, could not start together, if they were to arrive fairly simultaneously, and Susan on her tricycle was always the first to leave Tilling, and Diva followed. There was some competition for the honour of being the last to leave: Lucia, with the cachet of furious riding to her credit, waited till she thought the Padre must have started, while he was sure that his normal pace was faster than hers. In consequence, they usually both arrived very late and very hot. They all wondered how they could ever have confined physical exercise within the radius of pedestrianism, and pitied Elizabeth for the pride that debarred her from joining in these pleasant excursions.

CHAPTER SEVEN

Lucia had failed to convince the Directors of the Southern Railway that the Royal Fish Train was a practicable scheme. 'Should Their Majesties' so ran the final communication 'express Their Royal wish to be supplied with fish from Tilling, the Directors would see that the delivery was made with all expedition, but in their opinion the ordinary resources of the line will suffice to meet Their requirements, of which at present no intimation has been received.'

'A sad want of enterprise, Georgie,' said the Mayor as she read this discouraging reply. 'A failure to think municipally and to see the distinction of bringing an Elizabethan custom up to date. I shall not put the scheme before my Council at all.' Lucia dropped this unenterprising ultimatum into the waste paper basket. The afternoon post had just arrived and the two letters which it brought for her followed the ultimatum.

'My syllabus for a series of lectures at the Literary Institute is not making a good start,' she said. 'I asked Mr Desmond McCarthy to talk to us about the less known novelists of the time of William IV, but he has declined. Nor can Mr Noel Coward speak on the technique of the modern stage on any of the five nights I offered him. I am surprised that they should not have welcomed the opportunity to get more widely known.'

'Tar'some of them,' said Georgie sympathetically, 'such a chance for them.'

Lucia gave him a sharp glance, then mused for a while in silence over her scheme. Fresh ideas began to flood her mind so copiously that she could scarcely scribble them down fast enough to keep up with them.

'I think I will lecture on the Shakespearian drama myself,' she said. 'That should be the inaugural lecture, say April the fifteenth. I don't seem to have any engagement that night, and you will take the chair for me ... Georgie, we might act a short scene together, without dresses or scenery to illustrate the simplicity of the Elizabethan stage. Really, on reflection I think my first series of lectures had much better be given by local speakers. The Padre would address us one night on Free-Will or the Origin of Evil. Irene on the technique of fresco painting. Diva on catering for the masses. Then I ought to ask Elizabeth to lecture on something, though I'm sure I don't know on what subject she has any ideas of the slightest value. Ah! Instead, Major Benjy on tiger-shooting. Then a musical evening: the art of Beethoven, with examples. That would make six lectures; six would be enough. I think it would be expected of me to give the last as well as the first. Admission, a shilling, or five shillings for the series. Official, I think, under the patronage of the Mayor.'

'No,' said Georgie, going back to one of the earlier topics. 'I won't act any Shakespearian scene with you to illustrate Elizabethan simplicity. And if you ask me I don't believe people will pay a shilling to hear the Padre lecture on Free-Will. They can hear that sort of thing every Sunday morning for nothing but

169

the offertory.'

'I will consider that,' said Lucia, not listening and beginning to draw up a schedule of the discourses. 'And if you won't do a scene with me, I might do the sleep-walking from Macbeth by myself. But you must help me with the Beethoven evening. Extracts from the Fifth Symphony for four hands on the piano. That glorious work contains, as I have always maintained, the Key to the Master's soul. We must practise hard, and get our extracts by heart.'

Georgie felt the sensation, that was now becoming odiously familiar, of being hunted and harried. Life for him was losing that quality of leisure, which gave one time to feel busy and ready to take so thrilled an interest in the minute happenings of the day. Lucia was poisoning that eager fount by this infusion of Mayoral duties and responsibilities, and tedious schemes for educational lectures and lighting of the streets. True, the old pellucid spring gushed out sometimes: who, for instance, but she could have made Tilling bicycle-crazy, or have convinced Susan that Blue Birdie had gone to a higher sphere? That was her real *métier*, to render the trivialities of life intense for others. But how her schemes for the good of Tilling bored him!

Lucia finished sketching out her schedule, and began gabbling again.

'Yes, Georgie, the dates seem to work out all

right,' she said, 'though Mrs Simpson must check them for me. April the fifteenth: my inaugural lecture on Shakespeare: April the twenty-second: the Padre on Free-Will which I am convinced will attract all serious people, for it is a most interesting subject, and I don't think any final explanation of it has yet been given; April the twenty-ninth, Irene on the technique of fresco painting: May the sixth: Diva on tea-shops. I expect I shall have to write it for her. May the thirteenth: Major Benjy on tigers: May the twentieth: Beethoven, me again . . . I should like to see these little centres of enlightenment established everywhere in England, and I count it a privilege to be able, in my position, to set an example. The B.B.C., I don't deny, is doing good work, but lectures delivered viva-voce are so much more vivid. Personal magnetism. I shall always entertain the lecturer and a few friends to a plain supper-party here afterwards, and we can continue the discussion in the garden-room. I shall ask some distinguished expert on the subject to come down and stay the night after each lecture: the Bishop when the Padre lectures on Free-Will: Mr Gielgud when I speak about Shakespearian technique: Sir Henry Wood when we have our Beethoven night: and perhaps the Manager of Messrs Lyons after Diva's discourse. I shall send my Town Council complimentary seats in the first row for the inaugural lecture. How does that strike you for a rough sketch? You know how I value your judgment, and it is most important to get the initial steps right.'

Georgie was standing by her table, suppressing a yawn as he glanced at the schedule, and feeling in his waistcoat pocket for his gun-metal match-box with the turquoise latch. As he scooped for it, there dropped out the silver top of Major Benjy's riding-whip, which he always kept on his person. It fell noiselessly on the piece of damp sponge which Mrs Simpson always preferred to use for moistening postage-stamps, rather than the less genteel human tongue. Simultaneously the telephone-bell rang, and Lucia jumped up.

'That incessant summons!' she said. 'A perfect slavery. I think I must take my name off the exchange, and give my number to just a few friends ... Yes, yes, I am the Mayor of Tilling. Irene, is it? ... My dear how colossal! I don't suppose anybody in Tilling has ever had a picture in the Royal Academy before. Is that the amended version of your fresco, Venus with no clothes on coming to Tilling? I'm sure this one is far nicer. How I wish I had seen it before you sent it in, but when the Academy closes you must show it at our picture-exhibition here. Oh, I've put you down to give a lecture in my Mayoral course of Culture on the technique of painting in fresco. And you're going up to London for varnishing day? Do take care. So many pictures have been ruined

172

by being varnished too much.'

She rang off.

'Accepted, is it?' said Georgie in great excitement. 'There'll be wigs on the green if it's exhibited here. I believe I told you about it, but you were wrestling with the Royal Fish Express. Elizabeth, unmistakable, in a shawl and bonnet and striped skirt and button-boots, standing on an oyster-shell, and being blown into Tilling by Benjy in a top-hat among the clouds.'

'Dear me, that sounds rather dangerously topical,' said Lucia. 'But it's time to dress. The Mapp-Flints are dining, aren't they? What a coincidence!'

*   *   *

They had a most harmonious dinner, with never a mention of bicycles. Benjy readily consented to read a paper on tiger-shooting on May 13.

'Ah, what a joy,' said Lucia. 'I will book it. And some properties perhaps, to give vividness. The riding-whip with which you hit the tiger in the face. Oh, how stupid of me. I had forgotten about its mysterious disappearance which was never cleared up. Pass me the sugar, Georgie.'

There was a momentary pause, and Lucia grew very red in the face as she buried her orange in sugar. But that was soon over, and presently the Mayor and Mayoress went out to the garden-room with interlaced waists and arms. Lucia had told Georgie not to stop too long in the dining-room and Benjy made the most of his time and drank a prodigious quantity of a sound but inexpensive port. Elizabeth had eaten a dried fig for dessert, and a minute but adamantine fig-seed had lodged itself at the base of one of her beautiful teeth. She knew she would not have a tranquil moment till she had evicted it, and she needed only a few seconds unobserved.

'Dear Worship,' she said. 'Give me a treat, and let your hands just stray over the piano. Haven't heard you play for ever so long.'

Lucia never needed pressing and opened the lid of the instrument.

'I'm terribly rusty, I'm afraid,' she said, 'for I get no time for practising nowadays. Beethoven, dear, or a morsel of precious Mozart; whichever you like.'

'Oh, prettioth Mothart, pleath,' mumbled Elizabeth, who had effaced herself behind Lucia's business table. A moment sufficed, and her eye, as she turned round towards the piano again to drink in precious Mozart, fell on Mrs Simpson's piece of damp sponge. Something small and bright, long-lost and familiar, gleamed there. Hesitation would have been mere weakness (besides, it belonged to her husband). She reached out a stealthy hand, and put it inside her bead-bag.

174

It was barely eleven when the party broke up, for Elizabeth was totally unable to concentrate on cards when her bag contained the lock, if not the key to the unsolved mystery, and she insisted that dear Worship looked very tired. But both she and Benjy were very tired before they had framed and been forced to reject all the hypotheses which could account for the reappearance in so fantastic a place of this fragment of the riding-whip. If the relic had come to light in one of Diva's jam-puffs, the quality of the mystery would have been less baffling, for at least it would have been found on the premises where it was lost, but how it had got to Lucia's table was as inexplicable as the doctrine of Free-Will. They went over the ground five or six times.

'Lucia wasn't even present when it vanished,' said Elizabeth as the clock struck midnight. 'Often, as you know, I think Worship is not quite as above-board as I should wish a colleague to be, but here I do not suspect her.'

Benjy poured himself out some whisky. Finding that Elizabeth was far too absorbed in speculation to notice anything that was going on round her, he hastily drank it, and poured out some more.

'Pillson then,' he suggested.

'No; I rang him up that night from Diva's, as he was going to his bath,' said she, 'and he denied knowing anything about it. He's fairly truthful—far more truthful than Worship anyhow—as far as I've observed.'

'Diva then,' said Benjy, quietly strengthening his drink.

'But I searched and I searched, and she had not been out of my sight for five minutes. And where's the rest of it? One could understand the valuable silver cap disappearing—though I don't say for a moment that Diva would have stolen it—but it's just that part that has reappeared.'

'All mos' mysterious,' said Benjy. 'But wo'll you do next, Liz? There's the cruksh. Wo'll you do next?'

Benjy had not observed that the Mayoress was trembling slightly, like a motor-bicycle before it starts. Otherwise he would not have been so surprised when she sprang up with a loud crow of triumph.

'I have it,' she cried. '*Eureka!* as Worship so often says when she's thought of nothing at all. Don't say a word to anybody, Benjy, about the silver cap, but have a fresh cane put into it, and use it as a property (isn't that the word?) at your tiger-talk, just as if it had never been lost. That'll be a bit of puzzle-work for guilty persons, whoever they may be. And it may lead to something in the way of discovery. The thief may turn pale or red or betray himself in some way ... What a time of night!'

* * *

Puzzle-work began next morning.

'I can't make out what's happened to it,' said Georgie, in a state of fuss, as he came down very late to breakfast, 'and Foljambe can't either.'

Lucia gave an annoyed glance at the clock. It was five minutes to ten; Georgie was getting lazier and lazier in the morning. She gave the special peal of silvery laughter in which mirth played a minor part.

'Good afternoon, *caro*,' she said sarcastically. 'Quite rested? Capital!'

Georgie did not like her tone.

'No, I'm rather tired still,' he said. 'I shall have a nap after breakfast.'

Lucia abandoned her banter, as he did not seem to appreciate it.

'Well, I've finished,' she said. 'Poor Worship has got to go and dictate to Mrs Simpson. And what was it you and Foljambe couldn't find?'

'The silver top to Benjy's riding-whip. I was sure it was in my yesterday's waistcoat pocket, but it isn't, and Foljambe and I have been through all my suits. Nowhere.'

'Georgie, how very queer,' she said. 'When did you see it last?'

'Some time yesterday,' he said, opening a letter. A bill.

'It'll turn up. Things do,' said Lucia.

He was still rather vexed with her.

'They seem to be better at vanishing,' he

177

said. 'There was Blue Birdie—'

He opened the second of his letters, and the thought of riding-whip and Blue Birdie alike were totally expunged from his brain.

'My dear,' he cried. 'You'd never guess. Olga Bracely. She's back from her world-tour.'

Lucia pretended to recall distant memories. She actually had the most vivid recollection of Olga Bracely, and, not less, of Georgie's unbounded admiration of her in his bachelor days. She wished the world-tour had been longer.

'Olga Bracely?' she said vaguely. 'Ah, yes. Prima donna. Charming voice; some notes lovely. So she's got back. How nice!'

'—and she's going to sing at Covent Garden next month,' continued Georgie, deep in her letter. 'They're producing Cortese's opera, *Lucrezia*, on May the twentieth. Oh, she'll give us seats in her box. It's a gala performance. Isn't that too lovely? And she wants us to come and stay with her at Riseholme.'

'Indeed, most kind of her,' said Lucia. 'The dear thing! But she doesn't realize how difficult it is for me to get away from Tilling while I am Mayor.'

'I don't suppose she has the slightest idea that you are Mayor,' said Georgie, beginning to read the letter over again.

'Ah, I forgot,' said Lucia. 'She has been on a world-tour, you told me. And as for going up to hear *Lucrezia*—though it's very kind of

178

her—I think we must get out of it. Cortese brought it down to Riseholme, I remember, as soon as he had finished it, and dear Olga begged me to come and hear her sing the great scene—I think she called it—and, oh, that cacophonous evening! Ah! *Eureka!* Did you not say the date was May the twentieth? How providential! That's the very evening we have fixed for my lecture on Beethoven. Olga will understand how impossible it is to cancel that.'

'But that's quite easily altered,' said Georgie. 'You made out just the roughest schedule, and Benjy's tiger-slaying is the only date fixed. And think of hearing the gala performance in London! *Lucrezia's* had the hugest success in America and Australia. And in Berlin and Paris.'

Lucia's decisive mind wavered. She saw herself sitting in a prominent box at Covent Garden, with all her seed-pearls and her Mayoral badge. Reporters would be eager to know who she was, and she would be careful to tell the box-attendant, so that they could find out without difficulty. And at Tilling, what *réclame* to have gone up to London on the prima donna's invitation to hear this performance of the world-famous *Lucrezia*. She might give an interview to the *Hampshire Argus* about it when she got back.

'Of course we must go,' continued Georgie. 'But she wants to know at once.'

Still Lucia hesitated. It would be almost as

179

magnificent to tell Tilling that she had refused Olga's invitation, except for the mortifying fact that Tilling would probably not believe her. And if she refused, what would Georgie do? Would he leave her to lecture on Beethoven all by herself, or would he loyally stand by her, and do his part in the four-handed pianoforte arrangement of the Fifth Symphony? He furnished the answer to that unspoken question.

'I'm sorry if you find it impossible to go,' he said quite firmly, 'but I shall go anyhow. You can play bits of the Moonlight by yourself. You've often said it was another key to Beethoven's soul.'

It suddenly struck Lucia that Georgie seemed not to care two hoots whether she went or not. Her sensitive ear could not detect the smallest regret in his voice, and the prospect of his going alone was strangely distasteful. She did not fear any temperamental disturbance; Georgie's passions were not volcanic, but there was glitter and glamour in opera houses and prima donnas which might upset him if he was unchaperoned.

'I'll try to manage it somehow, dear, for your sake,' she said, 'for I know how disappointed you would be if I didn't join you in Olga's welcome to London. Dear me; I've been keeping Mrs Simpson waiting a terrible time. Shall I take Olga's letter and dictate a grateful acceptance from both of us?'

'Don't bother,' said Georgie. 'I'll do it. You're much too busy. And as for that bit of Benjy's riding-whip, I daresay it will turn up.'

*   *   *

The prospectus of the Mayoral series of cultural lectures at the Literary Institute was re-cast, for the other lecturers, wildly excited at the prospect, found every night equally convenient. Mrs Simpson was supplied with packets of tickets, and books of receipts and counterfoils for those who sent a shilling for a single lecture or five shillings for the whole course. She arrived now at half-past nine o'clock so as to be ready for the Mayor's dictation of official correspondence at ten, and had always got through this additional work by that time. Complimentary tickets in the front row were sent to Town Councillors for Lucia's inaugural lecture, with the request that they should be returned if the recipient found himself unable to attend. Apart from these, the sale was very sluggish. Mr John Gielgud could not attend the lecture on Shakespearian technique, and previous engagements prevented the Bishop and Sir Henry Wood from listening to the Padre on Free-Will and Lucia on Beethoven. But luckily the *Hampshire Argus* had already announced that they had received invitations.

'Charming letters from them all, Georgie,'

said Lucia, tearing them up, 'and their evident disappointment at not being able to come really touches me. And I don't regret, far from it, that apparently we shall not have very large audiences. A small audience is more *intime*; the personal touch is more quickly established. And now for my sleep-walking scene in the first lecture. I should like to discuss that with you. I shall give that with Elizabethan realism.'

'Not pyjamas?' asked Georgie, in an awestruck voice.

'Certainly not: it would be a gross anachronism. But I shall have all the lights in the room extinguished. Night.'

'Then they won't see you,' said Georgie. 'You would lose the personal touch.'

Lucia puzzled over this problem.

'Ah! I have it!' she said. 'An electric torch.'

'Wouldn't that be an anachronism, too?' interrupted Georgie.

'Rather a pedantic criticism, Georgie,' said Lucia.

'An electric torch: and as soon as the room is plunged in darkness, I shall turn it on to my face. I shall advance slowly, only my face visible suspended in the air, to the edge of the platform. Eyes open I think: I believe sleep-walkers often have their eyes open. Very wide, something like this, and unseeing. Filled with an expression of internal soul-horror. Have you half an hour to spare? Put the lights out, dear: I have my electric torch. Now.'

As the day for the inaugural lecture drew near and the bookings continued unsatisfactory except from the *intime* point of view, Lucia showered complimentary tickets right and left. Grosvenor and Foljambe received them and Diva's Janet. In fact, those who had purchased tickets felt defrauded, since so many were to be had without even asking for them. This discontent reached Lucia's ears, and in an ecstasy of fair-mindedness she paid Mrs Simpson the sum of one shilling for each complimentary ticket she had sent out. But even that did not silence the carpings of Elizabeth.

'What it really comes to, Diva,' she said, 'is that Worship is paying everybody to attend her lecture.'

'Nothing of the kind,' said Diva. 'She is taking seats for her lecture, and giving them to her friends.'

'Much the same thing,' said Elizabeth, 'but we won't argue. Of course she'll take the same number for Benjy's lecture and yours and all the others.'

'Don't see why, if, as you say, she's only paying people to go to hers. Major Benjy can pay people to go to his.'

Elizabeth softened at the thought of the puzzle that would rack the brains of Tilling when Benjy lectured.

'The dear boy is quite excited about it,' she said. 'He's going to have his tiger-skins hung up behind the platform to give local jungle-colour. He's copied out his lecture twice already and is thinking of having it typed. I daresay Worship would allow Mrs Simpson to do it for nothing to fill up her time a little. He read it to me: most dramatic. How I shuddered when he told how he had hit the man-slayer across the nose while he seized his rifle. Such a pity he can't whack that very tiger-skin with the riding-whip he used then. He's never quite got over its loss.'

Elizabeth eyed Diva narrowly and thought she looked very uncomfortable, as if she knew something about that loss. But she replied in the most spirited manner.

'Wouldn't be very wise of him,' she said. 'Might take a lot more of the fur off. Might hurt the dead tiger more than he hurt the live one.'

'Very droll,' said Elizabeth. 'But as the riding-whip vanished so mysteriously in your house, there's the end of it.'

*   *   *

Thanks to Lucia's prudent distribution of complimentary tickets, the room was very well filled at the inaugural lecture. Georgie for a week past had been threatened with a nervous

184

collapse at the thought of taking the chair, but he had staved this off by patent medicines, physical exercises and breakfast in bed. Wearing his ruby-coloured dinner-suit, he told the audience in a firm and audible voice that any introductory words from him were quite unnecessary, as they all knew the lecturer so well. He then revealed the astonishing fact that she was their beloved Mayor of Tilling, the woman whom he had the honour to call wife. She would now address them on the Technique of the Shakespearian Stage.

Lucia first gave them a brief and lucid definition of Drama as the audible and visible presentation of situations of human woe or weal, based on and developing from those dynamic individual forces which evoke the psychological clashes of temperament that give rise to action. This action (drama) being strictly dependent on the underlying motives which prompt it and on emotional stresses might be roughly summed up as Plot. It was important that her audience should grasp that quite clearly. She went on to say that anything that distracts attention from Plot or from the psychology of which it is the logical outcome, hinders rather than helps Drama, and therefore the modern craze for elaborate decorations and embellishments must be ruthlessly condemned. It was otherwise in Shakespeare's day. There was hardly any scenery for the setting of his masterpieces, and she ventured to put forward a theory which had hitherto escaped the acumen of more erudite Shakespearian scholars than she. Shakespeare was a staunch upholder of this simplicity and had unmistakably shewn that in *Midsummer Night's Dream.* In that glorious masterpiece a play was chosen for the marriage festival at Athens, and the setting of it clearly proved Shakespeare's conviction that the less distraction of scenery there was on the stage, the better for Drama. The moon appeared in this play within a play. Modern *decor* would have provided a luminous disk moving slowly across the sky by some mechanical device. Not so Shakespeare. A man came on with a lantern, and told them that his lantern was the moon and he the man in the moon. There he was static and undistracting. Again the lovers Pyramus and Thisbe were separated by a wall. Modern *decor* would have furnished a convincing edifice covered with climbing roses. Not so Shakespeare. A man came out of the wings and said 'I am the wall.' The lovers required a chink to talk through. The wall held up his hand and parted his fingers. Thus, in the guise of a jest the Master poured scorn on elaborate scenery.

'I will now,' said Lucia, 'without dress or scenery of any sort, give you an illustration of the technique of the Shakespearian Stage. Lady Macbeth in the sleep-walking scene.'

Foljambe, previously instructed, was sitting by the switch-board, and on a sign from Georgie, plunged the hall in darkness. Everybody thought that a fuse had gone. That fear was dispelled because Lucia, fumbling in the dark, could not find her electric torch, and Georgie called out 'Turn them on again, Foljambe.' Lucia found her torch and once more the lights went out. Then the face of the Mayor sprang into vivid illumination, suspended against the blackness, and her open, sleep-walking eyes gleamed with soul-horror in the focused light. A difficult moment came when she made the pantomimic washing of her hands for the beam went wobbling about all over the place and once fell full on Georgie's face, which much embarrassed him. He deftly took the torch from her and duly controlled its direction. At the end of the speech Foljambe restored the lights, and Lucia went on with her lecture.

Owing to the absence of distinguished strangers she did not give a supper-party afterwards, at which her subject could be further discussed and illuminated, but she was in a state of high elation herself as she and Georgie partook of a plain supper alone.

'From the first moment,' she said, waving a sandwich, 'I knew that I was in touch with my audience and held them in my hand. A delicious sensation of power and expansion,

187

Georgie; it is no use my trying to describe it to you, for you have to experience it to understand it. I regret that the *Hampshire Argus* cannot have a verbatim report in its issue this week. Mr McConnell—how he enjoyed it—told me that it went to press to-night. I said I quite understood, and should not think of asking him to hold it up. I gave him the full typescript for next week, and promised to let him have a close-up photograph of Lady Macbeth; just my face with the background blacked out. He thanked me most warmly. And I thought, didn't you, that I did the sleep-walking scene at the right moment, just after I had been speaking of Shakespearian simplicity. A little earlier than I had meant, but I suddenly felt that it came there. I *knew* it came there.'

'The very place for it,' said Georgie, vividly recalling her catechism after the Mayoral banquet.

'And that little *contretemps* about the light going out before I had found my torch—'

'That wasn't my fault,' said he. 'You told me to signal to Foljambe, when you said "sleep-walking scene." That was my cue.'

'My dear, of course it wasn't your fault,' said Lucia warmly. 'You were punctuality itself. I was only thinking how fortunate that was. The audience knew what was coming, and that made the suspense greater. The rows of upturned faces, Georgie; the suspense; I could see the strain in their eyes. And in the speech, I think I got, didn't I, that veiled timbre in my voice suggestive of the unconscious physical mechanism, sinking to a strangled whisper at "Out, damned spot!" That, I expect, was not quite original, for I now remember when I was quite a child being taken to see Ellen Terry in the part and she veiled her voice like that. A sub-conscious impression coming to the surface.'

She rose.

'You must tell me more of what you thought to-morrow, dear,' she said, 'for I must go to bed. The emotional strain has quite worn me out, though it was well worth while. Mere mental or physical exertion—'

'I feel very tired too,' said Georgie.

He followed Lucia upstairs, waiting while she practised the Lady Macbeth face in front of the mirror on the landing.

*　　　*　　　*

Benjy's lecture took place a week later. There was a palm tree beside his reading desk and his three tiger-skins hung on the wall behind. 'Very effective, Georgie,' said Lucia, as they took their seats in the middle of the front row. 'Quite the Shakespearian tradition. It brings the jungle to us, the heat of the Indian noonday, the buzz of insects. I feel quite stifled' ... He marched on to the platform, carrying a rifle, and wearing a pith helmet and saluted the audience. He described himself as a plain old campaigner, who had seen a good deal of shikarri in his time, and read them a series of exciting adventures. Then (what a climax!) he took up from his desk a cane riding-whip with a silver top and pointed to the third of the skins.

'And that old villain,' he said, 'nearly prevented my having the honour to speak to you to-night. I had just sat down to a bit of tiffin, putting my rifle aside, when he was on me.'

He whisked round and gave the head of the tiger-skin a terrific whack.

'I slashed at him, just like that, with my riding-whip which I had in my hand, and that gave me the half-second I needed to snatch up my rifle. I fired point-blank at his heart, and he rolled over dead. And this, ladies and gentlemen, is what saved my life. It may interest you to see it, though it is familiar to some of you. I will pass it round.'

He bowed to the applause and drank some whisky and a little soda. Lucia took the riding-whip from him, and passed it to Georgie, Georgie passed it to Diva. They all carefully examined the silver top, and the initials B. F. were engraved on it. There could be no doubt of its genuineness and they all became very still and thoughtful, forbearing to look at each other.

There was loud applause at the end of the lecture, and after making rather a long speech, thanking the lecturer, Lucia turned to Diva.

'Come to lunch to-morrow,' she whispered. 'Just us three. I am utterly puzzled ... Ah, Major Benjy, marvellous! What a treat! I have never been so thrilled. Dear Elizabeth, how proud you must be of him. He ought to have that lecture printed, not a word, not a syllable altered, and read it to the Royal Zoological Society. They would make him an honorary member at once.'

*   *   *

Next day at a secret session in the garden-room Georgie and Diva contributed their personal share in the strange history of the relic (Paddy's being taken for granted, as no other supposition would fit the facts of the case) and thus the movements of the silver cap were accounted for up to the moment of its disappearance from Georgie's possession.

'I always kept it in my waistcoat pocket,' he concluded, 'and one morning it couldn't be found anywhere. You remember that, don't you, Lucia?'

A look of intense concentration dwelt in Lucia's eyes: Georgie did not expect much from that, because it so often led to nothing at all. Then she spoke in that veiled voice which had become rather common with her since the sleep-walking scene.

'Yes, yes,' she murmured. 'It comes back to me. And the evening before Elizabeth and Benjy had dined with us. Did it drop out of your pocket, do you think, Georgie? ... She and I came into the garden-room after dinner, and ... and she asked me to play to her, which is unusual. I am always unconscious of all else when I am playing...'

Lucia dropped the veiled voice which was hard to keep up and became very distinct.

'She sat all by herself at my table here,' she continued. 'What if she found it on the floor or somewhere? I seem to sense her doing that. And she had something on her mind when we played Bridge. She couldn't attend at all, and she suggested stopping before eleven, because she said I looked so tired, though I was never fresher. Certainly we never saw the silver cap again till last night.'

'Well that is ingenious,' said Diva, 'and then I suppose they had another cane fitted to it, and Benjy said it was the real one. I do call that deceitful. How can we serve them out? Let's all think.'

They all thought. Lucia sat with her head on one side contemplating the ceiling, as was her wont when listening to music. Then she supplied the music, too, and laughed in the silvery ascending scale of an octave and a half.

'*Amichi*,' she said. 'If you will leave it to me, I think I can arrange something that will puzzle

192

Elizabeth. She and her accomplice have thought fit to try to puzzle us. I will contrive to puzzle them.'

Diva glanced at the clock.

'How scrumptious!' she said. 'Do be quick and tell us, because I must get back to help Janet.'

'Not quite complete yet,' answered Lucia. 'A few finishing touches. But trust me.'

Diva trundled away down the hill at top-speed. A party of clerical tourists were spending a day of pilgrimage in Tilling, and after being shewn round the church by the Padre were to refresh themselves at 'ye olde Tea-House.' The Padre would have his tea provided gratis as was customary with Couriers. She paused for a moment outside her house to admire the sign which quaint Irene had painted for her. There was nothing nude about it. Queen Anne in full regalia was having tea with the Archbishop of Canterbury, and decorum reigned. Diva plunged down the kitchen-stairs, and peeped into the garden where the tulips were now in flower. She wondered which tulip it was.

*   *   *

As often happened in Tilling, affairs of sensational interest overlapped. Georgie woke next morning to find Foljambe bringing in his early morning tea with the *Daily Mirror*.

193

'A picture this morning, sir, that'll make you jump,' she said. 'Lor', what'll happen?'

Off she went to fill his bath, and Georgie, still rather sleepy, began to look through the paper. On the third page was an article on the Royal Academy Exhibition, of which the Private View was to be held today.

'The Picture of the Year,' said our Art Editor, 'is already determined. For daring realism, for withering satire of the so-called Victorian age, for savage caricature of the simpering, guileless prettiness of such early Italian artists as Botticelli, Miss Irene Coles's—' Georgie read no more but turned to the centre-page of pictures. There it was. Simultaneously there came a rap on his door, and Grosvenor's hand, delicately inserted, in case he had got up, held a copy of the *Times*.

'Her Worship thought you might like to see the picture-page of the *Times*,' she said. 'And could you spare her the *Daily Mirror*, if it's got it in.'

The transfer was effected. There again was Elizabeth on her oyster-shell being wafted by Benjy up the river to the quay at Tilling, and our Art Editor gave his most serious attention to this arresting piece. He was not sure whether it was justifiable to parody a noble work of art in order to ridicule an age, which, in spite of its fantastic prudery, was distinguished for achievement and progress. But no one could question the vigour, the daring, the exuberant

194

vitality of this amazing canvas. Technically—

Georgie bounded out of bed. Thoughtful and suggestive though this criticism was, it was also lengthy, and the need for discussion with Lucia as to the reactions of Tilling was more immediate, especially since she had a committee meeting at ten. He omitted to have his bath at all, and nearly forgot about his *toupée.* She was already at breakfast when he got down, with the *Daily Mirror* propped up against the teapot in front of her, and seemed to continue aloud what she must have been saying to herself.

'—and in my position, I must—good morning, Georgie—be extremely careful. She *is* my Mayoress, and therefore, through me, has an official position, which I am bound to uphold if it is brought into ridicule. I should equally resent any ruthless caricature of the Padre, as he is my chaplain. Of course you've seen the picture itself, Georgie, which, alas, I never did, and it's hard to form a reasoned judgment from a reduced reproduction. Is it really like poor Elizabeth?'

'The image,' said Georgie. 'You could tell it a hundred miles off. It's the image of Benjy, too. But that thing in his hand, which looks so like the neck of a bottle is really the top of his umbrella.'

'No! I thought it was a bottle,' said Lucia. 'I'm glad of that. The other would have been a sad lack of taste.'

'Oh, it's all a lack of taste,' said Georgie, 'though I don't quite feel the sadness. On the other hand it's being hailed as a masterpiece. That'll sweeten it for them a bit.'

Lucia held the paper up to get a longer focus, and Georgie got his tea.

'A wonderful pose,' she said. 'Really, there's something majestic and dominant about Elizabeth, which distinctly flatters her. And look at Benjy with his cheeks puffed out, as when he's declared three no trumps, and knows he can't get them. A boisterous wind evidently, such as often comes roaring up the river. Waves tipped with foam. A slight want of perspective, I should have said, about the houses of Tilling ... One can't tell how Elizabeth will take it—'

'I should have thought one could make a good guess,' said Georgie.

'But it's something, as you say, to have inspired a masterpiece.'

'Yes, but Irene's real object was to be thoroughly nasty. The critics seem to have found in the picture a lot she didn't intend to put there.'

'Ah, but who can tell about the artist's mind?' asked Lucia, with a sudden attack of high-brow. 'Did Messer Leonardo really see in the face of La Gioconda all that our wonderful Walter Pater found there? Does not the artist work in a sort of trance?'

'No; Irene wasn't in a trance at all,' insisted

Georgie. 'Anything but. And as for your feeling that because Elizabeth is Mayoress you ought to resent it, that's thoroughly inconsistent with your theory that Art's got nothing to do with Life. But I'll go down to the High Street soon, and see what the general feeling is. You'll be late, dear, if you don't go off to your meeting at once. In fact, you're late already.'

Lucia mounted her bicycle in a great hurry and set off for the Town Hall. With every stroke of her pedals she felt growing pangs of jealousy of Elizabeth. Why, oh why, had not Irene painted her, the Mayor, the first woman who had ever been Mayor of Tilling, being wafted up the river, with Georgie blowing on her from the clouds?

Such a picture would have had a far greater historical interest, and she would not have resented the grossest caricature of herself if only she could have been the paramount figure in the Picture of the Year. The town in the background would be widely recognised as Tilling, and Lucia imagined the eager comments of the crowd swarming round the masterpiece ... 'Why that's Tilling! We spent a week there this summer. Just like! ...' 'And who can that woman be? Clearly a portrait' ... 'Oh, that's the Mayor, Lucia Pillson: she was pointed out to me. Lives in a lovely family house called Mallards' ... 'And the man in the clouds with the Vandyck beard and the red dinner-suit (what a colour!) must be her husband...'

'What fame!' thought Lucia with aching regret. 'What illimitable, immortal *réclame*. What publicity to be stared at all day by excited crowds!' At this moment the Private View would be going on, and Duchesses and Archbishops and Cabinet Ministers would soon be jostling to get a view of her, instead of Elizabeth and Benjy! 'I must instantly commission Irene to paint my portrait,' she said to herself as she dismounted at the steps of the Town Hall. 'A picture that tells a story I think. A sort of biography. In my robes by the front door at Mallards with my hand on my bicycle...'

She gave but scant attention to the proceedings at her Committee, and mounting again rang the bell all the way down the hill into the High Street on a secret errand to the haberdashery shop. By a curious coincidence she met Major Benjy on the threshold. He was carrying the reconstructed riding-whip and was in high elation.

'Good morning, your Worship,' he said. 'Just come to have my riding-whip repaired. I gave my old man-eater such a swipe at my lecture two nights ago, that I cracked it, by Jove.'

'Oh Major, what a pity!' said Lucia. 'But it was almost worth breaking it, wasn't it? You produced such a dramatic sensation.'

'And there's another sensation this morning,' chuckled Benjy. 'Have you seen the notice of the Royal Academy in the *Times*?'

Lucia still considered that the proper public line to take was her sense of the insult to her Mayoress, though certainly Benjy seemed very cheerful.

'I have,' she said indignantly. 'Oh, Major Benjy, it is monstrous! I was horrified: I should not have thought it of Irene. And the *Daily Mirror*, too—'

'No, really?' interrupted Benjy. 'I must get it.'

'Such a wanton insult to dear Elizabeth,' continued Lucia, 'and, of course, to you up in the clouds. Horrified! I shall write to Elizabeth as soon as I get home to convey my sympathy and indignation.'

'Don't you bother!' cried Benjy. 'Liz hasn't been so bucked up with anything for years. After all, to be the principal feature in the Picture of the Year is a privilege that doesn't fall to everybody. Such a leg up for our obscure little Tilling, too. We're going up to town next week to see it. Why, here's Liz herself.'

Elizabeth kissed her hand to Lucia from the other side of the street, and, waiting till Susan went ponderously by, tripped across, and kissed her (Lucia's) face.

'What a red-letter day, dear!' she cried. 'Quaint Irene suddenly becoming so world-wide, and your humble little Mayoress almost equally so. Benjy, it's in the *Daily Telegraph*, too. You'd better get a copy of every morning paper. Pop in, and tell them to mend your riding-whip, while I send a telegram of congratulation to Irene.—I should think Burlington House, London, would find her now—and meet me at the paper-shop. And do persuade Irene, Worship, to let us have the picture for our exhibition here, when the Academy's over, unless the Chantrey Bequest buys it straight away.'

Benjy went into the haberdashers's to get the riding-whip repaired. This meeting with him just here made Lucia's errand much simpler. She followed him into the shop and became completely absorbed in umbrellas till he went out again. Then, with an eye on the door, she spoke to the shopman in a confidential tone.

'I want you,' she said, 'to make me an exact copy of Major Mapp-Flint's pretty riding-whip. Silver top with the same initials on it. Quite private, you understand: it's a little surprise for a friend. And send it, please, to me at Mallards House, as soon as it's ready.'

Lucia mounted her bicycle and rode thoughtfully homewards. Since Elizabeth and Benjy both took this gross insult to her Mayoress as the highest possible compliment, and longed to have quaint Irene's libel on them exhibited here, there was no need that she should make herself indignant or unhappy for their sakes. Indeed, she understood their elation, and her regret that Irene had not caricatured her instead of Elizabeth grew very bitter: she would have borne it with a magnanimity fully equal to theirs. It was a slight consolation to know that the replica of the riding-whip was in hand.

She went out into the garden-room where patient Mrs Simpson was waiting for her. There were invitations to be sent out for an afternoon party next week to view the beauties of Lucia's spring-garden, for which she wanted to rouse the envious admiration of her friends, and the list must be written out. Then there was a letter to Irene of warm congratulation to be typed. Then the Committee of the Museum, of which the Mayor was Chairman was to meet on Friday, and she gave Mrs Simpson the key of the tin-box labelled 'Museum'.

'Just look in it, Mrs Simpson,' she said, 'and see if there are any papers I ought to glance through. A mountain of work, I fear, to-day.'

Grosvenor appeared.

'Could you see Mrs Wyse for a moment?' she asked.

Lucia knitted her brows, and consulted her engagement-book.

'Yes, just for ten minutes,' she said. 'Ask her to come out here.'

Grosvenor went back into the house to fetch Susan, and simultaneously Mrs Simpson gave a shriek of horror.

'The corpse of a blue parrakeet,' she cried,

'and an awful smell.'

Lucia sprang from her seat. She plucked Blue Birdie, exhaling disinfectant and decay, from the Museum box, and scudding across the room thrust it into the fire. She poked and battered it down among the glowing embers, and even as she wrought she cursed herself for not having told Mrs Simpson to leave it where it was and lock the Museum box again, but it was too late for that. In that swift journey to cremation Blue Birdie had dropped a plume or two, and from the fire came a vivid smell of burned feathers. But she was just in time and had resumed her seat and taken up her pen as Susan came ponderously up the steps into the garden-room.

'Good morning, dear,' said Lucia. 'At my eternal tasks as usual, but charmed to see you.'

She rose in welcome, and to her horror saw a long blue tail-feather (slightly tinged with red) on the carpet. She planted her foot upon it.

'Good morning,' said Susan. 'What a horrid smell of burned feathers.'

Lucia sniffed, still standing firm.

'I do smell something,' she said. 'Gas, surely. I thought I smelt it the other day. I must send for my town-surveyor. Do you not smell gas, Mrs Simpson?'

Lucia focused on her secretary the full power of her gimlet-eye.

'Certainly, gas,' said that loyal woman, locking the Museum box.

'Most disagreeable,' said Lucia, advancing on Susan. 'Let us go into the garden and have our little talk there. I know what you've come about: Irene's picture. The Picture of the Year, they say. Elizabeth is famous at last, and is skipping for joy. I am so pleased for her sake.'

'I should certainly have said burned feathers,' repeated Susan.

Dire speculations flitted through Lucia's mind: would Susan's vague but retentive brain begin to grope after a connection between burned feathers and her vanished bird? A concentration of force and volubility was required, and taking another step forward on to another blue feather, she broke into a gabble of topics as she launched Susan, like a huge liner, down the slip of the garden-room stairs.

'No, Susan, gas,' she said. 'And have you seen the reproduction of Irene's picture in the *Times*? Mrs Simpson, would you kindly bring the *Times* into the garden. You must stroll across the lawn and have a peep at my daffodils in my *giardino segreto*. Never have I had such a show. Those lovely lines "dancing with the daffodils." How true! I saw you in the High Street this morning, dear, on your tricycle. And such wallflowers; they will be in fullest bloom for my party next week, to which you and Mr Wyse must come. And Benjy in the clouds; so like, but Georgie says it isn't a bottle, but his umbrella. Tell me *exactly* what you think of it all. So important that I should know what Tilling feels.'

Unable to withstand such a cataract of subjects, Susan could hardly say 'burned feathers' again. She showed a tendency to drift towards the garden-room on their return, but Lucia, like a powerful tug, edged her away from dangerous shoal and towed her out to the front door of Mallards, where she cast her adrift to propel her tricycle under her own steam. Then returning to the garden-room, she found that the admirable Mrs Simpson had picked up a few more feathers, which she had laid on Lucia's blotting-pad.

Lucia threw them into the fire and swept up some half-burned fragments from the hearth.

'The smell of gas seems quite gone, Mrs Simpson,' she said. 'No need, I think, to send for my town-surveyor. It is such a pleasure to work with anyone who understands me as well as you ... Yes, the list for my garden-party.'

*　　　*　　　*

The replica of the riding-whip was delivered, and looked identical. Lucia's disposition of it was singular. After she had retired for the night, she tied it safely up among the foliage of the Clematis Montana which grew thickly up to the sill of her bedroom window. The silver top soon grew tarnished in this exposure, spiders spun threads about it, moisture dulled its varnished shaft, and it became a weathered

204

object. 'About ripe,' said Lucia to herself one morning, and rang up Elizabeth and Benjy, inviting them to tea at ye olde tea-house next day, with Bridge to follow. They had just returned from their visit to London to see the Picture of the Year, and accepted with pleasure.

Before starting for Diva's, Lucia took her umbrella up to her bedroom, and subsequently carried it to the tea-room, arriving there ten minutes before the others. Diva was busy in the kitchen, and she looked into the card-room. Yes: there was the heavy cupboard with claw feet standing in the corner; perfect. Her manoeuvres then comprised opening her umbrella and furling it again; and hearing Diva's firm foot on the kitchen stairs she came softly back into the tea-room.

'Diva, *what* a delicious smell!' she said. 'Oh, I want eighteen-penny teas. I came a few minutes early to tell you.'

'Reckoned on that,' said Diva. 'The smell is waffles. I've been practising. Going to make waffles at my lecture, as an illustration, if I can do them over a spirit-lamp. Hand them round to the front row. Good advertisement. Here are the others.'

The waffles were a greater success than Diva had anticipated, and the compliments hardly made up for the consumption. Then they adjourned to the card-room, and Lucia, leaning her umbrella against the wall let it slip behind the big cupboard.

'So clumsy!' she said, 'but never mind it now. We shall have to move the cupboard afterwards. Cut? You and I, Georgie. Families. Happy families.'

It was chatty Bridge at first, rich in agreeable conversation.

'We only got back from London yesterday,' said Elizabeth, dealing. 'Such a rush, but we went to the Academy three times; one no trump.'

'Two spades,' said Georgie. 'What did you think of the Picture?'

'Such a crowd round it! We had to scriggle in.'

'And I'm blest if I don't believe that they recognised Liz,' put in Major Benjy. 'A couple of women looked at her and then at the picture and back again, and whispered together, by Jove.'

'I'm sure they recognised me at our second visit,' said Elizabeth. 'The crowd was thicker than ever, and we got quite wedged in. Such glances and whisperings all round. Most entertaining, wasn't it, Benjy?'

Lucia tried to cork up her bitterness, but failed.

'I *am* glad you enjoyed it so much, dear,' she said. 'How I envy you your superb self-confidence. I should find such publicity quite insupportable. I should have scriggled out again at whatever cost.'

'Dear Worship, I don't think you would if you ever found yourself in such a position,' said Elizabeth. 'You would face it. So brave!'

'If we're playing Bridge, two spades was what I said. Ever so long ago,' announced Georgie.

'Oh, Mr Georgie; apologies,' said Elizabeth. 'I'm such a chatterbox. What do you bid, Benjy? Don't be so slow.'

'Two no trumps,' said Benjy. 'We made our third visit during lunch-time, when there were fewer people—'

'Three spades,' said Lucia. 'All I meant, dear Elizabeth, was that it is sufficient for me to tackle my little bit of public service, quietly and humbly and obscurely—'

'So like you, dear,' retorted Elizabeth, 'and I double three spades. That'll be a nice little bit for you to tackle quietly.'

Lucia made no reply, but the pleasant atmosphere was now charged with perilous stuff, for on the one side the Mayor was writhing with envy at the recognition of Elizabeth from the crowds round the Picture of the Year, while the Mayoress was writhing with exasperation at Lucia's pitiful assertion that she shunned publicity.

Lucia won the doubled contract and the game.

'So there's my little bit, Georgie,' she said, 'and you played it very carefully, though of course it was a sitter. I ought to have

207

redoubled: forgive me.'

'Benjy, your finesse was idiotic,' said Elizabeth, palpably wincing. 'If you had played your ace, they'd have been two down. Probably more.'

'And what about your doubling?' asked Benjy. 'And what about your original no-trump?'

'Thoroughly justified, both of them,' said Elizabeth, 'if you hadn't finessed. Cut to me, please, Worship.'

'But you've just dealt, dear,' cooed Lucia.

'Haw, Haw. Well tried, Liz,' said Benjy.

Elizabeth looked so deadly at Benjy's gentle fun that at the end of the hand Lucia loaded her with compliments.

'Beautifully played, dear!' she said. 'Did you notice, Georgie, how Elizabeth kept putting the lead with you? Masterly!'

Elizabeth was not to be appeased with that sort of blarney.

'Thank you, dear,' she said. 'I'm sorry, Benjy: I ought to have put the lead with Worship, and taken another trick.'

*　　*　　*

Diva came in as they were finishing the last rubber.

'Quite a lot of teas,' she said. 'But they all come in so late now. Hungrier, I suppose. Saves them supper. No more waffles for shilling teas. Not if I know it. Too popular.'

Lucia had won from the whole table, and with an indifferent air she swept silver and copper into her bag without troubling to count it.

'I must be off,' she said. 'I have pages of Borough expenditure to look through. Oh, my umbrella! I nearly forgot it.'

'Dear Worship,' asked Elizabeth. 'Do tell me what that means! Either you forget a thing, or you don't.'

'I let it slip behind your big cupboard, Diva,' said Lucia, not taking the slightest notice of her Mayoress. 'Catch hold of that end, Georgie, and we'll run it out from the wall.'

'Permit me,' said Benjy, taking Lucia's end. 'Now then, with a heave-ho, as they say in the sister service. One, two, three.'

He gave a tremendous tug. The cupboard, not so heavy as it looked, glided away from the wall with an interior rattle of crockery.

'Oh, my things!' cried Diva. 'Do be careful.'

'Here's your umbrella,' said Georgie. 'Covered with dust ... Why, what's this? Major Benjy's riding-whip, isn't it? Lost here ages ago. Well, that is queer!'

Diva simply snatched it from Georgie.

'But it is!' she cried. 'Initials, everything. Must have lain here all this time. But at your lecture the other day Major—'

Lucia instantly interrupted her.

'What a fortunate discovery!' she said. 'How

209

glad you will be, Major, to get your precious relic back. Why it's half-past seven! Good night everybody.'

She and Georgie let themselves out into the street.

'But you *must* tell me,' said he, as they walked briskly up the hill. 'I shall die if you don't tell me. How did you do it?'

'I? What do you mean?' asked the aggravating woman.

'You're too tar'some,' said Georgie crossly. 'And it isn't fair. Diva told you how she buried the silver cap, and I told you how I dug it up, and you tell us nothing. Very miserly!'

Lucia was startled at the ill-humour in his voice.

'My dear, I was only teasing you—' she began.

'Well it doesn't amuse me to be teased,' he snapped at her. 'You're like Elizabeth sometimes.'

'Georgie, what a monstrous thing to say to me! Of course, I'll tell you, and Diva, too. Ring her up and ask her to pop in after dinner.'

She paused with her hand on the door of Mallards.

'But never hint to the poor Mapp-Flints,' she said, 'as Diva did just now, that the riding-whip Benjy used at his lecture couldn't have been the real one. They knew that quite well, and they knew we know it. Much more excruciating for them *not* to rub it in.'

210

CHAPTER EIGHT

Lucia, followed by Georgie, and preceded by an attendant, swept along the corridor behind the boxes on the grand tier at Covent Garden Opera House. They had dined early at their hotel and were in good time. She wore her seed-pearls in her hair, her gold Mayoral badge, like an Order, on her breast, and her gown was of a rich, glittering russet hue like cloth of copper. A competent-looking lady, hovering about with a small note book and a pencil, hurried up to her as the attendant opened the door of the box.

'Name, please,' he said to Lucia.

'The Mayor of Tilling,' said Lucia, raising her voice for the benefit of the lady with the note book.

He consulted his list.

'No such name, ma'am,' he said. 'Madam has given strict orders—'

'Mr and Mrs Pillson,' suggested Georgie.

'That's all right, sir'; and in they went.

The house was gleaming with tiaras and white shoulders, and loud with conversation. Lucia stood for a minute at the front of the box which was close to the stage, and nodded and smiled as she looked this way and that, as if recognising friends ... But, oh, to think that she might have been recognised, too, if only

Irene had portrayed her in the Picture of the Year! They had been to see it this afternoon, and Georgie, also, had felt pangs of regret that it was not he with his Vandyck beard who sprawled windily among the clouds. But in spite of that he was very happy for in a few minutes now he would hear and see his adorable Olga again, and they were to lunch with her to-morrow at her hotel.

A burst of applause hailed the appearance of Cortese, composer, librettist and, to-night, conductor of *Lucrezia*. Lucia waggled her hand at him. He certainly bowed in her direction (for he was bowing in all directions), and she made up her mind to scrap her previous verdict on the opera and be enchanted with it.

The Royal party unfortunately invisible from Lucia's box arrived, and after the National Anthem the first slow notes of the overture wailed on the air.

'Divine!' she whispered to Georgie. 'How well I remember dear Signor Cortese playing it to me at Riseholme. I think he took it a shade faster … There! Lucrezia's motif, or is it the Pope's? Tragic splendour. The first composer in Europe.'

If Georgie had not known Lucia so well, he would scarcely have believed his ears. On that frightful evening, three years ago, when Olga had asked her to come and hear 'bits' of it, she had professed herself outraged at the hideous, modern stuff, but there were special circumstances on that occasion which conduced to pessimism. Lucia had let it be widely supposed that she talked Italian with ease and fluency, but when confronted with Cortese, it was painfully clear that she could not understand a word he said. An awful exposure ... Now she was in a prominent box, guest of the prima donna, at this gala performance, she could not be called upon to talk to Cortese without annoying the audience very much, and she was fanatic in admiration. She pressed Georgie's hand, emotion drowning utterance; she rose in her place at the end of Olga's great song in the first act, crying 'Brava! Brava!' in the most correct Italian, and was convinced that she led the applause that followed.

During the course of the second act, the box was invaded by a large lady, clad in a magnificent tiara, but not much else, and a small man, who hid himself at the back. Lucia felt justly indignant at this interruption, but softened when the box-attendant appeared with another programme, and distinctly said 'Your Grace' to the large lady. That made a difference, and during the interval Lucia talked very pleasantly to her (for when strangers were thrown together stiffness was ridiculous) and told her how she had heard her beloved Olga run through some of her part before the opera was produced, and that she had prophesied a huge success for it. She was agonising to know what the large lady was the Grace of, but could scarcely put so personal a question on such short acquaintance. She did not seem a brilliant conversationalist, but stared rather fixedly at Georgie ... At the end of the opera there was immense enthusiasm: Olga and Cortese were recalled again and again, and during these effusions, Her unidentified Grace and her companion left: Lucia presumed that they were husband and wife as they took no notice of each other. She regretted their disappearance, but consoled herself with the reflection that their names would appear in the dazzling list of those who would be recorded in the press to-morrow as having attended the first performance of *Lucrezia*. The competent female in the corridor would surely see to that.

Georgie lay long awake that night. The music had excited him, and, more than the music, Olga herself. What a voice, what an exquisite face and presence, what an infinite charm! He recalled his bachelor days at Riseholme, when Lucia had been undisputed Queen of that highly-cultured village and he her *cavaliere servente*, whose allegiance had been seriously shaken by Olga's advent. He really had been in love with her, he thought, and the fact that she had a husband alive then, to whom she was devoted, allowed a moral man like him to indulge his emotions in complete security. It had thrilled him with daring joy to imagine that, had Olga been free, he would have asked her to marry him, but even in those flights of fancy he knew that her acceptance of him would have put him in a panic. Since then, of course, he had been married himself, but his union with Lucia had not been formidable, as they had agreed that no ardent tokens of affection were to mar their union. Marriage, in fact, with Lucia might be regarded as a vow of celibacy. Now, after three years, the situation was reversing itself in the oddest manner. Olga's husband had died and she was free, while his own marriage with Lucia protected him. His high moral principles would never suffer him to be unfaithful to his wife. 'I am not that sort of man,' he said to himself. 'I must go to sleep.'

He tossed and turned on his bed. Visions of Olga as he had seen her to-night floated behind his closed eyelids. Olga as a mere girl at the fête of her infamous father Pope Alexander VI: Olga at her marriage in the Sistine Chapel to the Duke of Biseglia: his murder in her presence by the hired bravos of His Holiness and her brother. The scenery was fantastically gorgeous ('not Shakespearian at all, Georgie,' Lucia had whispered to him), but when Olga was on the stage, he was conscious of nothing but her. She outshone all the splendour, and never more so than when, swathed in black, she followed her husband's bier, and sang that lament—or was it a song of triumph?—'Amore misterioso, celeste, profondo.' . . . 'I believe I've got a very passionate nature,' thought Georgie, 'but I've always crushed it.'

It was impossible to get to sleep, and wheeling out of bed, he lit a cigarette and paced up and down his room. But it was chilly, and putting on a smart blue knitted pullover he got back into bed again. Once more he jumped up; he had no ashtray, but the lid of his soap-dish would do, and he reviewed Life.

'I know Tilling is very exciting,' he said to himself, 'for extraordinary things are always happening, and I'm very comfortable there. But I've no independence. I'm devoted to Lucia, but what with breakfast, lunch, tea and dinner, as well as a great deal in between . . . And then how exasperating she is as Mayor! What with her ceaseless jaw about her duties and position I get fed up. Those tin boxes with nothing in them! Mrs Simpson every morning with nothing to do! I want a change. Sometimes I almost sympathise with Elizabeth, when Lucia goes rolling along like the car of Juggernaut, squish-squash, whoever comes in her way. And yet it's she, I really believe, who makes things happen, just because she is Lucia, and I don't know where we should be without her. Good gracious, that's the second cigarette I've smoked in bed, and I had my full allowance before. Why didn't I bring up my embroidery? That often makes me sleepy. I shall be fit for nothing to-morrow, lying awake like this, and I must go shopping in the morning, and then we lunch with Olga, and catch the afternoon train back to That Hole. Damn everything!'

Georgie felt better in the morning after two cups of very hot tea brought him by Foljambe who had come up as their joint maid. He read his paper, breakfasting in his room, as in his comfortable bachelor days. There was a fervent notice of *Lucrezia*, but no indication, since there had been five Duchesses present, as to which their particular Grace was, who had rather embarrassed him by her fixed eye. But then Foljambe brought him another paper which Lucia wanted back. She had marked it with a blue pencil, and there he read that the Duke and Duchess of Sheffield and the Mayor of Tilling had attended the opera in Miss Bracely's box. That gave him great satisfaction, for all those folk who had looked at their box so much would now feel sure that he was the Mayor of Tilling ... Then he went out alone for his shopping, as Lucia sent word that she had received some agenda for the next Council meeting, which she must study, and thoroughly enjoyed it. He found some very pretty new ties and some nice underwear, and he could linger by attractive windows, instead of going to some improving exhibition which Lucia would certainly have wished to do. Then in eager trepidation he went to the Ritz for lunch, and found that Lucia had not yet

217

arrived. But there was Olga in the lounge, who hailed him on a high soprano note, so that everybody knew that he was Georgie, and might have guessed, from the *timbre*, that she was Olga.

'My dear, how nice to see you,' she cried. 'But a beard, Georgie! What does it mean? Tell me all about it. Where's your Lucia? She hasn't divorced you already, I hope? And have a cocktail? I insist, because it looks so bad for an elderly female to be drinking alone, and I am dying for one. And did you like the opera last night? I thought I sang superbly; even Cortese didn't scold me. How I love being in stuffy old London again; I'm off to Riseholme to-night for a week, and you must—Ah, here's Lucia! We'll go into lunch at once. I asked Cortese, but he can't come in till afterwards. Only Poppy Sheffield is coming, and she will probably arrive about tea-time. She'll be terribly taken up with Georgie, because she adores beards, and says they are getting so rare nowadays. Don't be alarmed, my lamb: she doesn't want to touch them, but the sight of them refreshes her in some psychic manner. Oh, of course, she was in your box last night. She hates music, and hears it only as a mortification of the flesh, of which she has plenty. Quite gaga, but so harmless.'

Olga was a long time getting to her table, because she made many greetings on the way, and Lucia began to hate her again. She was too

218

casual, keeping the Mayor of Tilling standing about like this, and Lucia, who had strong views about *maquillage*, was distressed to see how many women, Olga included, were sadly made-up. And yet how marvellous to thread her way through the crowded restaurant with the prima donna, not waiting for a Duchess: if only some Tillingites had been there to see! *Per contra*, it was rather familiar of Olga to put her hand on Georgie's shoulder and shove him into his place. Lucia stored up in separate packets resentment and the deepest gratification.

Asparagus. Cold and very buttery. Olga picked up the sticks with her fingers and then openly sucked them. Lucia used a neat little holder which was beside her plate. Perhaps Olga did not know what it was for.

'And you and Georgie must come to Riseholme for the week-end,' she said. 'I get down to-night, so join me to-morrow.'

Lucia shook her head.

'Too sweet of you,' she said, 'but impossible, I'm afraid. So many duties. To-morrow is Friday, isn't it? Yes: a prize-giving to-morrow afternoon, and something in the evening, I fancy. Borough Bench on Monday at ten. One thing after another; no end to them, day after day. It was only by the rarest chance I was able to come up yesterday.'

Georgie knew that this was utter rubbish. Lucia had not had a single municipal engagement for four days, and had spent her time in bicycling and sketching and playing Bridge. She just wanted to impress Olga with the innumerable duties of her position.

'Too bad!' said Olga. 'Georgie, you mustn't let her work herself to death like this. But you'll come, won't you, if we can't persuade her.'

Here was an opportunity for independent action. He strung himself up to take it.

'Certainly. Delighted. I should adore to,' he said with emphasis.

'Capital. That's settled then. But you must come, too, Lucia. How they would all love to see you again at Riseholme.'

Lucia wanted to go, especially since Georgie would otherwise go without her, and she would have been much disconcerted if her refusal had been taken as final. She pressed two fingers to her forehead.

'Let me think!' she said. 'I've nothing after Friday evening, have I, Georgie, till Monday's Council? I always try to keep Saturdays free. No: I don't think I have. I could come down with Georgie, on Saturday morning, but we shall have to leave again very early on Monday. Too tempting to refuse, dear Olga. The sweet place, and those busy days, or so they seemed then, but now, by comparison, what a holiday!'

Poppy appeared just as they had finished lunch, and Lucia was astonished to find that she had not the smallest idea that they had ever met before. When reminded, Poppy explained that when she went to hear music a total oblivion of all else seized her.

'Carried away,' she said. 'I don't know if I'm on my head or my heels.'

'If you were carried away you'd be on your back,' said Olga. 'What do you want to eat?'

'Dressed crab and plenty of black coffee,' said Poppy decidedly. 'That's what keeps me in perfect health.' She had just become conscious of Georgie, and had fixed her eye on his beard, when Cortese plunged into the restaurant and came, like a bore up the River Severn, to Olga's table, loudly lamenting in Italian that he had not been able to come to lunch. He kissed her hand, he kissed Poppy's hand, and after a short pause for recollection, he kissed Lucia's hand.

'Si, si,' he cried, 'it is the lady who came to hear the first trial of *Lucrezia* at your Riseholme, and spoke Italian with so pure an accent. *Come sta, signora?*' And he continued to prattle in Italian.

Lucia had a horrid feeling that all this had happened before, and that in a moment it would be rediscovered that she could not speak Italian. Lunch, anyhow, was over, and she could say a reluctant farewell. She summoned up a few words in that abhorred tongue.

'*Cara,*' she said to Olga, 'we must tear ourselves away. *A rivederci, non e vero, dopo domani.* But we must go to catch our train. A poor hard-worked Mayor must get back to the

221

call of duty.'

'Oh, is he a Mayor?' asked Poppy with interest. 'How very distinguished.'

There was no time to explain; it was better that Georgie should be temporarily enthroned in Poppy's mind as Mayor, rather than run any further risks, and Lucia threaded her way through the narrow passage between the tables. After all she had got plenty of material to work up into noble narrative at Tilling. Georgie followed and slammed the door of the taxi quite crossly.

'I can't think why you were in such a hurry,' he said. 'I was enjoying myself, and we shall only be kicking our heels at the station.'

'Better to run no risk of missing our train,' she said. 'And we have to pick up Foljambe and our luggage.'

'Not at all,' said Georgie. 'We particularly arranged that she should meet us with it at Victoria.'

'Georgie, how stupid of me!' said the shameless Lucia. 'Forgive me.'

*   *   *

Lucia found that she had no engagement for the next evening, and got up a party for dinner and Bridge in order casually to disseminate these magnificent experiences. Mr Wyse and Diva (Susan being indisposed) the Mapp-Flints and the Padre and Evie were her guests.

It rather surprised her that nobody asked any questions at dinner, about her visit to London, but, had she only known it, Tilling had seen in the paper that she and a Duke and Duchess had been in Olga's box, and had entered into a fell conspiracy, for Lucia's good, not to show the slightest curiosity about it. Thus, though her guests were starving for information, conversation at dinner had been entirely confined to other topics, and whenever Lucia made a casual allusion to the opera, somebody spoke loudly about something else. But when the ladies retired into the garden-room the strain on their curiosity began to tell, and Lucia tried again.

'So delightful to get back to peaceful Tilling,' she said, as if she had been away for thirty-six weeks instead of thirty-six hours, 'though I fear it is not for long. London was such a terrible rush. Of course the first thing we did was to go to the Academy to see the Picture of the Year, dear Elizabeth.'

That was crafty: Elizabeth could not help being interested in that.

'And could you get near it, dear?' she asked.

'Easily. Not such a great crowd. Technically I was a wee bit disappointed. Very vigorous, of course, and great *bravura*—'

'What does that mean?' asked Diva.

'How shall I say it? Dash, sensational effect, a too obvious dexterity,' said Lucia, gesticulating like a painter doing bold brush-

223

work. 'I should have liked more time to look at it, for Irene will long to know what I think about it, but we had to dress and dine before the opera. Dear Olga had given us an excellent box, a little too near the stage perhaps.'

It was more than flesh and blood could stand: the conspiracy of silence broke down.

'I saw in the paper that the Duke and Duchess of Sheffield were there, too,' said Evie.

'In the paper was it?' asked Lucia with an air of great surprise. 'How the press ferrets things out! He and Poppy Sheffield came in in the middle of the second act. I was rather cross, I'm afraid, for I hate such interruptions.'

Elizabeth was goaded into speech.

'Most inconsiderate,' she said. 'I hope you told her so, Worship.'

Lucia smiled indulgently.

'Ah, people who aren't *really* musical—poor Poppy Sheffield is not—have no idea of the pain they give. And what has happened here since Georgie and I left?'

'Seventeen to tea yesterday,' said Diva 'What was the opera like?'

'Superb. Olga sang the great scene to me years ago and I confess I did not do it justice. A little modern for my classical taste, but a very great work. Very. And her voice is still magnificent; perhaps a little sign of forcing in the top register, but then I am terribly critical.'

The conspiracy of silence had become a cross-examination of questions. These admissions were being forced from her.

'And then did you go out to supper?' asked Evie.

'Ah no! Music takes too much out of me. Back to the hotel and so to bed, as Pepys says.'

'And next morning, Worship, after such an exciting evening?' asked Elizabeth.

'Poor me! A bundle of agenda for the Council meeting on Monday. I had to slave at them until nearly lunch-time.'

'You and Mr Georgie in your hotel?' asked Diva.

'No: dear Olga insisted that we should lunch with her at the Ritz,' said Lucia in the slow drawling voice which she adopted when her audience were on tenterhooks. 'No party, just the four of us.'

'Who was the fourth?'

'The Duchess. She was very late, just as she had been at the opera. A positive obsession with her. So we didn't wait.'

Not waiting for a Duchess produced a stunning effect.

Diva recovered first.

'Good food?' she asked.

'Fair, I should have called it. Or do you mean Poppy's food? How you will laugh! A dressed crab and oceans of black coffee. The only diet on which she feels really well.'

'Sounds most indigestible,' said Diva. 'What an odd sort of stomach. And then?'

'How you all catechize me! Then Cortese

225

came in. He is the composer, I must explain, of *Lucrezia*, and conducted it. Italian, with all the vivaciousness of the South—'

'So you had a good talk in Italian to him, dear,' said Elizabeth viciously.

'Alas, no. We had to rush off almost immediately to catch our train. Hardly a word with him.'

'What a pity!' said Elizabeth. 'And just now you told us you were not going to be here long. Gadding off again?'

'Alas, yes; though how ungrateful of me to say "alas",' said Lucia still drawling. 'Dear Olga implored Georgie and me to spend the week-end with her at Riseholme. She would not take a refusal. It will be delicious to see the dear old place again. I shall make her sing to us. These great singers are always at their best with a small *intime* sympathetic audience.'

'And will there be some Duchesses there?' asked Elizabeth, unable to suppress her bitterness.

'*Chi lo sa?*' said Lucia with superb indifference. 'Ah, here come the men. Let us get to our Bridge.'

The men, who were members of this conspiracy, had shewn a stronger self-control than the women, and had not asked Georgie a single question about high-life, but they knew now about his new ties. Evie could not resist saying in an aside to her husband:

'Fancy, Kenneth, the Duchess of Sheffield

lives on dressed crab and black coffee.'

Who could resist such an alluring fragment? Certainly not the Padre.

'Eh, that's a singular diet,' he said, 'and has Mistress Mayor been telling you a' about it? An' what does she do when there's no crab to be had?'

From the eagerness in his voice, Lucia instantly guessed that the men had heard nothing, and were consumed with curiosity.

'Enough of my silly tittle-tattle,' she said. 'More important matters lie before us. Elizabeth, will you and the Padre and Mr Wyse play at my table?'

For a while cards overrode all other interests, but it was evident that the men were longing to know all that their vow of self-control had hidden from them: first one and then another, during the deals, alluded to shell-fish and Borgias. But Lucia was adamant: they had certainly conspired to show no interest in the great events of the London visit, and they must be punished. But when the party broke up, Mr Wyse insisted on driving Diva back in the Royce, and plied her with questions, and Major Benjy and the Padre, by the time they got home, knew as much as their wives.

*   *   *

Lucia and Georgie, with Grosvenor as maid (for it was only fair that she should have her share in these magnificent excursions) motored to Riseholme next morning. Lucia took among her luggage the tin box labelled 'Housing', in order to keep abreast of municipal work, but in the hurry of departure forgot to put any municipal papers inside it. She would have liked to take Mrs Simpson as well, but Grosvenor occupied the seat next her chauffeur, and three inside would have been uncomfortable. Olga gave a garden-party in her honour in the afternoon, and Lucia was most gracious to all her old friends, in the manner of a Dowager Queen who has somehow come into a far vaster kingdom, but who has a tender remembrance of her former subjects, however humble, and she had a kind word for them all. After the party had dispersed, she and Georgie and Olga sat on in the garden, and her smiles were touched with sadness.

'Such a joy to see all the dear, quaint folk again,' she said, 'but what a sad change has come over the place! Riseholme, which in old days used to be seething with every sort of interest, has become just like any other vegetating little village—'

'I don't agree at all,' said Georgie loudly. 'It's seething still. Daisy Quantock's got a French parlour-maid who's an atheist, and Mrs Antrobus has learned the deaf and dumb alphabet, as she's got so deaf that the most expensive ear-trumpet isn't any use to her.

Everybody has been learning it, too, and when Mrs Boucher gave a birthday party for her only last week, they all talked deaf and dumb to each other, so that Mrs Antrobus could understand what was being said. I call that marvellous manners.'

The old flame flickered for a moment in Lucia's breast.

'No!' she cried. 'What else?'

'I haven't finished this yet,' said Georgie. 'And they were all using their hands so much to talk, that they couldn't get on with their dinner, and it took an hour and a half, though it was only four courses.'

'Georgie, how thrilling!' said Olga. 'Go on.'

Georgie turned to the more sympathetic listener.

'You see, they couldn't talk fast, because they were only learning, but when Mrs Antrobus replied, she was so quick, being an expert, that nobody except Piggie and Goosie—'

Lucia tilted her head sideways, with a sidelong glance at Olga, busy with a looking-glass and lipstick.

'Ah; I recollect. Her daughters,' she said.

'Yes, of course. They could tell you what she said if they were looking, but if they weren't looking you had to guess, like when somebody talks fast in a foreign language which you don't know much of, and you make a shot at what he's saying.'

Lucia gave him a gimlet-glance. But of course, Georgie couldn't have been thinking of her and the Italian crisis.

'Their dear, funny little ways!' she said. 'But everyone I talked to was so eager to hear about Tilling and my Mayoral work, that I learned nothing about what was going on here. How they besieged me with questions! What else, Georgie?'

'Well, the people who have got your house now have made a swimming bath in the garden and have lovely mixed bathing parties.'

Lucia repressed a pang of regret that she had never thought of doing that, and uttered a shocked sort of noise.

'Oh, what a sad desecration!' she said. 'Where is it? In my pleached alley, or in Perdita's garden?'

'In the pleached alley, and it's a great success. I wish I'd brought my bathing-suit.'

'And do they keep up my tableaux and Elizabethan fêtes and literary circles?' she asked.

'I didn't hear anything about them, but there's a great deal going on. Very gay, and lots of people come down for week-ends from town.'

Lucia rose.

'And cocktail parties, I suppose,' she said. 'Well, well, one must expect one's traces to be removed by the hand of time. That wonderful sonnet of Shakespeare's about it. *Olga mia,*

230

will you excuse me till dinner-time? Some housing plans I have got to study, or I shall never be able to face my Council on Monday.'

*   *   *

Lucia came down to dinner steeped in the supposed contents of her tin box and with a troubled face.

'Those riband-developments!' she said. 'They form one of the greatest problems I have to tackle.'

Olga looked utterly bewildered.

'Ribands?' she asked. 'Things in hats.'

Lucia gave a bright laugh.

'Stupid of me not to explain, dear,' she said. 'How could you know? Building developments: dreadful hideous dwellings along the sweet country roads leading into Tilling. Red-brick villas instead of hedges of hawthorn and eglantine. It seems such desecration.'

Georgie sighed. Lucia had already told him what she meant to say to her Council on Monday afternoon, and would assuredly tell him what she had said on Monday evening.

'Caterpillars!' she cried with a sudden inspiration. 'I shall compare those lines of houses to caterpillars, hungry red caterpillars wriggling out across the marsh and devouring its verdant loveliness. A vivid metaphor like that is needed. But I know, dear Olga, that nothing I say to you will go any further. My Councillors have a right to know my views before anybody else.'

'My lips are sealed,' said Olga.

'And yet we must build these new houses,' said the Mayor, putting both her elbows on the table and disregarding her plate of chicken. 'We must abolish the slums in Tilling, and that means building on the roads outside. Such a multiplicity of conflicting interests.'

'I suppose the work is tremendous,' said Olga.

'Yes, I think we might call it tremendous, mightn't we, Georgie?' asked Lucia.

Georgie was feeling fearfully annoyed with her. She was only putting it on in order to impress Olga, but the more fervently he agreed, the sooner, it might be hoped, she would stop.

'Overwhelming. Incessant,' he asserted.

The hope was vain.

'No, dear, not overwhelming,' she said, eating her chicken in a great hurry. 'I am not overwhelmed by it. Working for others enlarges one's capacity for work. For the sake of my dear Tilling I can undertake without undue fatigue, what would otherwise render me a perfect wreck. *Ich Dien*. Of course I have to sacrifice other interests. My reading? I scarcely open a book. My painting? I have done nothing since I made a sketch of some gorgeous dahlias in the autumn, which Georgie didn't think too bad.'

'Lovely,' said Georgie in a voice of wood.

'Thank you, dear. My music? I have hardly played a note. But as you must know so well, dear Olga, music makes an imperishable store of memories within one: morsels of Mozart: bits of Beethoven all audible to the inward ear.'

'How well I remember you playing the slow movement of the Moonlight Sonata,' said Olga, seeking, like Georgie to entice her away from Mayoral topics. But the effect of this was appalling. Lucia assumed her rapt music-face, and with eyes fixed on the ceiling, indicated slow triplets on the table cloth. Her fingers faltered, they recovered; and nobody could guess how long she would continue: probably to the end of the movement, and yet it seemed rude to interrupt this symbolic recital. But presently she sighed.

'Naughty fingers,' she said, as if shaking the triplets off. 'So forgetful of them!'

Somehow she had drained the life out of the others, but dinner was over, and they moved into Olga's music-room. The piano stood open, and Lucia, as if walking in sleep, like Lady Macbeth, glided on to the music stool. The naughty fingers became much better, indeed they became as good as they had ever been. She dwelt long on the last note of the famous slow movement, gazing wistfully up, and they all sighed, according to the traditional usage when Lucia played the Moonlight.

'Thank you, dear,' said Olga. 'Perfect.'

Lucia suddenly sprang off the music-stool with a light laugh.

'Better than I had feared,' she said, 'but far from perfect. And now, dear Olga, dare I? Might we? One little song. Shall I try to accompany you?'

Olga thought she could accompany herself and Lucia seated herself on a sort of throne close beside her and resumed her rapt expression, as Olga sang the 'Ave' out of *Lucrezia*. That solemn strain seemed vaguely familiar to Lucia, but she could not place it. Was it Beethoven? Was it from *Fidelio* or from *Creation Hymn*? Perhaps it was wiser only to admire with emotion without committing herself to the composer.

'That wonderful old tune!' she said. 'What a treat to hear it again. Those great melodies are the very foundation-stone of music.'

'But isn't it the prayer in *Lucrezia*?' asked Georgie.

Lucia instantly remembered that it was.

'Yes, of course it is, Georgie,' she said. 'But in the plain-song mode. I expressed myself badly.'

'She hadn't the smallest idea what it was,' thought Olga, 'but she could wriggle out of a thumb-screw.' Then aloud:

'Yes, that was Cortese's intention,' she said. 'He will be pleased to know you think he has caught it. By the way, he rang up just before dinner to ask if he and his wife might come

234

down to-morrow afternoon for the night. I sent a fervent "yes".'

'My dear, you spoil us!' said Lucia ecstatically. 'That will be too delightful.'

*   *   *

In spite of her ecstasy, this was grave news, and as she went to bed she pondered it. There would be Cortese, whose English was very limited (though less circumscribed than her own Italian), there would be Olga, who, though she said she spoke Italian atrociously, was fluent and understood it perfectly, and possibly Cortese's wife knew no English at all. If she did not, conversation must be chiefly conducted in Italian, and Lucia's vivid imagination pictured Olga translating to her what they were all saying, and re-translating her replies to them. Then no doubt he would play to them, and she would have to guess whether he was playing Beethoven or Mozart or plain-song or Cortese. It would be an evening full of hazards and humiliations. Better perhaps, in view of a pretended engagement on Monday morning, to leave on Sunday afternoon, before these dangerous foreigners arrived. 'If only I could bring myself to say that I can neither speak nor understand Italian, and know nothing about music!' thought Lucia. 'But I can't after all these years.

It's wretched to run away like this, but I couldn't bear it.'

*   *   *

Georgie came down very late to breakfast. He had had dreams of Olga trying through a song to his accompaniment. She stood behind him with her hands on his shoulders, and her face close to his. Then he began singing, too, and their voices blended exquisitely ... Dressing was a festival with his tiled bathroom next door, and he debated as to which of his new ties Olga would like best. Breakfast, Grosvenor had told him, would be on the verandah, but it was such a warm morning there was no need for his cape.

The others were already down.

'Georgie, this will never do,' said Olga, as he came out. 'Lucia says she must go back to Tilling this afternoon. Keep her in order. Tell her she shan't.'

'But what's happened, Lucia?' he asked. 'If we start early to-morrow we shall be in heaps of time for your Council meeting.'

Lucia began to gabble.

'I'm too wretched about it,' she said, 'But when I went upstairs last night, I looked into those papers again which I brought down with me, and I find there is so much I must talk over with my Town Clerk if I am to be equipped for my Council in the afternoon. You know what Monday morning is, Georgie. I must not

236

neglect my duties though I have to sacrifice my delicious evening here. I must be adamant.'

'Too sad,' said Olga. 'But there's no reason why you should go, Georgie. I'll drive you back to-morrow. My dear, what a pretty tie!'

'I shall stop then,' said he. 'I've nothing to do at Tilling. I thought you'd like my tie.'

Lucia had never contemplated this, and she did not like it. But having announced herself as adamant, she could not instantly turn to putty. Just one chance of getting him to come with her remained.

'I shall have to take Grosvenor with me,' she said.

Georgie pictured a strange maid bringing in his tea, and getting his bath ready, with the risk of her finding his *toupée*, and other aids to juvenility. He faced it: it was worth it.

'That doesn't matter,' he replied. 'I shall be able to manage perfectly.'

CHAPTER NINE

Lucia was in for a run of bad luck, and it began that very afternoon. Ten minutes before she started with Grosvenor for Tilling, Cortese and his wife arrived. The latter was English and knew even less Italian than she did. And Cortese brought with him the first act of his new opera. It was too late to change her plans

237

and she drove off after a most affectionate parting from Olga, whom she charged to come and stay at Tilling any time at a moment's notice. Just a telephone message to say she was coming, and she could start at once sure of the fondest welcome … But it was all most tiresome, for no doubt Cortese would run through the first act of his opera to-night, and the linguistic panic which had caused her to flee from Riseholme as from a plague-stricken village, leaving her nearest and dearest there, had proved to be utterly foundationless.

For the present that was all she knew: had she known what was to occur half an hour after she had left, she would certainly have turned and gone back to the plague-stricken village again, trusting to her unbounded ingenuity to devise some reason for her reappearance. A phone-call from the Duchess of Sheffield came for Madame Cortese.

'Poor mad Cousin Poppy,' she said. 'What on earth can she want?'

'Dressed crab,' screamed Olga after her as she went to the telephone, 'Cortese, you darling, let's have a go at your *Diane de Poictiers* after dinner. I had no idea you were near the end of the first act.'

'Nor I also. It has come as smooth as margarine,' said Cortese, who had been enjoined by Madame to learn English with all speed, and never to dare to speak Italian in her presence. 'And such an aria for you. When you

238

hear it, you will jump for joy. I jump, you jumps, they jumpino. Dam' good.'

Madame returned from the telephone.

'Poppy asked more questions in half a minute than were ever asked before in that time,' she said. 'I took the first two or three and told her to wait. First, will we go to her awful old Castle to-morrow, to dine and stay the night. Second: who is here. Olga, I told her, and Cortese, and Mr Pillson of Tilling. "Why, of course I know him," said Poppy. "He's the Mayor of Tilling, and I met him at *Lucrezia*, and at lunch at the Ritz. Such a lovely beard". Thirdly—'

'But I'm not the Mayor of Tilling,' cried Georgie. 'Lucia's the Mayor of Tilling, and she hasn't got a beard—'

'Georgie, don't be pedantic,' said Olga. 'Evidently she means you—'

'*La Barba e mobile*,' chanted Cortese. '*Una barba per due. Scusi*. Should say "A beard for two," my Dorothea.'

'It isn't *mobile*,' said Georgie, thinking about his *toupée*.

'Of course it isn't,' said Olga. 'It's a fine, natural beard. Well, what about Poppy? Let's all go to-morrow afternoon.'

'No: I must get back to Tilling,' said Georgie. 'Lucia expects me—'

'Aha, you are a henpeck,' cried Cortese. 'And I am also a henpeck. Is it not so, my Dorothea?'

'You're coming with us, Georgie,' said Olga. 'Ring up Lucia in the morning and tell her so. Just like that. And tell Poppy that we'll all four come, Dorothy. So that's settled.'

*   *   *

Lucia, for all her chagrin, was thrilled at the news, when Georgie rang her up next morning. He laid special stress on the Mayor of Tilling having been asked, for he felt sure she would enjoy that. Though it was agonizing to think what she had missed by her precipitate departure yesterday, Lucia cordially gave him leave to go to Sheffield Castle, for it was something that Georgie should stay there, though not she, and she sent her love and regrets to Poppy. Then after presiding at the Borough Bench (which lasted exactly twenty seconds, as there were no cases) instead of conferring with her Town Clerk, she hurried down to the High Street to release the news like a new film.

'Back again, dear Worship,' cried Elizabeth, darting across the street. 'Pleasant visit?'

'Delicious,' said Lucia in the drawling voice. 'Dear Riseholme! How pleased they all were to see me. No party at Olga's; just Cortese and his wife, *très intime*, but such music. I got back last night to be ready for my duties to-day.'

'And not Mr Georgie?' asked Elizabeth.

'No. I insisted that he should stop. Indeed, I

240

don't expect him till to-morrow, for he has just telephoned that Duchess Poppy—a cousin of Madame Cortese—asked the whole lot of us to go over to Sheffield to-day to dine and sleep. Such short notice, and impossible for me, of course, with my Council meeting this afternoon. The dear thing cannot realise that one has duties which must not be thrown over.'

'What a pity. So disappointing for you, dear,' said Elizabeth, writhing under a sudden spasm of colic of the mind. 'But Sheffield's a long way to go for one night. Does she live in the town?'

Lucia emitted the musical trill of merriment.

'No, it's Sheffield Castle,' she said. 'Not a long drive from Riseholme, in one of Olga's Daimlers. A Norman tower. A moat. It was in *Country Life* not long ago ... Good morning, Padre.'

'An' where's your guide man?' asked the Padre.

Lucia considered whether she should repeat the great news. But it was more exalted not to, especially since the dissemination of it, now that Elizabeth knew, was as certain as if she had it proclaimed by the Town Crier.

'He joins me to-morrow,' she said. 'Any news here?'

'Such a lovely sermon from Reverence yesterday,' said Elizabeth, for the relief of her colic. 'All about riches and position in the world being only dross. I wish you could have

241

heard it, Worship.'

Lucia could afford to smile at this pitiable thrust, and proceeded with her shopping, not ordering any special delicacies for herself because Georgie would be dining with a Duchess. She felt that fate had not been very kind to her personally, though most thoughtful for Georgie. It was cruel that she had not known the nationality of Cortese's wife, and her rooted objection to his talking Italian, before she had become adamant about returning to Tilling, and this was doubly bitter, because in that case she would have still been on the spot when Poppy's invitation arrived, and it might have been possible (indeed, she would have made it possible) for the Deputy Mayor to take her place at the Council meeting to-day, at which her presence had been so imperative when she was retreating before the Italians.

She began to wonder whether she could not manage to join the Ducal party after all. There was actually very little business at the Council meeting; it would be over by half-past four, and if she started then she would be in time for dinner at Sheffield Castle. Or perhaps it would be safer to telephone to the Deputy Mayor, asking him to take her place, as she had been called away unexpectedly. The Deputy Mayor very willingly consented. He hoped it was not bad news and was reassured. All that there remained was to ring up Sheffield Castle, and say that the Mayor of Tilling was delighted to accept her Grace's invitation to dine and sleep, conveyed to her Worship by Mr Pillson. The answer was returned that the Mayor of Tilling was expected. 'And just for a joke,' thought Lucia, 'I won't tell them at Riseholme that I'm coming. Such a lovely surprise for them, if I get there first. I can start soon after lunch, and take it quietly.'

She recollected, with a trivial pang of uneasiness, that she had told Elizabeth that her duties at Tilling would have prevented her in any case from going to Sheffield Castle, but that did not last long. She would live it down or deny having said it, and she went into the garden-room to release Mrs Simpson, and, at the same time, to provide for the propagation of the tidings that she was going to her Duchess.

'I shall not attend the Council meeting this afternoon, Mrs Simpson,' she said, 'as there's nothing of the slightest importance. It will be a mere formality, so I am playing truant. I shall be leaving Tilling after lunch, to dine and sleep at the Duchess of Sheffield's, at Sheffield Castle. A moat and I think a drawbridge. Ring me up there if anything occurs that I must deal with personally, and I will give it my attention. There seems nothing that need detain you any more to-day. One of our rare holidays.'

On her way home Mrs Simpson met Diva's Janet, and told her the sumptuous news. Janet scuttled home and plunged down into the kitchen to tell her mistress who was making buns. She had already heard about Georgie from Elizabeth.

'Don't believe a word of it,' said Diva. 'You've mixed it up, Janet. It's Mr Georgie, if anybody, who's going to Sheffield Castle.'

'Beg your pardon, ma'am,' said Janet hotly, 'but I've mixed nothing up. Mrs Simpson told me direct that the Mayor was going, and talking of mixing you'd better mix twice that lot of currants, if it's going to be buns.'

The telephone bell rang in the tea-room above, and Diva flew up the kitchen-stairs, scattering flour.

'Diva, is that Diva?' said Lucia's voice. 'My memory is shocking; did I say I would pop in for tea to-day?'

'No. Why?' said Diva.

'That is all right then,' said Lucia. 'I feared that I might have to put it off. I'm joining Georgie on a one night's visit to a friend. I couldn't get out of it. Back to-morrow.'

Diva replaced the receiver.

'Janet, you're quite right,' she called down the kitchen stairs. 'Just finish the buns. Must go out and tell people.'

*　　　*　　　*

Lucia's motor came round after lunch. Foljambe (it was Foljambe's turn, and Georgie

244

felt more comfortable with her) was waiting in the hall with the jewel-case and a camera, and Lucia was getting the 'Slum Clearance' tin box from the garden-room to take with her, when the telephone bell rang. She had a faint presage of coming disaster as she said, 'Who is it?' in as steady a voice as she could command.

'Sheffield Castle speaking. Is that the Mayor of Tilling.'

'Yes,'

'Her Grace's maid speaking, your Worship. Her Grace partook of her usual luncheon to-day—'

'Dressed crab?' asked Lucia in parenthesis.

'Yes, your Worship, and was taken with internal pains.'

'I am terribly sorry,' said Lucia. 'Was it tinned?'

'Fresh, I understand, and the party is put off.'

Lucia gave a hollow moan into the receiver, and her Grace's maid offered consolation.

'No anxiety at all, your Worship,' she said, 'but she thought she wouldn't feel up to a party.'

The disaster evoked in Lucia the exercise of her utmost brilliance. There was such a fearful lot at stake over this petty indigestion.

'I don't mind an atom about the dislocation of my plans,' she said, 'but I am a little anxious about her dear Grace. I quite understand about the party being put off; so wise to spare her fatigue. It would be such a relief if I might come just to reassure myself. I was on the point of starting, my maid, my luggage all ready. I would not be any trouble. My maid would bring me a tray instead of dinner. Is it possible?'

'I'll see,' said her Grace's maid, touched by this devotion. 'Hold on.'

She held on; she held on, it seemed, as for life itself, till, after an interminable interval the reply came.

'Her Grace would be very happy to see the Mayor of Tilling, but she's putting off the rest of the party,' said the angelic voice.

'Thank you, thank you,' called Lucia. 'So good of her. I will start at once.'

She picked up Slum Clearance and went into the house only to be met by a fresh ringing of the telephone in the hall. A panic seized her lest Poppy should have changed her mind.

'Let it ring, Grosvenor,' she said. 'Don't answer it at all. Get in, Foljambe. Be quick.'

She leaped into the car.

'Drive on, Chapman,' she called.

The car rocked its way down to the High Street, and Lucia let down the window and looked out, in case there were any friends about. There was Diva at the corner, and she stopped the car.

'Just off, Diva,' she said. 'Duchess Poppy not very well, so I've just heard.'

'No! Crab?' asked Diva.

'Apparently, but not tinned, and there is no need for me to feel anxious. She insisted on my coming just the same. Such a lovely drive in front of me. Taking some work with me.'

Lucia pulled up the window again and pinched her finger but she hardly regarded that for there was so much to think about. Olga at Riseholme, for instance, must have been informed by now that the party was off, and yet Georgie had not rung up to say that he would be returning to Tilling to-day. A disagreeable notion flitted through her mind that, having got leave to go to Sheffield Castle, he now meant to stay another night with Olga, without telling her, and it was with a certain relief that she remembered the disregarded telephone call which had hurried her departure. Very likely that was Georgie ringing up to tell her that he was coming back to Tilling to-day. It would be a sad surprise for him not to find her there.

Her route lay through Riseholme, and passing along the edge of the village green, she kept a sharp look-out for familiar figures. She saw Piggie and Goosie with Mrs Antrobus: they were all three gesticulating with their hands in a manner that seemed very odd until she remembered that they must be speaking in deaf and dumb alphabet: she saw a very slim elegant young woman whom she conjectured to be Daisy Quantock's atheistic French maid, but there was no sign of Georgie or Olga. She debated a moment as to whether she should call at Olga's to find out for certain that he had gone, but dismissed the idea as implying a groundless suspicion. Beyond doubt the telephone call which she had so narrowly evaded was to say that he had done so, and she steadily backed away from the familiar scene in order to avoid seeing him if he was still here . . . Then came less familiar country, a belt of woods, a stretch of heathery upland glowing in the afternoon sun, positively demanding to be sketched in water-colours, and presently a turning with a sign-post 'To Sheffield Bottom'. Trees again, a small village of grey stone houses, and facing her a great castellated wall with a tower above a gateway and a bridge over a moat leading to it. Lucia stopped the car and got out, camera in hand.

'What a noble facade,' she said to herself. 'I wonder if my room will be in that tower.'

She took a couple of photographs, and getting back into the car, she passed over the bridge and through the gateway.

Inside lay a paved courtyard in a state of indescribable neglect. Weeds sprouted between the stones, a jungle of neglected flower-beds lay below the windows, here and there were moss-covered stone seats. On one of these close beside the huge discoloured door of blistered paint sat Poppy with her mouth open, fast asleep. As Lucia stepped out, she awoke, and looked at her with a dazed expression of strong disfavour.

'Who are you?' asked Poppy.

'Dear Duchess, so good of you to let me come,' said Lucia, thinking that she was only half-awake. 'Lucia Pillson, the Mayor of Tilling.'

'That you aren't,' said Poppy. 'It's a man, and he's got a beard.'

Lucia laughed brightly.

'Ah, you're thinking of my husband,' she said. 'Such a vivid description of him. It fits him exactly. But I'm the Mayor. We met at dear Olga's opera-box, and at the Ritz next day.'

Poppy gave a great yawn, and sat silent, assimilating this information.

'I'm afraid there's been a complete muddle,' she said. 'I thought it was he who was coming. You see I was much flattered at his eagerness to spend a quiet evening with me and my stomach-ache, and so I said yes. No designs on him of any kind I assure you. All clean as a whistle: he'd have been as safe with me as with his grandmother, if she's still alive. My husband's away, and I just wanted a pleasant companion. And to think that it was you all the while. That never entered my head. Fancy!'

It did not require a mind of Lucia's penetrative power to perceive that Poppy did not want her, and did not intend that she should stop. Her next remarks removed any possibility of doubt.

'But you'll have some tea first, *won't* you?'

she asked. 'Indeed I insist on your having some tea unless you prefer coffee. If you ring the door-bell, somebody will probably come. Oh, I see you've got a camera. Do take some photographs. Would you like to begin with me, though I'm not looking my best.'

In spite of the nightmarish quality of the situation, Lucia kept her head, and it was something to be given tea and to take photographs. Perhaps there was a scoop here, if she handled it properly, and first she photographed Poppy and the dismal courtyard, and then went to Poppy's bedroom to tidy herself for tea and snapped her washing-stand and the corner of her Elizabethan bed. After tea Poppy took her to the dining-room and the gaunt picture gallery and through a series of decayed drawing-rooms, and all the time Lucia babbled rapturous comments.

'Magnificent tapestry,' she said, 'ah, and a glimpse of the Park from the window. Would you stand there, Duchess, looking out with your dog on the window-seat? What a little love! Perfect. And this noble hall: the panelling by that lovely oriel window would make a lovely picture. And that refectory table.'

But now Poppy had had enough, and she walked firmly to the front-door and shook hands.

'Charmed to have seen you,' she said, 'though I've no head for names. You will have a pleasant drive home on this lovely evening.

Goodbye, or perhaps *au revoir*,'

'That would be much nicer,' said Lucia, cordial to the last.

* * *

She drove out of the gateway she had entered three quarters of an hour before, and stopped the car to think out her plans. Her first idea was to spend the night at the Ambermere Arms at Riseholme, and return to Tilling next morning laden with undeveloped photographs of Sheffield Castle and Poppy, having presumably spent the night there. But that was risky: it could hardly help leaking out through Foljambe that she had done nothing of the sort, and the exposure, coupled with the loss of prestige, would be infinitely painful. 'I must think of something better that that,' she said to herself, and suddenly a great illumination shone on her. 'I shall tell the truth,' she heroically determined, 'in all essentials. I shall say that Poppy's maid told me that I, the Mayor of Tilling was expected. That, though the party was abandoned, she still wanted me to come. That I found her asleep in a weedy courtyard, looking ghastly. That she evidently didn't feel up to entertaining me, but insisted that I should have tea. That I took photographs all over the place. All gospel truth, and no necessity for saying anything about that incredible mistake of hers in thinking that Georgie was the Mayor of Tilling.'

She tapped on the window.

'We'll just have dinner at the Ambermere Arms, at Riseholme, Chapman,' she called, 'and then go back to Tilling.'

*   *   *

It was about half-past ten when Lucia's car drew up at the door of Mallards. She could scarcely believe that it was still the same day as that on which she had awoken here, regretful that she had fled from Riseholme on a false alarm, had swanked about Georgie staying at Sheffield Castle, had shirked the Council meeting to which duty had called her, had wangled an invitation to the Castle herself, had stayed there for quite three quarters of an hour, and had dined at Riseholme. 'Quite like that huge horrid book by Mr James Joyce, which all happens in one day,' she reflected, as she stepped out of the car.

Looking up, she saw that the garden-room was lit, and simultaneously she heard the piano: Georgie therefore must have come home. Surely (this time) she recognised the tune: it was the prayer in *Lucrezia*. He was playing that stormy introduction with absolute mastery, and he must be playing it by heart, for he could not have the score, nor, if he had, could he have read it. And then that

252

unmistakeable soprano voice (though a little forced in the top register) began to sing. The wireless? Was Olga singing *Lucrezia* in London to-night? Impossible; for only a few hours ago during this interminable day, she was engaged to dine and sleep at Poppy's Castle. Besides, if this was relayed from Covent Garden, the orchestra, not the piano, would be accompanying her. Olga must be singing in the garden-room, and Georgie must be here, and nobody else could be here ... There seemed to be material for another huge horrid book by Mr James Joyce before the day was done.

'I shall be perfectly calm and ladylike whatever happens,' thought Lucia, and concentrating all her power on this genteel feat she passed through the hall and went out to the garden-room. But before entering, she paused, for in her reverence for Art, she felt she could not interrupt so superb a performance: Olga had never sung so gloriously as now when she was singing to Georgie all alone ... She perched on the final note pianissimo. She held it with gradual crescendo till she was singing fortissimo. She ceased, and it was as if a great white flame had been blown out.

Lucia opened the door. Georgie was sitting in the window: his piece of needlework had dropped from his hand, and he was gazing at the singer. 'Too marvellous,' he began, thinking that Grosvenor was coming in with drinks. Then, by some sixth sense, he knew it wasn't Grosvenor, and turning, he saw his wife.

In that moment he went through a selection of emotions that fully equalled hers. The first was blank consternation. A sense of baffled gallantry succeeded, and was followed by an overwhelming thankfulness that it was baffled. All evening he had been imagining himself delightfully in love with Olga, but had been tormented by the uneasy thought that any man of spirit would make some slight allusion to her magnetic charm. That would be a most perilous proceeding. He revelled in the feeling that he was in love with her, but to inform her of that might be supposed to lead to some small practical demonstration of his passion, and the thought made him feel cold with apprehension. She might respond (it was not likely but it was possible, for he had lately been reading a book by a very clever writer, which showed how lightly ladies in artistic professions, take an adorer's caresses), and he was quite convinced that he was no good at that sort of thing. On the other hand she might snub him, and that would wound his tenderest sensibilities. Whatever happened in fact, it would entirely mar their lovely evening. Taking it all in all, he had never been so glad to see Lucia.

Having pierced him with her eye, she turned her head calmly and gracefully towards Olga.

'Such a surprise!' she said. 'A delightful one of course. And you, no doubt, are equally

254

surprised to see me.'

Lucia was being such a perfect lady that Olga quaked and quivered with suppressed laughter.

'Georgie, explain at once,' she said. 'It's the most wonderful miracle that ever happened.'

'Well, it's like this,' said Georgie carefully. 'As I telephoned you this morning, we were all invited to go to Poppy's for the night. Then she was taken ill after lunch and put us off. So I rang up in order to tell you that I was coming back here and bringing Olga. You told her to propose herself whenever she felt inclined, and just start—'

Lucia bestowed a polite bow on Olga.

'Quite true,' she said. 'But I never received that message. Oh—'

'I know you didn't,' said Georgie. 'I couldn't get any answer. But I knew you would be delighted to see her, and when we got here not long before dinner, Grosvenor said you'd gone to dine and sleep at Poppy's. Why didn't you answer my telephone? And why didn't you tell us you were going away? In fact, what about you?'

During this brief but convincing narrative, the thwarted Muse of Tragedy picked up her skirts and fled. Lucia gave a little trill of happy laughter.

'Too extraordinary,' she said. 'A comedy of errors. Georgie, you told me this morning, very distinctly, that Poppy had invited the Mayor of

Tilling. Very well. I found that there was nothing that required my presence at the Council meeting, and I rang up Sheffield Castle to say I could manage to get away. I was told that I was expected. Then just as I was starting there came a message that poor Poppy was ill and the party was off.'

Lucia paused a moment to review her facts as already rehearsed, and resumed in her superior, drawling voice.

'I felt a little uneasy about her,' she said, 'and as I had no further engagement this afternoon, I suggested that though the party was off, I would run over—the motor was actually at the door—and stay the night. She said she would be so happy to see me. She gave me such a pleasant welcome, but evidently she was far from well, and I saw she was not up to entertaining me. So I just had tea; she insisted on that, and she took me round the Castle and made me snap a quantity of photographs. Herself, her bedroom, the gallery, that noble oriel window in the hall. I must remember to send her prints. A delicious hour or two, and then I left her. I think my visit had done her good. She seemed brighter. Then a snack at the Ambermere Arms; I saw your house was dark, dear Olga, or I should have popped in. And here we are. That lovely prayer from *Lucrezia* to welcome me. I waited entranced on the doorstep till it was over.'

It was only by strong and sustained effort

that Olga restrained herself from howling with laughter. She hadn't been singing the prayer from *Lucrezia* this time, but *Les feux magiques*, by Berlioz; Lucia seemed quite unable— though of course she had been an agitated listener—to recognise the prayer when she heard it. But she was really a wonderful woman. Who but she would have had the genius to take advantage of Poppy's delusion that Georgie was the Mayor of Tilling? Then what about Lucia's swift return from the Castle? Without doubt Poppy had sent her away when she saw her female, beardless guest, and the clever creature had made out that it was she who had withdrawn as Poppy was so unwell, with a gallery of photographs to prove she had been there. Then she recalled Lucia's face when she entered the garden-room a few minutes ago, the face of a perfect lady who, unexpectedly returns home to find a wanton woman, bent on seduction, alone with her husband. Or was Georgie's evident relief at her advent funnier still? Impossible to decide, but she must not laugh till she could bury her face in her pillow. Lucia had a few sandwiches to refresh her after her drive, and they went up to bed. The two women kissed each other affectionately. Nobody kissed Georgie.

* * *

Tilling next morning, unaware of Lucia's

return, soon began to sprout with a crop of conjectures which, like mushrooms, sprang up all over the High Street. Before doing any shopping at all, Elizabeth rushed into Diva's tea-shop to obtain confirmation that Diva had actually seen Lucia driving away with Foljambe and luggage on the previous afternoon *en route* for Sheffield Castle.

'Certainly I did,' said Diva. 'Why?'

Elizabeth contracted her brows in a spasm of moral anguish.

'I wish I could believe,' she said, 'that it was all a blind, and that Worship didn't go to Sheffield Castle at all, but only wanted to make us think so, and returned home after a short drive by another route. Deceitful though that would be, it would be far, far better than what I fear may have happened.'

'I suppose you're nosing out some false scent as usual,' said Diva. 'Get on.'

Elizabeth made a feint of walking towards the door at this rude speech, but gave it up.

'It's too terrible, Diva,' she said. 'Yesterday evening, it might have been about half-past six, I was walking up the street towards Mallards. A motor passed me, laden with luggage, and it stopped there.'

'So I suppose you stopped, too,' said Diva.

'—and out of it got Mr Georgie and a big, handsome—yes, she was very handsome—woman, though, oh, so common. She stood on the doorstep a minute looking round, and sang out, "Georgino! How *divino*!" Such a screech! I judge so much by voice. In they went, and the luggage was taken in after them, and the door shut. Bang. And Worship, you tell me, had gone away.'

'Gracious me!' said Diva.

'You may well say that. And you may well say that I stopped. I did, for I was rooted to the spot. It was enough to root anybody. At that moment the Padre had come round the corner, and he was rooted too. As I didn't know then for certain whether Worship had actually gone—it might only have been one of her grand plans of which one hears no more—I said nothing to him, because it is so wicked to start any breath of scandal, until one has one's facts. It looks to me very black, and I shouldn't have thought it of Mr Georgie. Whatever his faults—we all have faults—I did think he was a man of clean life. I still hope it may be so, for he has always conducted himself with propriety, as far as I know, to the ladies of Tilling, but I don't see how it possibly can.'

Diva gave a hoarse laugh.

'Not much temptation,' she said, 'from us old hags. But it is queer that he brought a woman of that sort to stay at Mallards on the very night Lucia was away. And then there's another thing. She told us all that *he* was going to stay at Poppy's last night—'

'I can't undertake to explain all that Worship tells us,' said Elizabeth. 'That is

259

asking too much of me.'

'—but he was here,' said Diva. 'Yet I shouldn't wonder if you'd got hold of the wrong end of the stick somehow. Habit of yours, Elizabeth. After all, the woman may have been a friend of Lucia's—'

'—and so Mr Georgie brought her when Lucia was away. I see,' said Elizabeth.

Her pensive gaze wandered to the window, and she stiffened like a pointing setter, for down the street from Mallards was coming Georgie with the common, handsome, screeching woman. Elizabeth said nothing to Diva, for something might be done in the way of original research, and she rose.

'Very dark clouds,' she said, 'but we must pray that they will break. I've done no shopping yet. I suppose Worship will be back some time to-day with a basket of strawberry leaves, if Poppy can spare her. Otherwise, the municipal life of Tilling will be suspended. Not that it matters two straws whether she's here or not. Quite a cypher in the Council.'

'Now that's not fair,' shouted Diva angrily after her. 'You can't have it both ways. Why she ever made you Mayoress—' but Elizabeth had shut the door.

Diva went down to her kitchen with an involuntary glow of admiration for Georgie, which was a positive shock to her moral principles. He and his *petit point*, and his little cape, and his old-maidish ways—was it possible that these cloaked a passionate temperament? Who could this handsome, common female be? Where had he picked her up? Perhaps in the hotel when he and Lucia had stayed in London, for Diva seemed to have heard that voluptuous assignations were sometimes made in the most respectable places. What a rogue! And how frightful for Lucia, if she got to know about it.

'I'm sure I hope she won't,' thought Diva, 'but it wouldn't be bad for her to be taken down a peg or two, though I should pity her at the same time. However, one mustn't rush to conclusions. But it's shocking that I've got a greater respect for Mr Georgie than I ever had before. Can't make it out.'

Diva got to work with her pastry-making, but some odd undercurrent of thought went trickling on. What a starvation diet for a man of ardent temperament, as Georgie now appeared, must his life in Tilling have been, where all the women were so very undecorative. If there had only been a woman with a bit of brilliance about her, whom he could admire and flirt with just a little, all this might have been averted. She left Janet to finish the shortbread, and went out to cull developments.

Elizabeth meantime had sighted her prey immediately, and from close at hand observed the guilty pair entering the photographer's. Were the shameless creatures, she wondered, going to be photographed together? That was the sort of bemused folly that sinning couples often committed, and bitterly rued it afterwards. She glided in after them, but Georgie was only giving the shopman a roll of negatives to be developed and printed and sent up to Mallards as soon as possible. He took off his hat to her very politely, but left the shop without introducing her to his companion which was only natural and showed good feeling. Certainly she was remarkably handsome. Beautifully dressed. A row of pearls so large that they could not be real. Hatless with waved hair. Rouge. Lipstick ... She went in pursuit again. They passed the Padre and his wife, who turned completely round to look at them; they passed Susan in her Royce (she had given up tricycling in this hot weather) who held her head out of the window till foot passengers blocked her view of them, and Diva, standing on her doorstep with her market-basket, was rooted to the spot as firmly as Elizabeth had been the night before. The woman was a dream of beauty with her brilliant colouring and her high, arched eyebrows. Recovering her powers of locomotion, Diva went into the hairdressing and toilet saloon.

Elizabeth bought some parsnips at Twistevant's, deep in thought. Bitter moralist though she was, she could not withhold her admiration for the anonymous female. Diva had rudely alluded to the ladies of Tilling as old hags, and was there not a grain of truth in it? They did not make the best of themselves. What brilliance that skilfully applied rouge and lipstick gave a face! Without it the anonymous might have looked ten years older and far less attractive. 'Hair, too,' thought Elizabeth, 'that soft brown, so like a natural tint. But fingernails, dripping with bright arterial blood: never!'

She went straight to the hair-dressing and toilet establishment. Diva was just coming out of the shop carrying a small packet.

'Little titivations, dear?' asked Elizabeth, reading her own thoughts unerringly.

'Tooth-powder,' said Diva without hesitation, and scooted across the road to where Susan was still leaning out of the window of her Royce and beckoning to her.

'I've seen her,' she said (there was no need to ask who 'she' was). 'And I recognised her at once from her picture in the *Tatler*. You'd never guess.'

'No, I know I shouldn't,' said Diva impatiently. 'Who?'

'The great prima donna. Dear me, I've forgotten her name. But the one Lucia went to hear sing in London,' said Susan. 'Bracelet, wasn't it?'

'Bracely? Olga Bracely?' cried Diva. 'Are you *quite* sure?'

'Positive. Quite lovely, and such hair.'

263

That was enough, and Diva twinkled back across the road to intercept Elizabeth who was just coming out of the hair-dressing and toilet shop with a pink packet in her hand, which she instantly concealed below the parsnips.

'Such a screechy voice, didn't you say, Elizabeth?' she asked.

'Yes, frightful. It went right through me like a railway whistle. Why?'

'It's the prima donna, Olga Bracely. That's all,' said Diva. 'Voice must have gone. Sad for her. Glad to have told you who she is.'

Very soon all Tilling knew who was the lovely *maquillée* woman with the pearls, who had stayed the night alone with Georgie at Mallards. Lucia had not been seen at all this morning, and it was taken for granted that she was still away on that snobbish expedition for which she had thrown over her Council meeting. Though Olga (so she said) was a dear friend, it would certainly be a surprise to her, when she returned to find her dear friend staying with her husband at her own house, when she had told Tilling that both Georgie and Olga were staying that night at Poppy's Castle. Or would Olga leave Tilling again before Lucia returned? Endless interpretations could be put on this absorbing incident, but Tilling was too dazzled with the prima donna herself, her pearls, her beauty, her reputation as the Queen of Song to sit in judgment on her.

What a dream of charm and loveliness she

was with her delicately rouged cheeks and vermilion mouth, and that air of joyous and unrepentant paganism! For Evie her blood-red nails had a peculiar attraction, and she too went to the hair-dressing and toilet establishment, and met Susan just coming out.

*   *   *

Lucia meantime had spent a municipal morning in the garden-room without showing herself even for a moment at the window. Her departmental boxes were grouped round her, but she gave them very little attention. She was completely satisfied with the explanation of the strange adventures which had led to the staggering discovery of Olga and Georgie alone in her house the night before, and was wondering whether Tilling need ever know how very brief her visit to Poppy had been. It certainly was not her business to tell her friends that a cup of tea had been the only hospitality she had received. Then her photographs (if they came out) would be ready by to-morrow, and if she gave a party in the evening she would leave her scrap-book open on the piano. She would not call attention to it, but there it would be, furnishing unshakable ocular evidence of her visit...

After lunch, accordingly, she rang up all her more intimate circle, and, without definitely stating that she had this moment returned to

Tilling from Sheffield Castle, let it be understood that such was the case. It had been such a lovely morning: she had enjoyed her drive so much: she had found a mass of arrears waiting for her, and she asked them all to dine next night at eight. She apologized for such short notice, but her dear friend Olga Bracely, who was here on a short visit, would be leaving the day after—a gala night at the opera—and it would give her such pleasure to meet them all. But, as she and Olga went up to dress next evening, she told Olga that dinner would be at eightish: say ten minutes past eight. There was a subtle reason for this, for the photographs of Sheffield Castle had arrived and she had pasted them into her scrap-book. Tilling would thus have time to admire and envy before Olga appeared: Lucia felt that her friends would not take much interest in them if she was there.

Never had any party in Tilling worn so brilliant and unexpected an appearance as that which assembled in the garden-room the following night. Evie and the Padre arrived first: Evie's finger nails looked as if she had pinched them all, except one, in the door, causing the blood to flow freely underneath each. She had forgotten about that one, and it looked frost-bitten. Elizabeth and Benjy came next: Elizabeth's cheeks were like the petals of wild roses, but she had not the nerve to incarnadine her mouth, which, by contrast, appeared to be afflicted with the cyanosis which precedes death. Diva, on the other hand, had been terrified at the aspect of blooming youth which rouge gave her, and she had wiped it off at the last moment, retaining the Cupid's bow of a vermilion mouth, and two thin arched eyebrows in charcoal. Susan, wearing the Order of the British Empire, had had her grey hair waved, and it resembled corrugated tin roofing: Mr Wyse and Georgie wore their velvet suits. It took them all a few minutes to get used to each other, for they were like butterflies which had previously only known each other in the caterpillar or chrysalis stage, and they smiled and simpered like new acquaintances in the most polite circles, instead of old and censorious friends. Olga had not yet appeared, and so they had time to study Lucia's album of snap-shots which lay open on the piano, and she explained in a casual manner what the latest additions were.

'A corner of the Courtyard of Sheffield Castle,' she said. 'Not come out very well. The Norman tower. The dining hall. The Duchess's bedroom; wonderful Elizabethan bed. The picture gallery. She is standing looking out of the window with her Pekingese. Such a sweet. It jumped up on the window-seat just before I snapped. The Duchess at the tea-table—'

'What a big cake!' interrupted Diva professionally. 'Sugared, too. So she does eat something besides dressed crab. Hope she didn't have much cake after her indigestion.'

'But what a shabby courtyard,' said Evie. 'I should have thought a Duke would have liked his Castle to look tidier. Why doesn't he tell his gardener to weed it?'

Elizabeth felt she would burst unless she put in a venomous word.

'Dear Worship, when you write to thank her Grace for your pleasant visit, you must say, just in fun, of course, that you expect the courtyard to be tidied up before you come next.'

Lucia was perfectly capable of dealing with such clumsy sarcasm.

'What a good idea!' she said. 'You always think of the right thing, Elizabeth. Certainly I will. Remind me, Georgie.'

So the photographs did their work. Tilling could not doubt that Lucia had been wrapped in the Norman embrace of Sheffield Castle, and determined silently and sternly never again to allude to the painful subject. That suited Lucia admirably, for there were questions that might be asked about her visit which would involve regrettable admissions if she was to reply quite truthfully. Just as her friends were turning surfeited and sad from the album a step was heard outside and Olga appeared in the doorway. A white gown, high at the neck, reeking of Molyneux and simplicity. A scarlet girdle, and pearls as before.

'Dear Lucia,' she cried, 'I see I'm late. Forgive me.'

'My own! I always forgive you as soon as I

268

see you, only there is never anything to forgive,' said Lucia effusively. 'Now I needn't say who you are, but this is Mrs Bartlett and our Padre, and here are Mr and Mrs Wyse, and this is Diva Plaistow, and here's my beloved Mayoress, Elizabeth Mapp-Flint and Major Mapp-Flint—'

Olga looked from Benjy to Elizabeth and back again.

'But surely I recognise them,' she said. 'That marvellous picture, which everybody raves about—'

'Yes, little me,' said the beaming Elizabeth, 'and my Benjy in the clouds. What an eye you've got, Miss Bracely!'

'And this is my husband,' went on Lucia with airy humour, 'who says he thinks he has met you before—'

'I believe we did meet somewhere, but ages ago, and he won't remember me,' said Olga. 'Oh, Georgie, I mustn't drink sherry, but as you've poured it out for me—'

'Dinner,' said Grosvenor rather sternly.

In the hard overhead light of the dining-room, the ladies of Tilling, novices in *maquillage*, looked strangely spurious, but the consciousness in each of her rejuvenated appearance, combined with Olga's gay presence, made them feel exceptionally brilliant. All round the table conversation was bright and eager, and they all talked at her, striving to catch her attention. Benjy, sitting next her, began telling her one of his adventures with a tiger, but instantly Susan raised her voice and spoke of her tricycle. Her husband chipped in, and with an eye on Olga told Lucia that his sister the Contessa di Faraglione was a passionate student of the age of Lucrezia Borgia. Diva, longing to get Olga to come to ye olde tea-house, spoke loudly about her new recipe for sardine tartlets, but Lucia overrode so commercial a subject by the introduction of the Mayoral Motif coupled with slums. Olga herself chattered and laughed, the only person present who was not anxious to make a favourable impression. She lit a cigarette long before dinner was over, and though Elizabeth had once called that 'a disgusting foreign habit' she lit one, too. Olga ate a cherry beginning with the end of the stalk and at once Benjy was trying to do the same, ejaculating, as it dropped into his finger bowl, 'Not so easy, by Jove.' There was no Bridge to-night, but by incessant harping on antique dances, Lucia managed to get herself asked to tread a minuet with Georgie. Olga accompanied them, and as she rose from the piano, she became aware that they were all looking at her with the expectant air of dogs that hope to be taken out for a walk.

'Yes, certainly if you want me to,' she said.

She sat down at the piano again. And she sang.

CHAPTER TEN

Though Tilling remained the same at heart, Olga's brief visit had considerably changed the decorative aspect of its leading citizenesses. The use of powder on the face on very hot days when prominent features were apt to turn crimson, or on very cold ones, when prominent features were apt to turn mauve, had always been accepted, but that they should embellish themselves with rouge and lipstick and arched eyebrows was a revolution indeed. They had always considered such aids to loveliness as typical of women who shamelessly advertised their desire to capture the admiration of males, and that was still far from their intentions. But Diva found that arched eyebrows carefully drawn where there were none before gave her a look of high-bred surprise: Elizabeth that the rose-mantled cheeks she now saw in her looking-glass made her feel (not only appear) ten years younger: Susan that her corrugated hair made her look like a French *marquise*. Irene, who had been spending a fortnight of lionization in London, was amazed at the change when she returned, and expressed her opinion of it, by appearing in the High Street with the tip of her nose covered with green billiard-chalk.

She at once got to work on the portrait

which Lucia had commissioned. She had amplified Lucia's biographical suggestion, and it represented her in full Mayoral robes and chain and a three-cornered hat playing the piano in the garden-room. Departmental boxes were piled in the background, a pack of cards and a paint-box lay on the lid of the piano, and her bicycle leaned against it.

'Symbols, beloved,' said the artist, 'indicating your marvellous many-sidedness. I know you don't ride your bicycle in the garden-room, nor play cards on your piano, nor wear your robes when you're at your music, but I group your completeness round you. Ah! Hold that expression of indulgent disdain for the follies of the world for a moment. Think of the Tilling hags and their rouge.'

'Like that?' asked Lucia, curling her upper lip.

'No, not at all like that. Try another. Be proud and calm. Think of spending an evening with your Duchess—darling, why are you such a snob?—or just think of yourself with all your faults and splendours. Perfect!'

Irene stepped back from her easel.

'And I've got it!' she cried. 'There's not a living artist and very few dead ones who could have seized that so unerringly. How monstrous that my work should be hated just because I am a woman!'

'But your picture was the picture of the year,' said Lucia, 'and all the critics cracked it up.'

'Yes, but I felt the undercurrent of hostility. Men are such self-centred brutes. Wait till I publish my memoirs.'

'But aren't you rather young for that?'

'No, I'm twenty-five, and by that age everyone has experienced all that matters, or anyhow has imagined it. Oh, tell me the truth about what all the painted hags are whispering. Georgie and Olga Bracely being alone here. What happened really? Did you arrange it all for them? How perfect of you! Nobody but you would be so modern and open-minded. And Tilling's respect for Georgie has gone up enormously.'

Lucia stared at her a moment, assimilating this monstrous suggestion, then sprang to her feet with a gasp of horror.

'Oh, the poisonous tongues!' she cried 'Oh, the asps. And besides—'

She stopped. She found herself entangled in the web she herself had woven, and never had any spider known to natural history so completely encircled itself. She had told Tilling that she was going to dine and sleep at Poppy's Castle, and had shewn everybody those elegant photographs as tacit evidence that she had done so. Tilling therefore, had concluded that Olga and Georgie had spent the night alone at Mallards, and here was Irene intolerably commending her for her open-mindedness not only in condoning but in promoting this assignation. The fair fame, the unsullied morality of herself and Georgie, not to mention Olga, was at stake, and (oh, how it hurt!) she would be forced to give the utmost publicity to the fact that she had come back to Tilling the same evening. That would be a frightful loss of prestige, but there was no choice. She laughed scornfully.

'Foolish of me to have been indignant for a single moment at such an idea!' she said. 'I never heard such rubbish. I found poor Poppy very unwell, so I just had tea with her, cheered her up and took some photographs and came home at once. Tilling is really beyond words!'

'Darling, what a disappointment!' said Irene. 'It would have been so colossal of you. And what a come-down for poor Georgie. Just an old maid again.'

The news was very soon known, and Tilling felt that Lucia and Georgie had let them down. Everything had been so exciting and ducal and compromising, and there was really nothing left of it. Elizabeth and Diva lost no time in discussing it in Diva's tea-room next morning when marketing was done, and were severe.

'The deceitfulness of it is what disgusts me most,' said the Mayoress. 'Far worse than the snobbishness. Worship let it be widely known that she was staying the night with Poppy, and then she skulks back, doesn't appear at all next morning to make us think that she was still away—'

'And shows us all those photographs,' chimed in Diva, 'as a sort of ... what's the word?'

'Can't say, dear,' said Elizabeth, regarding her rose-leaf cheeks with high approval in the looking-glass over the mantelpiece.

'Affidavit, that's it, as testifying that she had stayed with Poppy. Never told us she hadn't.'

'My simple brain can't follow her conjuring tricks,' said Elizabeth, 'and I should be sorry if it could. But I'm only too thankful she did come back. It will be a great relief to the Padre, I expect, to be told that. I wonder, if you insist on knowing what I think, whether Mr Georgie somehow decoyed that lovely creature to Tilling, telling her that Lucia was here. That's only my guess, and if so we must try to forgive him, for if anything is certain in this bad business, it is that he's madly in love with her. I know myself how a man looks—'

Diva gave a great gasp, but her eyebrows could not express any higher degree of astonishment.

'Oh, Elizabeth!' she cried. 'Was a man ever madly in love with you? Who was it? Do tell me!'

'There are things one can't speak of even to an old friend like you,' said Elizabeth. 'Yes, he's madly in love with her, and I think Worship knows it. Did you notice her demonstrations of affection to sweet Olga? She was making the best of it, I believe; putting on a brazen—no, let us say a brave face. How worn and anxious she looked the other night when we were all so gay. That pitiful little minuet! I'm sorry for her. When she married Mr Georgie, she thought life would be so safe and comfortable. A sad awakening, poor thing ... Oh, another bit of news. Quaint Irene tells me she is doing a portrait of Worship. Quite marvellous, she says, and it will be ready for our summer exhibition. After that Lucia means to present it to the Borough, and have it hung in the Town Hall. And Irene's Academy picture of Benjy and me will be back in time for our exhibition, too. Interesting to compare them.'

*   *   *

Lucia bore her loss of prestige with characteristic gallantry. Indeed, she seemed to be quite unconscious that she had lost any, and continued to let her album of snap-shots remain open on the piano at the Sheffield Castle page, and airily talked about the Florentine mirror which just did not come into the photograph of Poppy's bedroom. Occasionally a tiresome moment occurred, as when Elizabeth, being dummy at a Bridge-party in the garden-room, pored over the Castle page, and came back to her place, saying,

'So clever of you, Worship, to take so many pretty photographs in so short a time.'

Lucia was not the least disconcerted.

'They were all very short exposures, dear,' she said. 'I will explain that to you sometime.'

Everybody thought that a very fit retort, for now the Poppy-crisis was no longer recent, and it was not the custom of Tilling to keep such incidents alive too long: it was not generous or kind, and besides, they grew stale. But Lucia paid her back in her own coin, for next day, when playing Bridge at the Mapp-Flints, she looked long and earnestly at Benjy's tiger-whip, which now hung in its old place among bead-aprons and Malayan creases.

'Is that the one he broke at his interesting lecture, dear Elizabeth,' she asked, 'or the one he lost at Diva's tea-rooms?'

Evie continued to squeak in a disconcerting manner during the whole of the next hand, and the Poppy-crisis (for the present) was suffered to lapse.

*　　*　　*

The annual Art Exhibition moved into the foreground of current excitements, and the Tilling artists sent in their contributions: Lucia her study of dahlias, entitled '*Belli fiori*', and a sketch of the courtyard of Sheffield Castle, which she had weeded for purposes of Art. She called it 'From Memory', though it was really from her photograph, and, without specifying the Castle, she added the motto

277

'The splendour falls on Castle walls.'

Elizabeth sent in 'A misty morning on the Marsh'. She was fond of misty mornings, because the climatic conditions absolutely prohibited defined draughtsmanship. Georgie (without any notion of challenging her) contributed 'A sunny morning on the Marsh', with sheep and dykes and clumps of ragwort very clearly delineated: Mr Wyse, one of his usual still-life studies of a silver tankard, a glass half-full of (probably) Capri wine, and a spray of nasturtiums: Diva another piece of still life, in pastel, of two buns and a tartlet (probably sardine) on a plate. This was perhaps an invasion of Mr Wyse's right to reproduce still life, but Diva had to be in the kitchen so much, waiting for kettles to boil and buns to rise, that she had very little leisure for landscape. Susan Wyse sent a mystical picture of a budgerigar with a halo above its head, and rays of orange light emanating from the primary feathers of its spread wings: 'Lost Awhile' was the touching title. But in spite of these gems, the exhibition was really Irene's show. She had been elected an honorary member of the hanging committee, and at their meetings she showed that she fully appreciated this fact.

'My birth of Venus,' she stated, 'must be hung quite by itself at one end of the room, with all the studies I made for it below. They are of vast interest. Opposite it, also by itself, must be my picture of Lucia. There were no studies for that; it was an inspiration, but none of your potty little pictures must be near it. Hang them where you like—oh, darling Lucia, you don't mind your dahlias and your Castle walls being quite out of range, do you? But those are my terms, and if you don't like them, I shall withdraw my pictures. And the walls behind them must be painted duck's egg green. Take it or leave it. Now I can't bother about settling about the rest, so I shall go away. Let me know what you decide.'

There was no choice. To reject the picture of the year and that which Irene promised them should be the picture of next year was inconceivable. The end walls of the studio where the exhibition was held were painted duck's egg green, a hydrangea and some ferns were placed beneath each, and in front of them a row of chairs. Lucia, as Mayor, opened the show and made an inaugural speech, tracing the history of pictorial Art from earliest times, and, coming down to the present, alluded to the pictures of all her friends, the poetical studies of the marsh, the loving fidelity of the still life exhibits, the spiritual uplift of the budgerigar. 'Of the two great works of Miss Coles,' she concluded, 'which will make our exhibition so ever-memorable, I need not speak. One has already acquired world-wide fame, and I hope it will not be thought egotistic of me if I confidently prophesy that the other will also. I am violating no secrets if I say that it will remain in Tilling in some conspicuous and public place, the cherished possession for ever of our historic town.'

She bowed, she smiled, she accepted a special copy of the catalogue, which Georgie had decorated with a blue riband, and, very tactfully, instead of looking at the picture of herself, sat down with him in front of that of Elizabeth and Benjy, audibly pointing out its beauties to him.

'Wonderful brush-work,' she said, waving her catalogue as if it was a paintbrush. 'Such life and movement! The waves. Venus's button boots. Quite Dutch. But how Irene has developed since then! Presently we will look at the picture of me with this fresh in our minds.'

Elizabeth and Benjy were compelled, by the force of Lucia's polite example, to sit in front of her picture, and they talked quietly behind their catalogues.

'Can't make head or tail of it,' murmured Benjy. 'I never saw such a jumble.'

'A little puzzling at first,' said Elizabeth, 'but I'm beginning to grasp it. Seated at her piano you see, to show how divinely she plays. Scarlet robe and chain, to show she's Mayor. Cards littered about for her Bridge. Rather unkind. Bicycle leaning against the piano. Her paint-box because she's such a great artist. A pity the whole thing looks like a jumble-sale, with

Worship as auctioneer. And such a sad falling off as a work of Art. I'm afraid success has gone to Irene's head.'

'Time we looked at our own picture,' said Benjy. 'Fancy this daub in the Town Hall, if that's what she meant by some conspicuous and public place.'

'It hasn't got there yet,' whispered Elizabeth. 'As a Councillor, I shall have something to say to that.'

They crossed over to the other side of the room, passing Lucia and Georgie on the way, as if in some figure of the Lancers. Evie and the Padre were standing close in front of the Venus and Evie burst into a series of shrill squeaks.

'Oh, dear me! Did you ever, Kenneth!' she said. 'Poor Elizabeth. What a face and so like!'

'Well indeed!' said Kenneth. 'Surely the puir oyster-shell canna' bear that weight, and down she'll go and get a ducking. An' the Major up in the clouds wi' his wee bottle ... Eh, and here's Mistress Mapp-Flint herself and her guid man. A proud day for ye. Come along wifie.'

Irene had not been at the opening, but now she entered in her shorts and scarlet jersey. Her eye fell on the hydrangea below the Venus.

'Take that foul thing away,' she screamed. 'It kills my picture. What, another of them under my Lucia! Throw them into the street, somebody. By whose orders were they put there? Where's the hanging Committee? I summon the hanging Committee.'

The offending vegetables were borne away by Georgie and the Padre, and Irene, having cooled down, joined Benjy and Elizabeth by the Venus. She looked from it to them and from them to it.

'My God, how I've improved since I did that!' she said. 'I think I must repaint some of it, and put more character into your faces.'

'Don't touch it, dear,' said Elizabeth nervously. 'It's perfect as it is. Genius.'

'I know that,' said Irene, 'but a few touches would make it more scathing. There's rouge on your cheeks now, Mapp, and that would give your face a hungry impropriety. I'll see to that this afternoon when the exhibition closes for the day.'

'But not while it's on view, quaint one,' argued Elizabeth. 'The Committee accepted it as it was. Most irregular.'

'They'll like it far better when I've touched it up,' said Irene. 'You'll see;' and she joined Lucia and Georgie.

'Darling, it's not unworthy of you, is it?' she asked. 'And how noble you are to give it to the Borough for the Town Hall. It must hang just above the Mayor's chair. That's the only place for it.'

'There'll be no difficulty about that,' said Lucia.

*　　　*　　　*

282

She announced her gift to the Town Council at their next meeting, coupled with the artist's desire that it should be hung on the wall behind the Mayor's chair. Subdued respectful applause followed her gracious speech and an uncomfortable silence, for most of her Councillors had already viewed the work of Art with feelings of bewildered stupefaction. Then she was formally thanked for her generous intention and the Town-Clerk intimated that before the Borough accepted any gift, a small committee was always appointed to inspect it. Apart from Elizabeth, who said she would be honoured to serve on it, some diffidence was shown; several Councillors explained that they had no knowledge of the pictorial art, but eventually two of them said they would do their best.

This Committee met next morning at the exhibition, and sat in depressed silence in front of the picture. Then Elizabeth sighed wistfully and said 'Tut, tut' and the two others looked to her for a lead. She continued to gaze at the picture.

'Me to say something, gentlemen?' she asked, suddenly conscious of their scrutiny, 'Well, if you insist. I trust you will disagree with what I feel I'm bound to say, for otherwise I fear a very painful duty lies in front of us. So generous of our beloved Mayor, and so like her, isn't it? But I don't see how it is possible for us to recommend the Council to accept her gift.

I wouldn't for the world set up my opinion against yours, but that's what I feel. Most distressing for me, you will well understand, being so intimate a friend of hers, but private affection cannot rank against public responsibility.' A slight murmur of sympathy followed this speech, and the committee found that they were of one mind in being conscientiously unable to recommend the Council to accept the Mayor's gift.

'Very sad,' said Elizabeth, shaking her head. 'Our proceedings, I take it, are confidential until we communicate them officially to the Council.'

When her colleagues had gone, the Mayoress strolled round the gallery. A misty morning on the marsh really looked very well: its vague pearly opalescence seemed to emphasize the faulty drawing in Georgie's sunny morning on the marsh and Diva's tartlets. Detaching herself from it, she went to the Venus, and a horrified exclamation burst from her. Quaint Irene had carried out her awful threat, had tinged her cheeks with unnatural colour, and had outlined her mouth with a thin line of vermilion, giving it a coyly beckoning expression. So gross a parody of her face and indeed of her character could not be permitted to remain there: something must be done, and, leaving the gallery in great agitation, she went straight to Mallards, for no one but Lucia had the smallest influence with that quaint and venomous young person.

The Mayor had snatched a short respite from her incessant work, and was engaged on a picture of some fine hollyhocks in her garden. She was feeling very buoyant, for the Poppy-crisis seemed to be quite over, and she knew that she had guessed correctly the purport of her Mayoress's desire to see her on urgent business. Invisible to mortal eye, there was a brazier of coals of fire on the lawn beside her, which she would presently pour on to the Mayoress's head.

'Good morning, dear Elizabeth,' she said. 'I've just snatched half an hour while good Mrs Simpson is typing some letters for me. Susan and Mr Wyse have implored me to do another little flower-study for our *esposizione*, to fill up the vacant place by my dahlias. I shall call it "Jubilant July". As you know, I am always at your disposal. What good wind blows you here?'

'Lovely of you to spare the time,' said Elizabeth. 'I've just been to the *esposizione*, and I felt it was my duty to see you at once. Quaint Irene has done something too monstrous. She's altered my face; she's given it a most disgusting expression. The picture can't be allowed to remain there in its present condition. I wondered if you with your great influence—'

Lucia half-closed her eyes, and regarded her sketch with intolerable complacency.

'Yes: that curious picture of Irene's,' she said at length. 'What a Puck-like genius! I went with her to our gallery a couple of hours ago, to see what she had done to the Venus: she was so eager to know what I thought about her little alterations.'

'An outrage, an abomination!' cried Elizabeth.

'I should not put it quite as strongly as that,' said Lucia, returning to her hollyhocks and putting in a vein on one of the leaves with exquisite delicacy. 'But I told her that I could not approve of those new touches. They introduced, to my mind, a note of farce into her satire, which was out of place, though amusing in itself. She agreed with me after a little argument into which I need not go. She will remove them again during the lunch hour.'

'Oh thank you, dear,' said Elizabeth effusively. 'I always say what a true friend you are. I was terribly upset.'

'Nothing at all,' said Lucia sucking her paint-brush. 'Quite easy.'

Elizabeth turned her undivided attention to the holly-hocks.

'What a lovely sketch!' she said. 'How it will enrich our exhibition. Thank you, dear, again. I won't keep you from your work any longer. How you find time for all you do is a constant amazement to me.'

She ambled swiftly away. It would have been awkward if, at such a genial moment, Lucia

286

had asked whether the artistic committee appointed by the Council had inspected Irene's other masterpiece yet.

* * *

The holiday months of August and September were at hand, when the ladies of Tilling were accustomed to let their houses and move into smaller houses themselves at a cheaper rent than what they received. Diva, for instance, having let her own house, was accustomed to move into Irene's, who took a remote cottage on the marsh, where she could pursue her art and paint nude studies of herself in a looking-glass. But this year Diva refused to quit ye olde tea-house, when, with the town full of visitors, she would be doing so roaring a business; the Wyses decided not to go to Italy to stay with the Contessa, since international relations were so strained, and Lucia felt it her duty as Mayor, to remain in Tilling. The only letting done, in fact, was by the Padre, who left his curate in charge, while he and Evie took a prolonged holiday in bonnie Scotland, and let the Vicarage to the Mapp-Flints who had a most exciting tenant. This was a Miss Susan Leg, who, so Tilling was thrilled to learn from an interview she gave to a London paper, was none other than the world-wide novelist, Rudolph da Vinci. Miss Leg (so she stated in this piece of self-revelation) never took a holiday. 'I shall not rest,' she finely observed, 'till the shadows of life's eventide close round me,' and she went on to explain that she would be studying, in view of a future book, this little centre of provincial English life. 'I am well aware,' said Miss Leg, 'that my readers expect of me an aristocratic setting for my romances, but I intend to prove to them that life is as full of human interest in any simple, humble country village as in Belgravia and the country-houses of the nobility.'

Lucia read this interview aloud to Georgie. It seemed to suggest possibilities. She veiled these in her usual manner.

'Rudolph da Vinci,' she said musingly. 'I have heard her name now I come to think of it. She seems to expect us all to be yokels and bumpkins. I fancy she will have to change her views a little. No doubt she will get some introduction to me, and I shall certainly ask her to tea. If she is as uppish and superior as she appears to be, that would be enough. We don't want best-sellers to write up our cultured vivid life here. So cheap and vulgarising; not in accordance with our traditions.'

There was nothing, Georgie knew, that would fill Lucia with deeper pride than that traditions should be violated and life vulgarised, and even while she uttered these high sentiments a vision rose in her mind of Rudolph da Vinci writing a best-seller, with the scene laid in Tilling, and with herself, quite undisguised, as head of its social and municipal activities.

'Yet one must not prejudge her,' she went on, as this vision grew brighter. 'I must order a book of hers and read it, before I pass judgment on her work. And we may find her a very pleasant sort of woman. Perhaps I had better call on her, Georgie, for I should not like her to think that I slighted her, and then I will ask her to dine with us, *très intime*, just you and she and I. I should be sorry if her first impressions of Tilling were not worthy of us. Diva, for instance, it would be misleading if she saw Diva with those extraordinary eyebrows, bringing up teas from the kitchen, purple in the face, and thought her representative of our social life. Or if Elizabeth with her rouged cheeks asked her to dine at the Parsonage, and Benjy told his tiger-stories. Yes, I will call on her as soon as she arrives, and get hold of her. I will take her to our Art Exhibition, allow her to sign the Mayor's book as a distinguished visitor, and make her free of my house without ceremony. We will show her our real, inner life. Perhaps she plays Bridge: I will ascertain that when I call. I might almost meet her at the station, if I can find out when she arrives. Or it might be better if you met her at the station as representing me, and I would call on her at Grebe half an hour afterwards. That would be more regular.'

'Elizabeth told me that she arrives by the

289

three-twenty-five to-day,' said Georgie. 'And she has hired a motor and is meeting her.'

It did not require so keen a nose as Lucia's to scent rivalry, but she gave no hint of that.

'Very proper,' she said. 'Elizabeth no doubt will drive her to Grebe, and show her tenant the house.'

Lucia bicycled to Grebe about tea-time, but found that Miss Leg had driven into the town, accompanied by the Mayoress, to have tea. She left her official card, as Mayor of Tilling, and went straight to the Vicarage. But Elizabeth was also out, and Lucia at once divined that she had taken Miss Leg to have tea at Diva's. She longed to follow and open operations at once, but decided to let the Mayoral card do its work. On her way home she bought a copy of the 25th edition of the novelist's *Kind Hearts and Coronets*, and dipped into it. It was very sumptuous. On the first page there was a Marchioness who had promised to open a village bazaar and was just setting off to do so, when a telephone message arrived that a Royal Princess would like to visit her that afternoon. 'Tell her Royal Highness,' said that kind-hearted woman, 'that I have a long-standing engagement, and cannot disappoint my people. I will hurry back as soon as the function is over...' Lucia pictured herself coming back rather late to entertain Miss Leg at lunch—Georgie would be there to receive her—because it was her day for reading to the inmates of the workhouse. She would return with a copy of *Kind Hearts and Coronets* in her hand, explaining that the dear old bodies implored her to finish the chapter. The idea of Miss Leg writing a best-seller about Tilling became stupefyingly sweet.

Georgie came in, bringing the evening post.

'A letter from Olga,' he said, 'and she's written to me too, so it's sure to be the same. She wants us to go to Riseholme to-morrow for two days, as she's got music. A string quartette coming down.'

Lucia read her letter.

'Yes, most kind of her,' she said. 'But how can I get away? Ah, she anticipates that, and says that if I'm too busy she will understand. And it would look so marked if I went away directly after Miss Leg had arrived.'

'That's for you to judge,' he said. 'If you think she matters, I expect you're right, because Elizabeth's getting a pretty firm hold. I've been introduced to her: Elizabeth brought her in to tea at Diva's.'

'I imagined that had happened,' said Lucia. 'What about her?'

'A funny little round red thing, rather like Diva. Swanky. She's brought a butler and a footman, she told us, and her new Daimler will get down late to-night. And she asked if any of the nobility had got country seats near Tilling—'

'Did you tell her that I dined and slept—that

291

Duchess Poppy asked me to dine and sleep at the Castle?' interrupted Lucia.

'No,' said Georgie. 'I thought of it, but then I judged it was wiser not to bring it up again. She ate a whole lot of buns, and she was very gracious to Diva, (which Diva didn't like much) and told her she would order her *chef*— her very words—to send her a recipe for cream-wafers. Elizabeth's toadying her like anything. She said "Oh, how kind, Miss Leg. You are lucky, dear Diva." And they were going on to see the church afterwards, and Leg's dining with the Mapp-Flints tomorrow.'

Lucia reviewed this rather sinister intelligence.

'I hate to disappoint dear Olga,' she said, 'but I think I had better stop here. What about you?'

'Of course I shall go,' said Georgie.

*　　　*　　　*

Georgie had to leave for Riseholme next morning without a maid, for in view of the entertainment that might be going on at Mallards, Lucia could not spare either Foljambe or Grosvenor. She spent a long time at the garden-room window that afternoon, and told her cook to have a good tea ready to be served at a moment's notice, for Miss Leg would surely return her call to-day. Presently a large car came bouncing up the street: from its size Lucia thought at first that it was Susan's, but there was a man in livery sitting next the chauffeur, and at once she guessed. The car stopped at Mallards, and from behind her curtain Lucia could see that Elizabeth and another woman were inside. A podgy little hand was thrust out of the window, holding a card, which the man-servant thrust into the letter box. He rang the bell, but before it was answered he mounted again, and the car drove on. A hundred pages of stream-of-consciousness fiction could not have explained the situation more exhaustively to Lucia than her own flash of insight. Elizabeth had evidently told the novelist that it would be quite sufficient to leave a card on the Mayor and have done with her. What followed at the Parsonage that evening when Miss Leg dined with the Mapp-Flints bore out the accuracy of Lucia's intuition.

'A very plain simple dinner, dear Miss Leg,' said Elizabeth as they sat down. 'Just pot luck, as I warned you, so I hope you've got a country appetite.'

'I know I have, Liz,' said Benjy heartily. 'A round of golf makes me as hungry as I used to be after a day's tiger-shooting in the jungle.'

'Those are trophies of yours at Grebe, then,' said Miss Leg. 'I consider tiger-shooting a manly pursuit. That's what I mean by sport, taking your life in your hand instead of sitting in an arm chair and firing into flocks of hand-reared pheasants. That kind of "sportsman" doesn't even load his own gun, I believe. Butchers and poulterers; that's what I call them in one of my books.'

'Withering! scathing!' cried Elizabeth. 'And how well-deserved! Benjy gave such a wonderful lecture here the other day about his hair-breath escapes. You could have heard a pin drop.'

'Ah, that's an old story now,' said Benjy. 'My shikarri days are over. And there's not a man in Tilling who's even seen a tiger except through the bars at the Zoo. Georgie Pillson, for instance—'

'Whom I presented to you at tea yesterday, Miss Leg,' put in Elizabeth. 'Husband of our dear Mayor. Pointed beard. Sketches quite prettily, and does exquisite needlework. My wicked Benjy once dubbed him Miss Milliner Michael-Angelo.'

'And that was very withering too,' said Miss Leg, eating lumps of expensive middle-cut salmon with a country appetite.

'Well, well, not very kind, I'm afraid, but I like a man to be a man,' said Benjy. 'I'll take a bit more fish, Liz. A nice fresh-run fish. And what are you going to give us next?'

'Just a brace of grouse,' said Elizabeth.

'Ah, yes. A few old friends with Scotch moors haven't quite forgotten me yet, Miss Leg. Dear old General!'

'Your Miss Milliner has gone away, Benjy,' said Elizabeth. 'Staying with Miss Olga

Bracely. Probably you know her, Miss Leg. The prima donna. Such a fascinating woman.'

'Alone? Without his wife?' asked Miss Leg. 'I do not approve of that. A wife's duty, Mayor or not, is to be always with her husband and vice versa. If she can't leave her home, she ought to insist on his stopping with her.'

'Dear Lucia is a little slack in these ways,' said Elizabeth regretfully. 'But she gives us to understand that they're all old friends.'

'The older the better,' said Miss Leg epigrammatically, and they all laughed very much.

'Tell me more about your Lucia,' she ordered, when their mirth subsided.

'I don't fancy you would find very much in common with her,' said Elizabeth thoughtfully. 'Rather prone we think, to plot and intrigue in a way we regret. And a little superior at times.'

'It seems to have gone to her head to be Mayor,' put in Benjy. 'She'd have made a sad mess of things without you to steady her, Liz.'

'I do my best,' sighed Elizabeth, 'though it's uphill work sometimes. I am her Mayoress and a Councillor, Miss Leg, and she does need assistance and support. Oh, her dear, funny little ways! She's got a curious delusion that she can play the piano, and she gives us a treat sometimes, and one doesn't know which way to look. And not long ago—how you'll scream, Miss Leg, she told us all, several times over, that she was going to stay with the Duchess of Sheffield, and when she came back she showed us quantities of photographs of the Castle to prove she had been there—'

'I went to a Charity Concert of the Duchess's in her mansion in Grosvenor Square not long ago,' said Miss Leg. 'Five-guinea seats. Does she live near here?'

'No, many miles away. There's the cream of it. It turned out that Worship only went to tea. A three hours' drive each way to get a cup of tea! So odd. I almost suspect that she was never asked at all really; some mistake. And she always alludes to her as Poppy; whether she calls her that to her face is another question.'

'Evidently a snob,' said Miss Leg. 'If there's one thing I hate it's snobbishness.'

'Oh, you mustn't call her a snob,' cried Elizabeth. 'I should be so vexed with myself if I had conveyed that impression.'

'And is that a family house of her husband's where I left my card to-day?' asked Miss Leg.

Elizabeth sighed.

'Oh, what a tragic question!' she said. 'No, they're quite *parvenus* in Tilling; that beautiful house—such a garden—belonged to my family. I couldn't afford to live there, and I had to sell it. Lucia gave me a pitiful price for it, but beggars can't be choosers. A cruel moment!'

'What a shame,' said Miss Leg. 'All the old homes of England are going to upstarts and interlopers. I hope you never set foot in it.'

'It's a struggle to do so,' said Elizabeth, 'but I feel that both as Mayoress and as a friend of Lucia, I must be neighbourly. Neither officially nor socially must I fail to stand by her.'

They made plans for next day. Elizabeth was very sarcastic and amusing about the morning shopping of her friends.

'Such fun!' she said. 'Quite a feature of life here, you must not miss it. You'll see Diva bolting in and out of shops like a rabbit, Benjy says, when a ferret's after it, and Susan Wyse perhaps on a tricycle, and Lucia and quaint Irene Coles who painted the picture of the year, which is in our exhibition here; you must see that. Then we could pop in at the Town Hall, and I would show you our ancient charters and our wonderful Elizabethan plate. And would you honour us by signing your name in the Mayor's book for distinguished visitors?'

'Certainly, very glad,' said Miss Leg, 'though I don't often give my autograph.'

'Oh, that is kind. I would be ready for you at ten—not too early?—and take you round. Must you really be going? Benjy, see if Miss Leg's beautiful Daimler is here. Au reservoir!'

'O what?' asked Miss Leg.

'Some of the dear folk here say "au reservoir" instead of "au revoir",' explained Elizabeth.

'Why do they do that?' asked Miss Leg.

*   *   *

Lucia, as she dined alone, had been thinking over the hostilities which she felt were imminent. She was quite determined to annex Miss Leg with a view to being the central figure in her next best-seller, but Elizabeth was determined to annex her too, and Lucia was aware that she and her Mayoress could not run in harness over this job; the feat was impossible. Her pride forbade her to get hold of Miss Leg through Elizabeth, and Elizabeth, somehow or other, must be detached. She sat long that night meditating in the garden-room, and when next morning the Mayoress rang her up as usual at breakfast time, she went to the telephone ready for anything.

'Good morning, dear Worship,' said that cooing voice. 'What a beautiful day.'

'Lovely!' said Lucia.

'Nothing I can do for you, dear?'

'Nothing, thanks,' said Lucia, and waited.

'I'm taking Miss Leg—'

'Who?' asked Lucia.

'Susan Leg: Rudolph da Vinci: my tenant,' explained Elizabeth.

'Oh, yes. She left a card on me yesterday, Foljambe told me. So kind. I hope she will enjoy her visit.'

'I'm taking her to the Town Hall this morning. So would you be a very sweet Worship and tell the Serjeant to get out the Corporation plate, which she would like to see.

We shall be there by half-past ten, so if it is ready by a quarter past there'll be no delay. And though she seldom gives her autograph, she's promised to sign her name in Worship's book.'

Lucia gave a happy sigh. She had not dared to hope for such a rash move.

'My dear, how very awkward,' she said. 'You see, the Corporation plate is always on view to the public on Tuesdays at three p.m.—or it may be two p.m.; you had better make certain—and it is such a business to get it out. One cannot do that for any casual visitor. And the privilege of signing the Mayor's book is reserved for really distinguished strangers, whose visit it is an honour to record. Olga, for instance.'

'But, dear Worship,' said Elizabeth. 'I've already promised to show her the plate.'

'Nothing simpler. At two p.m. or three p.m., whichever it is, on Tuesday afternoon.'

'And the Mayor's book: I've asked her to sign it.'

Lucia laughed gaily.

'Start a Mayoress's book, dear,' she said. 'You can get anybody you like to sign that.'

*   *   *

Lucia remained a moment in thought after ringing off. Then she rang up the Town Hall.

'Is that the Serjeant?' she said. 'The Mayor speaking. Serjeant, do not get out the

Corporation plate or produce my visitors' book without direct orders from me. At present I have given none. What a lovely morning.'

Lucia gave Mrs Simpson a holiday, as there was nothing for her to do, and went down to the High Street for her marketing. Her mind resembled a modern army attended by an air force and all appliances. It was ready to scout and skirmish, to lay an ambush, to defend or to attack an enemy with explosives from its aircraft or poison gas (which would be only a reprisal, for she was certain it had been used against her). Diva was watching at her window, evidently waiting for her, and threw it open.

'Have you seen her?' she asked.

There was only one 'her' just now.

'Only her hand,' said Lucia. 'She put it out of her motor—a podgy sort of hand—yesterday afternoon. She left a card on me, or rather her footman popped it into my letter box, without asking if I was in. Elizabeth was with her. They drove on.'

'Well, I do call that rude,' said Diva, warmly. 'High and lofty, that's what she is. She told me her *chef* would send me a recipe for cream-wafers. I tried it. Muck. I gave one to Paddy, and he was sick. And she rang me up just now to go to tea with her this afternoon. Did she think I was going out to Grebe, just when I was busiest, to eat more muck? Not I. She dined at

300

Elizabeth's last night, and Janet heard from Elizabeth's parlour-maid what they had. Tomato soup, middle-cut of salmon sent over from Hornbridge, a brace of grouse from Rice's, Melba peaches, but only bottled with custard instead of cream, and tinned caviare. And Elizabeth called it pot-luck! I never had such luck there, pot or unpot. Elizabeth's meaning to run her, that's what it is. Let 'em run! I'll come out with you and do my shopping. Just see how Paddy is, but I think he's got rid of it. Cream-wafers, indeed! Wait a sec.'

While Lucia waited a sec., Susan Wyse's Royce, with her husband and herself inside, hooted its ponderous way into the High Street. As it drew up at the fishmonger's, Lucia's eagle eye spied Elizabeth and a round, fat little woman, of whose identity there could be no doubt, walking towards it. Mr Wyse had got out and Elizabeth clearly introduced him to her companion. He stood hatless, as was his polite habit when he talked to ladies under God's blue sky, or even in the rain, and then led her towards the open door of the Royce, where Elizabeth was chatting to Susan.

Lucia strolled towards them, but the moment Elizabeth saw her, she wheeled round without smile or greeting, and, detaching Miss Leg, moved away up the street to where Irene in her usual shorts and scarlet pullover, had just set up her easel at the edge of the pavement.

'Good morning, dear Susan,' called Lucia. 'Oh, Mr Wyse, pray put your hat on; such a hot sun. Who was that odd little woman with my Mayoress, who spoke to you just now?'

'I think your Mayoress said Miss Leg,' observed Mr Wyse. 'And she told my Susan that if she asked Miss Leg to dine to-night she would probably accept. Did you ask her, dear? If so, we must order more fish.'

'Certainly I didn't,' said Susan. 'Who is this Leg? Why should Elizabeth foist her friends on me? Most unheard of.'

'Leg? Leg?' said Lucia vaguely. 'Ah, of course. Elizabeth's tenant. The novelist. Does she not call herself Rudolph da Vinci?'

'A very self-satisfied little woman, whatever she calls herself,' said Susan with unusual severity, 'and she's not going to dine with me. She can dine with Elizabeth.'

Diva had trundled up and overheard this.

'She did. Last night,' she said. 'All most sumptuous and grand. But fancy her leaving a card on Lucia without even asking whether she was at home! So rude.'

'Did she indeed?' asked Mr Wyse in a shocked voice. 'We are not accustomed to such want of manners in Tilling. You were very right, Susan, not to ask her to dine. Your intuition served you well.'

'I thought it strange,' said Lucia, 'but I daresay she's a very decent, homely little

302

woman, when left to herself. Elizabeth was with her, when she honoured me with her card.'

'That accounts for it,' interrupted Diva and Susan simultaneously.

'—and Elizabeth rang me up at breakfast and asked to give orders that the Corporation plate should be ready for her little friend's inspection this morning at 10-30. And the Mayor's book for her to sign.'

'Well, I never!' said Diva. 'And the church-bells ringing, I suppose. And the Town Band playing the Italian National Anthem for Rudolph da Vinci. What did you say?'

'Very polite regrets.'

Irene's voice from a few yards away, loud and emphatic, broke in on their conversation.

'No, Mapp!' she cried. 'I will not come to the Exhibition to show you and your friend—I didn't catch her name—my pictures. And I can't bear being looked over when I'm sketching. Trot along.'

There seemed nothing else for them to do, and Lucia walked on to Irene.

'Did you hear?' asked Irene. 'I sent Mapp and her friend about their business. Who is the little guy?'

'A Miss Leg, I am told,' said Lucia. 'She writes novels under some foreign name. Elizabeth's tenant: she seems to have taken her up with great warmth.'

'Poor wretch. Mapp-kissed, like raisins. But the most exciting news, beloved. The directors of the Carlton Gallery in Bond Street have asked me if I will let them have my Venus for their autumn exhibition. Also an enquiry from an American collector, if it's for sale. I'm asking a thumping price for it. But I shall show it at the Carlton first, and I shall certainly put back Mapp's rouge and her cocotte smile. May I come up presently to Mallards?'

'Do dear. I have a little leisure this morning.'

Lucia passed on with that ever-recurring sense of regret that Irene had not painted her on the oyster-shell and Georgie in the clouds, and, having finished her shopping, strolled home by the Town Hall. The Serjeant was standing on the steps, looking a little flushed.

'The Mayoress and a friend have just been here, your Worship,' he said. 'She told me to get out the Corporation plate and your Worship's book. I said I couldn't without direct orders from you. She was a bit threatening.'

'You did quite right, Serjeant,' said Lucia very graciously. 'The same reply always, please.'

*   *   *

Meantime Elizabeth and Miss Leg, having been thwarted at the Town Hall, passed on to the Exhibition where Elizabeth demanded free admittance for her as a distinguished visitor. But the door-keeper was as firm as the Serjeant had been, and Elizabeth produced a sixpence and six coppers. They went first to look at the Venus, and Elizabeth had a most disagreeable surprise, for the eminent novelist highly disapproved of it.

'An irreverent parody of that great Italian picture by Botticelli,' she said. 'And look at that old hag on the oyster-shell and that boozy navvy in a top-hat. Most shocking! I am astonished that you allowed it to be exhibited. And by that rude unsexed girl in shorts? Her manners and her painting are on a par.'

After this pronouncement Elizabeth did not feel equal to disclosing that she was the hag and Benjy the navvy. But she was pleased that Miss Leg was so severe on the art of the rude girl in shorts, and took her to the portrait of Lucia.

'There's another picture of Miss Coles's' she said, 'which is much worse than the other. Look: it reminds me of an auctioneer at a jumble sale. Bicycle, piano, old packs of cards, paint-box—'

Miss Leg burst into loud cries of pleasure and admiration.

'A magnificent work!' she said. 'That's something to look at. Glorious colour, wonderful composition. And what an interesting face. Who is it?'

'Our Mayor: our dear Lucia whom we chatted about last night,' said Elizabeth.

'Your chat misled me. That woman has great character. Please ask her to meet me, and the artist too. She has real talent in spite of her other picture. I could dine with you this evening: just a plain little meal as we had last night. I never mind what I eat. Or tea. Tea would suit me as well.'

Agitated thoughts darted through the Mayoress's mind. She was still desperately anxious to retain her proprietary rights over Miss Leg, but another plain little meal could not be managed. Moreover it could not be expected that even the most exalted Christian should forgive, to the extent of asking Lucia to dinner, her monstrous rudeness about the Corporation plate and the Mayor's book, and it would take a very good Christian to forgive Irene. Tea was as far as she could go, and there was always the hope that they would refuse.

'Alas, Benjy and I are both engaged to-night,' she said. 'But I'll ask them to tea as soon as I get home.'

They strayed round the rest of the gallery: the misty morning on the marsh, Elizabeth thought, looked very full of poetry.

'The usual little local daubs,' observed Miss Leg, walking by it without a glance. 'But the hollyhocks are charming, and so are the dahlias. By Miss Coles, too, I suppose.'

Elizabeth simply could not bear that she should know who the artist was.

'She does exquisite flower-studies,' she said.

*　　*　　*

Irene was in the garden-room with Lucia when Elizabeth's call came through.

'Just been to the Exhibition, dear Worship, with Miss Leg. She's so anxious to know you and quaint Irene. Would you pop in for a cup of tea this afternoon? She will be there.'

'So kind!' said Lucia. 'I must consult my engagement book.'

She covered the receiver with her hand, and thought intensely for a moment.

'Irene,' she whispered. 'Elizabeth asks us both to go to tea with her and meet Miss Leg. I think I won't. I don't want to get at her *via* Elizabeth. What about you?'

'I don't want to get at Leg *via* anybody,' said Irene.

Lucia uncovered the receiver.

'Alas!' she said. 'As I feared I am engaged. And Irene is with me and regrets she can't come either. Such a pity. Goodbye.'

'Why my regrets?' asked Irene. 'And what's it all about?'

Lucia sighed. 'All very tiresome,' she said, 'but Elizabeth forces me, in mere self-defence, to descend to little schemings and intrigues. How it bores me!'

'Darling, it's the breath of your life!' said Irene, 'and you do it so beautifully!'

*　　　*　　　*

307

In the course of that day and the next Miss Leg found that she was not penetrating far into the life of Tilling. She attended shopping parade next morning by herself. Diva and the Wyses were talking together, but gave her no more than cold polite smiles, and when she had passed, Irene joined them and there was laughter. Further on Lucia, whom she recognised from Irene's portrait was walking with a tall man with a Vandyck beard, whom she guessed to be the truant husband returned. Elizabeth was approaching, all smiles; surely they would have a few words together, and she would introduce them, but Lucia and the tall man instantly crossed the road. It was all very odd: Lucia and Irene would not come to tea at the Mapp-Flints, and the Wyses had not asked her to dinner, and Diva had refused to go to tea at Grebe, and Elizabeth had not produced the Corporation plate and the Mayor's book. She began to wonder whether the Mapp-Flints were not some species of pariah whom nobody would know. This was a dreadful thought; perhaps she had got into wrong hands, and, while they clutched her, Tilling held aloof. She remembered quite a large percentage of Elizabeth's disparaging remarks about Lucia at the plain little meal, and of Benjy's comments on Georgie, and now they assumed a different aspect. Were they prompted by malice and jealousy and impotence to climb into Tilling society? 'I've not got any copy at

308

present,' thought Miss Leg. 'I must do something. Perhaps Mrs Mapp-Flint has had a past, though it doesn't look likely.'

It was a very hot day, and Georgie and Lucia settled to go bicycling after tea. The garden-room, till then, was the coolest place and after lunch they played the piano and sat in the window overlooking the street. He had had two lovely days at Riseholme, and enlarged on them with more enthusiasm than tact.

'Olga was too wonderful,' he said. 'Singing divinely and inspiring everybody. She enjoys herself simply by giving enjoyment to other people. A concert both evenings at seven, with the Spanish quartette and a few songs by Olga. Just an hour and a half and then a delicious supper in the garden, with everybody in Riseholme asked, and no Duchesses and things at all. Just for Riseholme: that's so like her: she doesn't know what the word "snob" means. And I had the room I had before, with a bathroom next door, and my breakfast on the balcony. And none of those plots and intrigues we used to be always embroiled in. It *was* a change.'

A certain stoniness had come into Lucia's face, which Georgie, fired with his subject, did not perceive.

'And she asked down a lot of the supers from Covent Garden,' he went on, 'and put them up at the Ambermere Arms. And her kindness to all her old friends: dull old me, for instance.

She's taken a villa at Le Touquet now, and she's asked me there for a week. I shall cross from Seaport, and there are some wonderful anti-sick tablets—'

'Did dearest Olga happen to mention if she was expecting me as well?' asked Lucia in a perfectly calm voice.

Georgie descended, like an aeroplane with engine-trouble, from these sunlit spaces. He made a bumpy landing.

'I can't remember her doing so,' he said.

'Not a thing you would be likely to forget,' said Lucia. 'Your wonderful memory.'

'I daresay she doesn't want to bother you with invitations,' said Georgie artfully. 'You see, you did rub it in a good deal how difficult it was for you to get away, and how you had to bring tin boxes full of municipal papers with you.'

Lucia's face brightened.

'Very likely that is it,' she said.

'And you promised to spend Saturday till Monday with her a few weeks ago,' continued Georgie, 'and then left on Sunday because of your Council meeting, and then you couldn't leave Tilling the other day because of Miss Leg. Olga's beginning to realize, don't you think, how busy you are—What's the matter?'

Lucia had sprung to her feet.

'Leg's motor coming up the street,' she said. 'Georgie, stand at the door, and, if I waggle my thumb at you, fly into the house and tell

Grosvenor I'm at home. If I turn it down—those Roman gladiators—still fly, but tell her I'm out. It all depends on whether Elizabeth is with her. I'll explain afterwards.'

Lucia slid behind the window-curtain, and Georgie stood at the door, ready to fly. There came a violent waggling of his wife's thumb, and he sped into the house. He came flying back again, and Lucia motioned him to the piano, on the music-stand of which she had already placed a familiar Mozart duet. 'Quick! Top of the page,' she said. '*Uno, due, tre*. Pom. Perfect!'

They played half a dozen brilliant bars, and Grosvenor opened the door and said, 'Miss Leg'. Lucia took no notice but continued playing, till Grosvenor said 'Miss Leg!' much louder, and then, with a musical exclamation of surprise, she turned and rose from her seat.

'Ah, Miss Leg, so pleased!' she said, drawling frightfully. 'How-de-do? Have you met Miss Leg, Georgie? Ah, yes, I think you saw her at Diva's one afternoon. Georgie, tell somebody that Miss Leg—you will, won't you—will stop to tea ... My little garden-room, which you may have noticed from outside. I'm told that they call it the Star Chamber—'

Miss Leg looked up at the ceiling, as if expecting to see the hosts of heaven depicted there.

'Indeed. Why do they call it that?' she asked.

Lucia had, of course, just invented that name for the garden-room herself. She waved her hand at the pile of Departmental tin boxes.

'Secrets of municipal business,' she said lightly. 'The Cabal, you know: Arlington, Bolingbroke ... Shall we go out into the garden, until tea is ready? A tiny little plot, but so dear to me, the red brick walls, the modest little house.'

'You bought it quite lately from Mrs Mapp-Flint, I understand,' said Miss Leg.

Clever Lucia at once guessed that Elizabeth had given her version of that.

'Yes, poor thing,' she said. 'I was so glad to be able to get her out of her difficulties. It used to belong to an aunt of hers by marriage. What a state it was in! The garden a jungle of weeds, but I am reclaiming it. And here's my little secret garden: when I am here and the door is shut, I am not to be disturbed by anybody. Busy folk, like you and me, you with your marvellous creative work, and me with my life so full of interruptions, must have some inviolable sanctuary, must we not? ... Some rather fine hollyhocks.'

'Charming!' said Miss Leg, who was disposed to hate Lucia with her loftiness and her Star Chamber, but still thought she might be the Key to Tilling. 'I have a veritable grove of them at my little cottage in the country. There was a beautiful study of hollyhocks at your little exhibition. By Miss Coles, I think

Mrs Mapp-Flint said.'

Lucia laughed gaily.

'Oh, my sweet, muddle-headed Mayoress!' she cried. 'Georgie, did you hear? Elizabeth told Miss Leg that my picture of hollyhocks was by Irene. So like her. Tea ready?'

Harmony ripened. Miss Leg expressed her great admiration for Irene's portrait of Lucia, and her withering scorn for the Venus, and promised to pay another visit to study the features of the two principal figures: she had been so disgusted with the picture that one glance was enough. Before she had eaten her second bun, Lucia had rung up the Serjeant at the Town Hall, and asked him to get out the Corporation plate and the Mayor's book, for she would be bringing round a distinguished visitor very shortly: and before Miss Leg had admired the plate and signed the book ('Susan Leg' and below, 'Rudolph da Vinci'), she had engaged herself to dine at Mallards next day. 'Just a few friends,' said Lucia, 'who would be so much honoured to meet you.' She did not ask Elizabeth and Benjy, for Miss Leg had seen so much of them lately, but, for fear they should feel neglected, she begged them to come in afterwards for a cup of coffee and a chat. Elizabeth interpreted this as an insult rather than an invitation, and she and Benjy had coffee and a vivacious chat by themselves.

The party was very gay, and a quantity of little anecdotes were told about the absentees.

At the end of most of them Lucia cried out:

'Ah, you mustn't be so ill-natured about them,' and sometimes she told another. It was close on midnight when the gathering broke up, and they were all bidden to dine with Miss Leg the next night.

'Such a pleasant evening, may I say "Lucia?"' said she on the doorstep, as she put up her round red face for the Mayor to deal with as she liked.

'Indeed do, dear Susan,' she said. 'But I think you must be Susanna. Will you? We have one dear Susan already.'

They kissed.

CHAPTER ELEVEN

George continued to be tactless about Olga's manifold perfections, and though his chaste passion for her did not cause Lucia the smallest anxiety (she knew Georgie too well for that) she wondered what Tilling would make of his coming visit to Le Touquet without her. Her native effrontery had lived the Poppy-crisis down, but her rescue of Susan Leg, like some mature Andromeda, from the clutches of her Mayoress, had raised the deepest animosity of the Mapp-Flints, and she was well aware that Elizabeth would embrace every opportunity to be nasty. She was therefore prepared for

314

trouble, but, luckily for her peace of mind, she had no notion what a tempest of tribulation was gathering ... Georgie and Foljambe left by a very early train for Seaport so that he might secure a good position amidships on the boat, for the motion was felt less there, before the continental express from London arrived, and each of them had a tube of *cachets* preventive of sea-sickness.

Elizabeth popped into Diva's for a chat that morning.

'They've gone,' she said. 'I've just met Worship. She was looking very much worried, poor thing, and I'm sure I don't wonder.'

Diva had left off her eyebrows. They took too long, and she was tired of always looking surprised when, as on this occasion, she was not surprised.

'I suppose you mean about Mr Georgie going off alone,' she said.

'Among other worries. Benjy and I both grieve for her. Mr Georgie's infatuation is evidently increasing. First of all there was that night here—'

'No: Lucia came back,' said Diva.

'Never quite cleared up, I think. And then he's been staying at Riseholme without her, unless you're going to tell me that Worship went over every evening and returned at cock-crow for her duties here.'

'Olga asked them both, anyhow,' said Diva.

'So we've been told, but did she? And this

315

time Lucia's certainly not been asked. It's mounting up, and it must be terrible for her. All that we feared at first is coming true, as I knew it would. And I don't believe for a moment that he'll come back at the end of a week.'

'That would be humiliating,' said Diva.

'Far be it from me to insinuate that there's anything wrong,' continued Elizabeth emphatically, 'but if I was Lucia I shouldn't like it, any more than I should like it if you and Benjy went for a week and perhaps more to Le Touquet.'

'And I shouldn't like it either,' said Diva. 'But I'm sorry for Lucia, too.'

'I daresay she'll need our sympathy before long,' said Elizabeth darkly. 'And how truly grateful I am to her for taking that Leg woman off my hands. Such an incubus. How she managed it I don't enquire. She may have poisoned Leg's mind about me, but I should prefer to be poisoned than see much more of her.'

'Now you're getting mixed, Elizabeth,' protested Diva. 'It was Leg's mind you suggested was poisoned, not you.'

'That's a quibble, dear,' said Elizabeth decidedly. 'You'll hardly deny that Benjy and I were most civil to the woman. I even asked Lucia and Irene to meet her, which was going a long way considering Lucia's conduct about the Corporation plate and the Mayor's book.

316

But I couldn't have stood Leg much longer, and I should have had to drop her ... I must be off; so busy to-day, like Worship. A Council meeting this afternoon.'

*   *   *

Lucia always enjoyed her Council meetings. She liked presiding, she liked being suave and gracious and deeply conscious of her own directing will. As she took her seat to-day, she glanced at the wall behind her, where before long Irene's portrait of her would be hanging. Minutes of the previous meeting were read, reports from various committees were received, discussed and adopted. The last of these was that of the Committee which had been appointed to make its recommendation to the Council about her portrait. She had thought over a well-turned sentence or two: she would say what a privilege it was to make this work of genius the permanent possession of the Borough. Miss Coles, she need hardly remind the Council was a Tillingite of whom they were all proud, and the painter also of the Picture of the Year, in which there figured two of Tilling's most prominent citizens, one being a highly honoured member of the Council. ('And then I shall bow to Elizabeth,' thought Lucia, 'she will appreciate that.')

She looked at the agenda.

'And now we come to our last business,

ladies and gentlemen,' she said. 'To receive the report of the Committee on the Mayor's offer of a portrait of herself to the Council, to be hung in the Town Hall.'

Elizabeth rose.

'As Chairman of this Committee,' she said, 'it is my duty to say that we came to the unanimous conclusion that we cannot recommend the Council to accept the Mayor's most generous gift.'

The gracious sovereignty of Lucia's demeanour did not suffer the smallest diminution.

'Those in favour of accepting the findings of the Committee?' she asked. 'Unanimous, I think.'

*　　　*　　　*

Never, in all Lucia's triumphant career, had she suffered so serious a reverse, nor one out of which it seemed more impossible to reap some incidental advantage. She had been dismissed from Sheffield Castle at the shortest notice, but she had got a harvest of photographs. Out of her inability to find the brake on her bicycle, thus madly scorching through a crowded street, she had built herself a monument for dash and high athletic prowess. She always discovered silver linings to the blackest of clouds, but now, scrutinize them as she might, she could detect in them none but the most

318

sombre hues. Her imagination had worked out a dazzling future for this portrait. It would hang on the wall behind her; the Corporation, at her request, would lend it (heavily insured) to the Royal Academy exhibition next May, where it would be universally acclaimed as a masterpiece far outshining the Venus of the year before. It would be lithographed or mezzo-tinted, and she would sign the first fifty pulls. Visitors would flock to the Town Hall to see it; they would recognise her as she flashed by them on her bicycle or sat sketching at some picturesque corner; admiring the mellow front of Mallards, the ancestral home of the Mayor, they would be thrilled to know that the pianist, whose exquisite strains floated out of the open window of the garden-room, was the woman whose portrait they had just seen above her official chair. Such thoughts as these were not rigidly defined but floated like cloud-castles in the sky, forming and shifting and always elegant.

Now of those fairy edifices there was nothing left. The Venus was to be exhibited at the Carlton Gallery and then perhaps to form a gem in the collection of some American millionaire, and Elizabeth would go out into all lands and Benjy to the ends of the earth, while her own rejected portrait would be returned to Mallards, with the best thanks of the Committee, like Georgie's sunny morning on the marsh, and Susan's budgerigar, and Diva's sardine tartlet. (And where on earth should she hang this perpetual reminder of defeated dreams?) ... Another aspect of this collapse struck her. She had always thought of herself as the beneficent director of municipal action, but now the rest of her Council had expressed unanimous agreement with the report of a small malignant Committee, instead of indignantly rallying round her and expressing their contempt of such base ingratitude. This was a snub to which she saw no possible rejoinder except immediate resignation of her office, but that would imply that she felt the snub, which was not to be thought of. Besides, if her resignation was accepted, there would be nothing left at all.

*　　*　　*

Her pensive steps, after the Council meeting was over, had brought her to the garden-room, and the bright japanned faces of tin-boxes labelled 'Museum' 'Fire Brigade' or 'Burial Board' gave her no comfort: their empty expressions seemed to mock her. Had Georgie been here, she could have confided the tragedy to him without loss of dignity. He would have been sympathetic in the right sort of way: he would have said 'My dear, how tar'some! That foul Elizabeth: of course she was at the bottom of it. Let's think of some plan to serve her out.' But without that encouragement she was too flattened out to think of Elizabeth at all. The

320

only thing she could do was to maintain, once more, her habitual air of prosperous self-sufficiency. She shuddered at the thought of Tilling being sorry for her, because, communing with herself, she seemed to sense below this superficial pity, some secret satisfaction that she had had a knock. Irene, no doubt, would be wholly sincere, but though her prestige as an artist had suffered indignity, what difference would it make to her that the Town Council of Tilling had rejected her picture, when the Carlton Gallery in London had craved the loan of her Venus, and an American millionaire was nibbling for its purchase? Irene would treat it as a huge joke; perhaps she would design a Christmas card showing Mapp, as a nude, mature, female Cupid, transfixing Benjy's heart with a riding-whip. For a moment, as this pleasing fantasy tickled Lucia's brain, she smiled wanly. But the smile faded again: not the grossest insult to Elizabeth would mend matters. A head held high and a total unconsciousness that anything disagreeable had happened was the only course worthy of the Mayor.

The Council meeting had been short, for no reports from Committees (especially the last) had raised controversy, and Lucia stepped briskly down the hill to have tea in public at Diva's, and exhibit herself as being in cheerful or even exuberant spirits. Just opposite the door was drawn up a monstrous motor, behind which was strapped a dress-basket and other substantial luggage with the initials P.S. on them. 'A big postscript,' thought Lucia, lightening her heavy heart with humorous fancies, and she skirted round behind this ponderous conveyance, and so on to the pavement. Two women were just stepping out of ye olde tea-shop: one was Elizabeth dripping with unctuous smiles, and the other was Poppy Sheffield.

'And here's sweet Worship herself,' said Elizabeth. 'Just in time to see you. How fortunate!'

Some deadly misgiving stirred in Lucia's heart as Poppy turned on her a look of blank unrecognition. But she managed to emit a thin cry of welcome.

'Dear Duchess!' she said. 'How naughty of you to come to my little Tilling without letting me know. It was *au revoir* when we parted last.'

Poppy still seemed puzzled, and then (unfortunately, perhaps) she began to remember.

'Why, of course!' she said. 'You came to see me at the Castle, owing to some stupid misunderstanding. My abominable memory. Do tell me your name.'

'Lucia Pillson,' said the wretched woman. 'Mayor of Tilling.'

'Yes, how it all comes back,' said Poppy, warmly shaking hands. 'That was it. I thought your husband was the Mayor of Tilling, and I was expecting him. Quite. So stupid of me. And then tea and photographs, wasn't it? I trust they came out well.'

'Beautifully. Do come up to my house—only a step—and I'll show you them.'

'Alas! not a moment to spare. I've spent such a long time chatting to all your friends. Somebody—somebody called Leg, I think—introduced them to me. She said she had been to my house in London which I daresay was quite true. One never can tell. But I'm catching, at least I hope so, the evening boat at Seaport on my way to stay with Olga Bracely at Le Touquet. Such a pleasure to have met you again.'

Lucia presented a brave front.

'Then do come and dine and sleep here to break your journey on your return,' she said. 'I shall expect you to propose yourself at any time, like all my friends. Just a wire or a telephone call. Georgie and I are sure to be here. Impossible for me to get away in these crowded months—'

'That *would* be nice,' said Poppy. 'Good-bye: Mrs Pillson, isn't it? Quite. Charmed, I'm sure: so pleasant. Drive straight on to the quay at Seaport,' she called to her chauffeur.

Lucia kissed her hand after the car.

'How lucky just to have caught her for a moment,' she drawled to Elizabeth, as they went back into ye olde tea-house. 'Naughty of her not to have let me know. How dreadfully bad her memory is becoming.'

'Shocking,' said Elizabeth. 'You should persuade her to see somebody about it.'

Lucia turned on the full horse-power of her courage for the coming encounter in ye olde tea-house. The moment she saw the faces of her friends assembled there, Evie and Leg and Diva, she knew she would need it all.

'You've just missed an old friend, Lucia,' said Susanna. (Was there in her words a touch of the irony for which Rudolph da Vinci was celebrated?)

'Too unfortunate, dear Susanna,' said Lucia. 'But I just got a word with her. Off to stay at Le Touquet, she said. Ah! I never told her she would find Georgie there. My memory is getting as bad as hers. Diva, may I have a one and sixpenny?'

Diva usually went down to the kitchen to see to the serving of a one and sixpenny, but she only called the order down the stairs to Janet. And her face lacked its usual cordiality.

'You've missed such a nice chat,' she said.

There was a silence pregnant with trouble. It was impossible, thought Lucia, that her name should not have figured in the nice chat, or that Poppy should not have exhibited that distressing ignorance about her which had been so evident outside. In any case Elizabeth would soon promulgate the news with the addition of that hideous detail, as yet undiscovered, that she had been asked to

324

Sheffield Castle only because Poppy thought that Georgie was Mayor of Tilling. Brave cheerfulness was the only possible demeanour.

'Too unfortunate,' she repeated, 'and I could have been here half an hour ago, for we had quite a short Council meeting. Nothing controversial: all went so smoothly—'

The memory of that uncontroversial rejection of her portrait brought her up short. Then the sight of Elizabeth's wistful, softly smiling face lashed her forward again.

'How you will laugh, Susanna,' she said brightly, 'when I tell you that the Council unanimously refused to accept my gift of the portrait Irene painted of me which you admired so much. A small Committee advised them against it. And *ecco*!'

Susanna's laugh lacked the quality of scorn and contempt for the Council, for which Lucia had hoped. It sounded amused.

'Well, that was a pity,' she said. 'They just didn't like it. But you can't get people to like what they don't like by telling them that they ought to.'

The base desertion was a shock. Lucia looked without favour at the sumptuous one and sixpenny Janet had brought her, but her voice remained calm.

'I think I was wrong to have offered it them at all,' she said. 'I ought to have known that they could not understand it. What fun Irene and I will have over it when I tell her. I can hear her scream "Philistines! Vandals!" and burst into shrieks of laughter. And what a joy to have it back at Mallards again!'

Elizabeth continued to smile.

'No place like home is there, dear?' she said. 'Where will you hang it?'

Lucia gave up the idea of eating her sardine tartlet. She had intended to stay on, until Susanna and Elizabeth left, and find out from Diva what had been said about her before she came in. She tried a few light topics of general interest, evoking only short replies of paralyzing politeness. This atmosphere of veiled hostility was undermining her. She knew that if she went away first, Elizabeth would pour out all that Poppy had let slip on the doorstep, but perhaps the sooner that was known the better. After drinking her tea and scalding her mouth she rose.

'I must be off,' she said. 'See you again very soon, Susanna. One and sixpence, Diva? Such a lovely tea.'

Elizabeth continued smiling till the door closed.

'Such odd things happened outside,' she said. 'Her Poppy didn't recognise her. She asked her who she was. And Worship wasn't invited to Sheffield Castle at all. Poppy thought that Mr Georgie was the Mayor, and the invitation was for him. That was why Worship came back so soon.'

'Gracious, what a crash!' said Diva.

326

'It always comes in time,' said Elizabeth thoughtfully. 'Poor thing, we must be very gentle with her, but what a lot of things we must avoid talking about!'

She enumerated them on her plump fingers. 'Duchesses, Castles, photographs—I wonder if they were picture postcards—prima-donnas, for I'm sure she'd have gone to Le Touquet, if she had been asked—portraits—it was my duty to recommend the Council not to accept that daub—gad-about husbands—I haven't got enough fingers. Such a lot of subjects that would tear old wounds open, and she's brought it all on herself, which makes it so much more bitter for her.'

Diva, who hated waste (and nothing would keep in this hot weather) ate Lucia's sardine tartlet.

'Don't gloat, Elizabeth!' she commanded. 'You may say sympathetic things, but there's a nasty tone in the way you say them. I'm really rather sorry for her.'

'Which is just what I have been trying to express,' retorted Elizabeth.

'Then you haven't expressed it well. Not that impression at all. Goodness, here's a fresh party coming in. Janet!'

Lucia passed by the fishmonger's, and some stir of subconscious cerebration prompted her to order a dressed crab that she saw in the window. Then she went home and out into the garden-room. This second blow falling so fast

327

on the heels of the first, caused her to reel. To all the dismal reflections occasioned by the rejection of her portrait there were added those appropriate to the second, and the composite mental picture presented by the two was appalling. Surely some malignant Power, specially dedicated to the service of her discomfiture, must have ordained the mishaps (and their accurate timing) of this staggering afternoon: the malignant Power was a master of stage-craft. Who could stand up against a relentless tragedian? Lucia could not, and two tears of self-pity rolled down her cheeks. She was much surprised to feel their tickling progress, for she had always thought herself incapable of such weakness, but there they were. The larger one fell on to her blotting-pad, and she dashed the smaller aside.

She pulled herself together. Whatever humiliations were heaped on her, her resolve to continue sprightly and dominant and unsubdued was as firm as ever, and she must swallow pity or contempt without apparently tasting them. She went to her piano, and through a slightly blurred vision had a good practice at the difficult treble part of the duet Georgie and she had run through before his departure. She did a few bracing physical exercises, and a little deep breathing. 'I have lost a great deal of prestige,' she said to herself as she held her breath and puffed it out again, 'but that shall not upset me. I shall recover it all. In a fortnight's time, if not less, I shall be unable to believe that I could ever have felt so abject and have behaved so weakly. *Sursum corda!* I shall—'

Her telephone bell rang. It required a strong call on her courage to answer it, for who could tell what fresh calamity might not be sprung on her? When she heard the name of the speaker, she nearly rang off, for it seemed so impossible. Probably some infamous joke was being played on her. But she listened.

'I've just missed my boat,' said the voice, 'and sleeping in a hotel makes me ill for a week. Would you be wonderfully kind and let me dine and sleep? You were so good as to suggest that this afternoon. Then I can catch the early boat to-morrow.'

A sob of joy rose in Lucia's throat.

'Delighted, Duchess,' she answered. 'So glad you took me at my word and proposed yourself.'

'Many thanks. I shall be with you in an hour or so.'

Lucia skipped to the bell, and kept her finger on it till Grosvenor came running out.

'Grosvenor, the Duchess of Sheffield will be here in about an hour to dine and sleep,' cried Lucia, still ringing. 'What is there for dinner?'

'Couldn't say, except for a dressed crab that's just come in—' began Grosvenor.

'Yes, I ordered it,' cried Lucia excitedly, ceasing to ring. 'It was instinctive, Grosvenor, it was a leading. Things like that often happen to me. See what else, and plenty of strong coffee.'

Grosvenor went into the house, and the music of triumphant meditations poured through Lucia's brain.

'Shall I ask Benjy and Elizabeth?' she thought. 'That would crush Elizabeth for ever, but I don't really wish her such a fate. Diva? No. A good little thing, but it might seem odd to Poppy to meet at dinner a woman to whom she had paid a shilling for her tea, or perhaps eighteen-pence. Susanna Leg? No: she was not at all kind about the picture. Shall I send for the Mayor's book and get Poppy to write in it? Again, no. It would look as if I wanted to record her visit officially, whereas she only just drops in. We will be alone, I think. Far more *chic*.'

Grosvenor returned with the modest menu, and Lucia added a savoury.

'And I shan't dress, Grosvenor,' she said. 'Her Grace (rich words!) will be leaving very early, and she won't want to unpack, I expect.'

Her Grace arrived. She seemed surprised not to find Georgie there, but was pleased to know that he was staying with Olga at Le Touquet. She went to bed very soon after dinner, and left at eight next morning. Never had Lucia waited so impatiently for the shopping hour, when casually, drawlingly she would diffuse the news.

330

* * *

The first person she met was Elizabeth herself, who hurried across the street with an odious smile of kindly pity on her face.

'So lonely for you, Worship, all by yourself without Mr Georgie,' she said. 'Pop in and dine with us to-night.'

Lucia could have sung aloud to think how soon that kindly pity would be struck from the Mayoress's face. She pressed a finger to her forehead.

'Let me think,' she said. 'I'm afraid ... No, that's to-morrow ... Yes, I am free. Charmed.' She paused, prolonging the anticipation of the wonderful disclosure.

'And I had such a queer little surprise last night,' she drawled. 'I went home after tea at Diva's,—of course you were there—and played my piano a while. Then the eternal telephone rang. Who do you think it was who wanted to dine and sleep at such short notice?'

Elizabeth curbed her longing to say 'Duchess Poppy', but that would have been too unkind and sarcastic.

'Tell me, dear,' she said.

'The Duchess,' said Lucia. 'I begged her, do you remember, when we three met for a minute yesterday, just to propose herself ... And an hour afterwards, she did. Dear vague thing! She missed her boat and can't bear hotels and

331

telephoned. A pleasant quiet evening. She went off again very early to-day, to catch the morning boat. I wonder if she'll succeed this time. Eight o'clock this evening then? I shall look forward to it.'

Lucia went into a shop, leaving Elizabeth speechless on the pavement, with her mouth wide open. Then she closed it, and it assumed its grimmest aspect. She began to cross the street, but leaped back to the pavement again on the violent hooting, almost in her ear, of Susan's Royce.

'So sorry if it made you jump,' said Susan, putting her face out of the window, 'but I hear that Lucia's Duchess was here yesterday and didn't know her from Adam. Or Eve. Either of them. Can it be true?'

'I was there,' said Elizabeth. 'She hadn't the slightest idea who Worship was.'

'That's odd, considering all those photographs.'

'There's something odder yet,' said Elizabeth. 'Worship has just told me she had a visitor to dine and sleep, who left very early this morning. Guess who that was!'

'I never can guess, as you know,' said Susan. 'Who?'

'She!' cried Elizabeth shrilly. 'And Lucia had the face to tell me so!'

Mr Wyse, concealed behind the immense bulk of his wife, popped his head round the corner of her shoulder. The Mayoress's savage countenance so terrified him that he popped it back again.

'How Worship's conscience will let her tell such whoppers, is her concern and not mine, thank God,' continued the Mayoress. 'What I deplore is that she should think me idiotic enough to believe them. Does one woman ask another woman, whom she doesn't know by sight, to let her dine and sleep? *Does* she?'

Mr Wyse always refused to be drawn into social crises. 'Drive on,' he said in a low voice down the speaking-tube, and the car hooted and moved away. Elizabeth screamed '*Does* she,' after it.

The news spread fast, and there was only one verdict on it. Obviously Lucia had invented the story to counter the mortification of being unrecognised by Poppy the day before. 'So silly,' said Diva, when Elizabeth plunged into the tea-house and told her. 'Much better to have lived it down. We've all got to live things down sometimes. She's only made it much harder for herself. What's the good of telling lies which nobody can believe? When you and I tell lies, Elizabeth, it's in the hope anyhow— What is it Janet?'

'Please ma'am, Grosvenor's just told me there was a visitor at Mallards last night, and who do you think—'

'Yes, I've heard,' said Diva. 'I'll be down in the kitchen in a minute.'

'And making poor Grosvenor her

333

accomplice,' said Elizabeth. 'Come and dine to-night, Diva. I've asked Worship, and you must help Benjy and me to get through the evening. You must help us to keep her off the subject, or I shall lose my self-control and forget that I'm a lady and tell her she's a liar.'

Lucia spent a wonderfully happy day. She came straight home after telling Elizabeth her news, for it was far more lofty not to spread it herself and give the impression that she was gratified, and devoted herself to her music and her reading, as there was no municipal business to occupy her. Long before evening everyone would know, and she would merely make casual allusions at dinner to her visitor, and inflame their curiosity. She went out wearing her seed-pearls in the highest spirits.

'Dear host and hostess,' she said as she swept in. 'So sweet of you to take compassion on my loneliness. No, Major Benjy, no sherry thanks, though I really deserve some after my long day. Breakfast at half-past seven—'

'Fancy! That was early!' interrupted Elizabeth. Diva entered.

'So sorry,' she said. 'A bit late. Fearfully busy afternoon. Worn out. Yes, Major Benjy: just half a glass.'

'I was just saying that I had had a long day, too,' said Lucia. 'My guest was off at eight to catch the early boat at Seaport—'

'Such a good service,' put in Benjy. 'Liz and I went by that route on our honeymoon.'

'—and would get to Le Touquet in time for lunch.'

'Well, dinner, dinner,' said Benjy, and in they went.

* * *

'I've not seen Susan Leg to-day,' remarked Diva. 'She usually drops in to tea now.'

'She's been writing hard,' said Elizabeth. 'I popped in for a minute. She's got some material *now*, she told me.'

This dark saying had a bright lining for Lucia. Her optimistic mind concluded that Susanna knew about her visitor, and she laughed gaily as dressed crab was handed to her.

'Such a coincidence,' she said. 'Last night I had ordered dressed crab before—dear Elizabeth, I never get tired of it—before I was rung up from Seaport. Was not that lucky? Her favourite food.'

'And how many teas did you say you served to-day, Diva?' asked Elizabeth.

'Couldn't tell you yet. Janet hadn't finished counting up. People still in the garden when I left.'

'I heard from Georgie to-day,' said Lucia. 'He'll be back from Le Touquet on Saturday. The house was quite full already, he said, and he didn't know where Olga would put another guest.'

'Such lovely September weather,' said Elizabeth. 'So good for the crops.'

Lucia was faintly puzzled. They had all been so eager to hear about her visit to Sheffield Castle, and now whenever she brought up kindred topics, Elizabeth or Diva changed the subject with peculiar abruptness. Very likely Elizabeth was a little jealous, a little resentful that Lucia had not asked her to dine last night. But she could explain that.

'It was too late, alas,' she said, 'to get up a small party,' she said, 'as I should have so much liked to do. Simply no time. We didn't even dress.'

Elizabeth rose.

'Such a short visit,' she said, 'and breakfast at half-past seven. Fancy! Let us have a rubber, as we needn't get up so early to-morrow.'

*　　　*　　　*

Lucia walked home in the bright moonlight, making benevolent plans. If Poppy broke her return journey by staying a night here she must certainly have a party. She vaguely regretted not having done so last night: it would have given pleasure, and she ought to welcome all opportunities of making treats for her friends ... They were touchy folk; to-night they had been harsh with each other over Bridge, but to her they had been scrupulously polite, receiving all her criticisms of their play in meek

336

silence. Perhaps they were beginning to perceive at last that she was a different class of player from them. As she caressed this vainglorious thought, she stopped to admire the chaste whiteness of the moonlight on the church-tower, which seemed to point skywards as if towards her own serene superiority among the stars. Then quite suddenly a violent earthquake happened in her mind, and it collapsed.

'They don't believe that Poppy ever stayed with me at all,' she moaned. 'They think I invented it. Infamous!'

CHAPTER TWELVE

For the whole of the next day no burgess of Tilling, except Mrs Simpson and the domestic staff, set eyes on the Mayor. By a strong effort of will Lucia took up her market-basket after breakfast with the intention of shopping, but looking out from the window of her hall, she saw Elizabeth on the pavement opposite, sketching the front of the ancestral house of her aunt by marriage. She could not face Elizabeth yet, for that awful mental earthquake in the churchyard last night had shattered her nerve. The Mayor was a self-ordained prisoner in her own house, as Popes had been at the Vatican.

She put down her basket and went back into the garden-room. She must show Elizabeth though not by direct encounter, that she was happy and brilliant and busy. She went to her piano and began practising scales. Arpeggios and roulades of the most dazzling kind followed. Slightly exhausted by this fine display she crept behind the curtain and peered out. Elizabeth was still there, and, in order to continue the impression of strenuous artistic activity, Lucia put on a gramophone record of the Moonlight Sonata. At the conclusion of that she looked out again; Elizabeth had gone. It was something to have driven that baleful presence away from the immediate neighbourhood, but it had only taken its balefulness elsewhere. She remembered how Susanna had said with regard to the rejected portrait (which no longer seemed to matter an atom) 'You can't get people to like what they don't like by telling them that they ought to'; and now a parallel aphorism suggested itself to Lucia's harassed brain.

'You can't get people to believe what they won't believe by telling them that it's true,' she whispered to herself. 'Yet Poppy did stay here: she did, she did! And it's *too* unfair that I should lose more prestige over that, when I ought to have recovered all that I had lost ... What is it, Grosvenor?'

Grosvenor handed her a telegram.

'Mr Georgie won't be back till Monday

instead of Saturday,' said Lucia in a toneless voice. 'Anything else?'

'Shall Cook do the shopping, ma'am, if you're not going out? It's early closing.'

'Yes. I shall be alone for lunch and dinner,' said Lucia, wishing that it were possible for all human affairs to shut down with the shops.

She glanced at Georgie's telegram again, amazed at its light-heartedness. 'Having such fun,' it ran. 'Olga insists I stop till Monday. Know you won't mind. Devoted Georgie.'

She longed for devoted Georgie, and fantastic ideas born of pure misery darted through her head. She thought of replying: 'Come back at once and stand by me. Nobody believes that Poppy slept here.' She thought of asking the B.B.C. to broadcast an S.O.S.: 'Will George Pillson last heard of to-day at Le Touquet, return at once to Tilling where his wife the Mayor—' No, she could not say she was dangerously ill. That would alarm him; besides he would find on arrival that she was perfectly well. He might even come by air, and then the plane might crash and he would be burned to death. She realised that such thoughts were of the most morbid nature, and wondered if a glass of sherry would disperse them. But she resisted. 'I won't risk becoming like Major Benjy,' she said to herself, 'and I've got to stick it alone till Monday.'

The hours crept dismally by: she had lunch,

tea and dinner by herself. One fragment of news reached her through Grosvenor and that was not encouraging. Her cook had boasted to Elizabeth's parlour-maid that she had cooked dinner for a Duchess, and the parlour-maid with an odd laugh, had advised her not to be so sure about that. Cook had returned in a state of high indignation, which possibly she had expressed by saturating Lucia's soup with pepper, and putting so much mustard into her devilled chicken that it might have been used as a plaster for the parlour-maid. Perhaps these fiery substances helped to kindle Lucia again materially, and all day psychical stimulants were at work: pride which refused to surrender, the extreme boredom of being alone, and the consciousness of rectitude. So next morning, after making sure that Elizabeth was not lurking about, Lucia set forth with her market-basket. Irene was just coming out of her house, and met her with a grave and sympathetic face.

'Darling, I am so sorry about it,' she said.

Lucia naturally supposed that she was referring to the rejection of the portrait.

'Don't give it another thought,' she said. 'It will be such a joy to have it at Mallards. They're all Goths and Vandals and Elizabeths.'

'Oh that!' said Irene. 'Who cares? Just wait till I've touched up Elizabeth and Benjy for the Carlton Gallery. No, about this septic Duchess. Why did you do it? So unwise!'

Lucia wondered if some fresh horror had

ripened, and her mouth went dry.

'Why did I do what?' she asked.

'Say that she'd been to stay with you, when she didn't even know you by sight. So futile!'

'But she did stay with me!' cried Lucia.

'No, no,' said Irene soothingly. 'Don't go on saying it. It wounds me. Naturally, you were vexed at her not recognising you. You *had* seen her before somewhere, hadn't you?'

'But this is preposterous!' cried Lucia. 'You *must* believe me. We had dressed crab for dinner. She went to bed early. She slept in the spare room. She snored. We breakfasted at half-past seven—'

'Darling, we won't talk about it any more,' said Irene. 'Whenever you want me, I'll come to you. Just send for me.'

'I shall want you,' said Lucia with awful finality, 'when you beg my pardon for not believing me.'

Irene uttered a dismal cry, and went back into her house. Lucia with a face of stone went on to the High Street. As she was leaving the grocer's her basket bumped against Diva's, who was entering.

'Sorry,' said Diva. 'Rather in a hurry. My fault.'

It was as if an iceberg, straight from the North Pole, had apologized. Mr Wyse was just stepping on to the pavement, and he stood hatless as she hailed him.

'Lovely weather, isn't it?' she said. 'Georgie

writes to me that they're having the same at Le Touquet. We must have some more Bridge parties when he gets back.'

'You enjoy your Bridge so much, and play it so beautifully,' said Mr Wyse with a bow. 'And, believe me, I shall never forget your kindness over Susan's budgerigar.'

In Lucia's agitated state, this sounded dreadfully like an assurance that, in spite of all, she hadn't lost his friendship. Then with an accession of courage, she determined to stick to her guns.

'The Duchess's visit to me was at such short notice,' she said, 'that there was literally not time to get a few friends together. She would so much have liked to see you and Susan.'

'Very good of you to say so. I—I heard that she had spent the night under your hospitable roof. Ah! I see Susan beckoning to me.'

Lucia's shopping had not raised her spirits, and when she went up the street again towards Mallards, there was Elizabeth on the pavement opposite, at her easel. But now the sight of her braced Lucia. It flashed through her mind that her dear Mayoress had selected this subject for her sketch in order to keep an eye on her, to observe, as through a malicious microscope, her joyless exits and entrances and report to her friends how sad and wan she looked: otherwise Elizabeth would never have attempted anything which required the power to draw straight lines and some knowledge,

342

however elementary, of perspective. All the more reason, then, that Lucia should be at her very best and brightest and politest and most withering.

Elizabeth out of the corner of her eye saw her approaching and kissed the top end of her paint-brush to her.

'Good morning, dear Worship,' she said. 'Been shopping and chatting with all your friends? Any news?'

'Good morning, *sindaca mia*,' she said. 'That means Mayoress, dear. Oh, what a promising sketch! But have you quite got the mellow tone of the bricks in my garden-room? I should suggest just a touch of brown-madder.'

Elizabeth's paint-brush began to tremble.

'Thank you, dear,' she said 'Brown-madder. I must remember that.'

'Or a little rose-madder mixed with burnt sienna would do as well,' continued Lucia. 'Just stippled on. You will find that will give the glowing effect you want.'

Elizabeth wondered whether Lucia could have realised that nobody in Tilling believed that Poppy had ever stayed with her and yet remain so complacent and superior. She hoped to find an opportunity of introducing that topic. But she could find something to say on the subject of Art first.

'So lovely for quaint Irene to have had this great success with her picture of me,' she said. 'The Carlton Gallery, she tells me, and then perhaps an American purchaser. Such a pity that masterpieces have to leave the country. Luckily her picture of you is likely to remain here.'

'That was a terrible set-back for Irene,' said Lucia, as glibly as if she had learned this dialogue by heart, 'when your Committee induced the Council to reject it.'

'Impossible to take any other view,' said Elizabeth. 'A daub. We couldn't have it in our beautiful Town Hall. And it didn't do you justice, dear.'

'How interesting that you should say that!' said Lucia. 'Dear Irene felt just that about her picture of you. She felt she had not put enough character into your face. She means to make some little alterations in it before she sends it to the Carlton Galleries.'

That was alarming: Elizabeth remembered the 'little alterations' Irene had made before. But she did not allow that to unnerve her.

'Sometimes I am afraid she will never rise to the level of her Venus again,' she sighed. 'Her high-water mark. Her picture of you, for instance. It might have been out of Mr Wyse's pieces of still life: bicycle, piano, packs of cards.'

'Some day when I can find time, I will explain to you the principles of symbolism,' Lucia promised.

Elizabeth saw her way to the desired topic.

'Thank you, dear,' she said fervently. 'That

344

would be a treat. But I know how busy you are with all your duties and all your entertaining. Have you had any more visitors to dine and sleep and go away very early next morning before they had seen anything of our lovely Tilling?'

The blow was wholly unexpected and it shook Lucia. She pulled herself together.

'Let me think,' she said. 'Such a succession of people dropping in. No! I think the dear Duchess was my last guest.'

'What a lovely evening you must have had,' said Elizabeth. 'Two old friends together. How I love a *tête-à-tête*, just like what we're having now with nobody to interrupt. Roaming over all sorts of subjects, like bees sipping at flowers. How much you always teach me, Worship. Rose-madder and burnt sienna to give luminousness—'

Lucia clutched at the return of this topic, and surveyed Elizabeth's sketch.

'So glad to have given you that little tip,' she said. 'Immense improvement, isn't it? How the bricks glow now—'

'I haven't put any madder on yet, brown or rose,' cooed Elizabeth, 'but so glad to know about it. And is poor Duchess's memory really as bad as it seemed? How dreadful for you if she had forgotten her own name as well as yours.'

Quite suddenly Lucia knew that she had no more force left in her. She could only just manage a merry laugh.

'What a delicious social crisis that would be!' she said. 'You ought to send it to some comic paper. And what a pleasant talk we have had! I could stay stay here all morning chatting, but alas, I have a hundred arrears to get through. *Addio, cara sindaca.*'

She walked without hurrying up the steps to her door and tottered out into the garden-room. Presently she crept to the observation post behind the curtain and looked out. Benjy had joined the Mayoress, and something she said caused him to laugh very heartily ... And even devoted Irene did not believe that Poppy had ever stayed here.

Next day was Sunday. As Lucia listened to the joyful peal of the bells she wondered whether, without Georgie, she could meet the fresh ordeal that awaited her, when after the service Tilling society assembled outside the south porch of the church for the Sunday morning chat which took the place of the week-day shopping. To shirk that would be a tacit confession that she could not face her friends: she might just as well, from the social point of view, not go to church at all. But though the *débâcle* appeared so complete, she knew that her essential spirit was unbroken: it would be 'given her,' she felt, to make that manifest in some convincing manner.

She sang very loud in the hymns and psalms, she winced when the organist had a slight misunderstanding with the choir, she let ecclesiastical smiles play over her face when she found herself in sympathy with the doctrine of the curate's sermon, she gave liberally to the offertory. When the service was over she waited outside the south porch. Elizabeth followed close behind, and behind Elizabeth were other familiar faces. Lucia felt irresistibly reminded of the hymn she had just been singing about the hosts of Midian who 'prowled and prowled around' ... So much the worse for the hosts of Midian.

'Good morning, dear,' said Elizabeth. 'No Mr Georgie in church? Not ill I hope?'

'No, particularly well,' said Lucia, 'and enjoying himself so much at Le Touquet that he's staying till Monday.'

'Sweet of you to allow him,' responded Elizabeth, 'for you must be so lonely without him.'

At that precise moment there took possession of Lucia an emotion to which hitherto she had been a stranger, namely sheer red rage. In all the numerous crises of her career her brain had always been occupied with getting what she wanted and with calm triumph when she got it, or with devising plans to extricate herself from tight places and with scaring off those who had laid traps for her. Now all such insipidities were swept away; rage at the injustice done her thrilled every fibre of her being, and she found the sensation delicious. She began rather gently.

'Lonely?' she asked. 'I don't know the word. How could I be lonely with my books and my music and my work, above all with so many loving loyal friends like yourself, dear Elizabeth, so close about me?'

'That's the stuff to give her. That made her wince,' she thought, and opening the furnace doors she turned to the group of loving loyal friends, who had emerged from church, and were close about her.

'I'm still the deserted wife, you see,' she said gaily. 'My Georgie can't tear himself away from the sirens at Le Touquet, Olga and Poppy and the rest. Oh, Mr Wyse, what a cold you've got! You must take care of yourself: your sister the Contessa Amelia di Faraglione would never have allowed you to come out! Dear Susan! No Royce? Have you actually walked all the way from Porpoise Street? You mustn't overdo it! Diva, how is Paddy? He's not been sick again, I hope, after eating one of your delicious sardine tartlets. Yes, Georgie's not back yet. I am thinking of going by aeroplane to Le Touquet this afternoon, just to dine and sleep—like Poppy—and return with him tomorrow. And Susanna! I hear you've been so busy with your new story about Tilling. I do hope you will get someone to publish it when it's finished. Dear Diva, what a silly mistake I've made: of course it was the recipe for cream-wafers which Susanna's *chef* gave you which made Paddy so unwell. Irene? You in church? Was it not a lovely sermon, all about thinking evil of your friends? Good morning, Major Benjy. You must get poor Mr Wyse to try your favourite cure for colds. A tumbler of whisky, isn't it, every two hours with a little boiling water according to taste. Au revoir, dear ones: See you all to-morrow I hope.'

She smiled and kissed her hand, and walked off without turning her head, a little out of breath with this shattering eloquence, but rejoicing and rejuvenated.

'That *was* a pleasure,' she said to herself, 'and to think that I was ever terrified of meeting them! What a coward! I don't think I left anybody out: I insulted each one in the presence of all the rest. That's what they get for not believing that Poppy stayed here, and for thinking that I was down and out. I've given them something else to think about. I've paid them back, thank God, and now we'll see what will happen next.'

* * *

Lucia, of course, had no intention of flying to Le Touquet, but she drove to Seaport next morning to meet Georgie. He was wearing a new French yachting costume with a double-breasted jacket and brass buttons.

'My dear, how delightful of you to come and meet me!' he said. 'Quite a smooth crossing.

Do you like my clothes?'

'Too smart for anything, Georgie, and I am so glad to see you again. Such a lot to tell you which I couldn't write.'

'Elizabeth been behaving well?' he asked.

'Fiendishly. A real crisis, Georgie, and you've come into the middle of it. I'll tell you all about it as we go.'

Lucia gave an unbiassed and lucid sketch of what had happened, peppered by indignant and excited comments from him:

'Poppy's imbecile—yes I call her Poppy to her face, she asked me to—Fancy her forgetting you: just the sort of thing for that foul Mapp to make capital of—And so like her to get the Council to reject the picture of you—My dear, you cried? What a shame, and how very unlike you—And they don't believe Poppy stayed with you? Why of course she did! She talked about it—Even Irene?—How utterly poisonous of them all!—Hurrah, I'm glad you gave it them hot after church. Capital! We'll do something stunning, now that we can put our heads together about it. I must hear it all over again bit by bit. And here we are in the High Street. There's Mapp, grinning like a Cheshire cat. We'll cut her anyhow, just to make a beginning: we can't go wrong over that.'

Georgie paused a moment.

'And, do you know, I'm very glad to be back,' he said. 'Olga was perfectly sweet, as she
350

always is, but there were other things. It would have been far better if I'd come home on Saturday.'

'Georgie, how thrilling!' cried Lucia, forgetting her own crisis for a brief second. 'What is it?'

'I'll tell you afterwards. Hullo, Grosvenor, how are you? Yes, I think I'll have a warm bath after my journey and then rest till tea-time.'

They had tea in his sitting-room after he had rested, where he was arranging his bibelots, for Grosvenor had not put them back, after dusting them, exactly as he wished. This done, he took up his needle-work and his narration.

'It's been rather upsetting,' he said. 'Poppy was terribly ill on her crossing, and I didn't see her till next day, after I had settled to stop at Olga's over the Sunday, as I telegraphed. And then she was very queer. She took hold of my hand under the table at dinner, and trod on my foot and smiled at me most oddly. She wouldn't play Bridge, but came and sat close up against me. One thing after another—'

'Georgie, what a horrid woman,' said Lucia. 'How could she dare? Did she try—'

'No,' said Georgie hastily. 'Nothing important. Olga assured me she didn't mean anything of the sort, but that she always behaved like that to people with beards. Olga wasn't very sympathetic about it: in fact she came to my room one night, and simply went into fits of laughter.'

'Your bedroom, Georgie?' asked Lucia.

'Yes. She often did when we went upstairs and talked for a bit. But Poppy was very embarrassing. I'm not good at that sort of thing. And yesterday, she made me go for a walk with her along the beach, and wanted to paddle with me. But I was quite firm about that. I said I should go inland at once if she went on about it.'

'Quite right, dear. Just what I should have done myself,' said Lucia appreciatively.

'And so those last two days weren't so pleasant. I was uncomfortable. I wished I'd come back on Saturday.'

'Very tiresome for you, dear,' said Lucia. 'But it's all over now.'

'That's just what I'm not so sure about,' said he. 'She's leaving Olga's to-morrow, and she's going to telegraph to you, asking if you would let her stay here for a couple of nights. Apparently you begged her to propose herself. You must really say your house is full or that you're away. Though Olga says she means no harm, it's most disagreeable.'

Lucia sprang from her chair.

'Georgie, how absolutely providential!' she cried. 'If only she came, it would kill that despicable scandal that she hadn't stayed here before. They would be forced to believe that she had. Oh! What a score!'

'Well, I couldn't stop here if she came,' said Georgie firmly. 'It got on my nerves. It made

352

me feel very jumpy.'

'But then she mightn't stop if she found you weren't here' pleaded Lucia. 'Besides, as Olga says, she doesn't mean anything, I shall be with you; surely that will be sufficient protection, and I won't leave you alone with her a minute all day. And if you're nervous, you may sleep in my room. Just while she's here, of course.'

'Oh, I don't think either of us would like that,' said Georgie, 'and Foljambe would think it so odd.'

'Well, you could lock your door. Oh, Georgie, it isn't really much to ask, and it will put me on a higher pinnacle than ever, far, far above their base insinuations. They will eat their hearts out with shame.'

Grosvenor entered.

'A telegram for you, ma'am. Prepaid.'

With trembling hands Lucia tore it open, and, for Grosvenor's benefit, assumed her drawling voice.

'From the Duchess, dear,' she said. 'She wants to come here to-morrow for two nights, on her way back from Le Touquet. I suppose I had better say yes, as I did ask her to propose herself.'

'Oh, very well,' said Georgie.

Lucia scribbled a cordial reply, and Grosvenor took it away with the tea-tray.

'Georgino, you're an angel,' said she. 'My dear, all the time that I was so wretched here, I knew it would all come right as soon as you got back, and see what has happened! Now let us make our plans at once. I think we'll ask nobody the first night she is here—'

'Nor the second either I should hope,' said Georgie. 'Give them a good lesson. Besides, after the way you talked to them yesterday after church, they probably wouldn't come. That would be a knock.'

Lucia regarded an angle of the ceiling with that far away abstracted expression with which she listened to music.

'About their coming, dear,' she said, 'I will wager my knowledge of human nature that they will without exception. As to my asking them, you know how I trust your judgment, but here I'm not sure that I agree. Don't you think that to forgive them all, and to behave as if nothing had happened, would be the most devastating thing I could do? There's nothing that stings so much as contemptuous oblivion. I have often found that.'

'You don't mean to say that you'll ask Elizabeth Mapp-Flint to dine?' asked Georgie.

'I think so, Georgie, poor soul. If I don't she will feel that she has hurt me, that I want to pay her out. I shouldn't like her to feel that. I don't want to leave her a leg to stand on. Up till now I have never desired quite to crush her, but I feel I have been too lenient. If she is to become a better woman, I must give her a sharper lesson than merely ignoring her. I may remind her by some little impromptu touch of what she tried to do to me, but I shall trust to the inspiration of the moment about that.'

Georgie came round to Lucia's view of the value of vindictive forgiveness, while for himself he liked the idea of calling a Duchess by her Christian name before Mapp and Co. He would not even mind her holding his hand if there were plenty of people there.

'It ought to be a wonderful party,' he said. 'Even better than the party you gave for Olga. I'm beginning to look forward to it. Shall I help you with writing the invitations?'

'Not necessary, dear, thank you,' said Lucia. 'I shall ask them all quite casually by telephone on the afternoon of our dinner. Leave it to me.'

*   *   *

Poppy arrived next evening, again prostrated by seasickness and far from amorous. But a good night restored her, and the three took a morning stroll in the High Street, so that everybody saw them. Lucia, absolutely certain that there would be a large dinner-party at Mallards that night, ordered appropriate provisions. In the afternoon they went for a motor-drive: just before starting Lucia directed Foljambe to ring up the whole circle of friends, asking them to excuse such short notice and take pot-luck with her, and not a word was Foljambe to say about Duchesses. They knew.

While the ducal party traversed the country

roads, the telephone bells of Tilling were ringing merrily. For the Wyses were engaged to dine and play Bridge with the Mapp-Flints, and Susan, feeling certain that she would not meet the Mapp-Flints anyhow at Mallards, rang up Elizabeth to say that she was not feeling at all well and regretted not being able to come. Algernon, she said, did not like to leave her. To her surprise Elizabeth was all cordiality: dear Susan must not think of going out, it was no inconvenience at all, and they would arrange another night. So, with sighs of relief, they both rang up Mallards, and found that the line was engaged, for Susan Leg, having explained to Diva that she had made a stupid mistake, and had meant to ask her for tomorrow not for to-night, was telling Foljambe that she would be charmed to come. Diva got the line next, and fussing with this delay, Elizabeth sent Benjy round to Mallards to say how pleased. Then to make certain, they all wrote formal notes of acceptance. As for Irene, she was so overcome with remorse at having ever doubted Lucia's word, and so overwhelmed by her nobility in forgiving her, that she burst into tears, and forgot to answer at all.

Poppy was very late for dinner, and all Lucia's guests had arrived before she appeared. They were full of a timid yet eager cordiality, as if scarcely believing that such magnanimity was possible, and their hostess was graciousness itself. She was particularly kind to Elizabeth and made enquiries about her sketch. Then as Poppy still lingered she said to Georgie: 'Run up to Poppy's room, dear, and tell her she must be quick.' She had hardly got that pleasant sentence out when Poppy entered.

'Naughty!' said Lucia, and took her arm to introduce the company. 'Mr and Mrs Wyse, Miss Leg (Rudolph da Vinci, you know, dear), Miss Irene Coles—the picture of the year—and Mrs Plaistow: didn't you have one of her delicious teas when you were here? And my Mayoress, Mrs Mapp-Flint, I don't think you met her when you stayed with me last week. And Major Mapp-Flint. Now everybody knows everybody. Sherry, dear Poppy?'

Georgie kept his hands on the table during dinner, and Poppy intermittently caressed the one nearest her in a casual manner; with so many witnesses and in so bright a light, Georgie liked it rather than otherwise. Her attempt to stroll with him alone in the garden afterwards was frustrated, for Lucia, as bound by her promise, instantly joined them, and brought them back to the garden-room. She was induced to play to them, and Poppy, sitting close to Georgie on the sofa, fell into a refreshing slumber. At the cessation of the music, she woke with a start and asked what the time was. A most distinguished suavity prevailed, and though the party lacked the gaiety and lightness of the Olga-festival, its quality was far more monumental. Then the guests dispersed; Lucia had a kind word for each and she thanked them all for having excused her giving them such short notice.

Elizabeth walked home in silence with Benjy. Her exaltation evaporated in the night-air like the fumes of wine, leaving behind an irritated depression.

'Well, there's no help for it,' she said bitterly, as he fumbled with the latch-key of the Vicarage. 'But I daresay before long—Do be quick.'

* * *

Half an hour later at Mallards, Lucia, having seen Poppy well on the way to bed, tapped discreetly at Georgie's door. That gave him a terrible fright, till he remembered he had locked it.

'No, you can't come in,' he said. 'Good night, Poppy. Sleep well.'

'It's me, Georgie,' said Lucia in a low voice. 'Open the door: only a chink. She isn't here.'

Georgie unlocked it.

'Perfect!' she whispered. 'Such a treat for them all! They will remember this evening. Perfect.'

We hope you have enjoyed this Large Print book. Other Chivers Press or Thorndike Press Large Print books are available at your library or directly from the publishers.

For more information about current and forthcoming titles, please call or write, without obligation, to:

Chivers Press Limited
Windsor Bridge Road
Bath BA2 3AX
England
Tel. (01225) 335336

OR

Thorndike Press
P.O. Box 159
Thorndike, Maine 04986
USA
Tel. (800) 223–2336

All our Large Print titles are designed for easy reading, and all our books are made to last.